IMPERIAL YELLOW

Other Sunstone Books by Douglas Atwill

Why I Won't Be Going to Lunch Anymore

The Galisteo Escarpment

Creep Around the Corner

IMPERIAL YELLOW

A NOVEL

DOUGLAS ATWILL

SANTA FE

Sunstone books may be purchased for educational, business, or sales
promotional use. For information please write:
Special Markets Department, Sunstone Press,
P.O. Box 2321, Santa Fe, New Mexico 87504-2321.

Book design ▶ Vicki Ahl
Body typeface ▶ Book Antiqua
Printed on acid free paper

Library of Congress Cataloging-in-Publication Data

Atwill, Douglas.
 Imperial yellow : a novel / Douglas Atwill.
    p. cm.
 ISBN 978-0-86534-702-1 (pbk. : alk. paper)
 1. Orphans--Fiction. 2. Boys--Fiction. 3. Grandparent and child--Fiction.
 4. Grandmothers--Fiction. 5. Painters--Fiction. I. Title.
 PS3601.T85I44 2009
 813'.6--dc22

                                2009005430

WWW.SUNSTONEPRESS.COM
SUNSTONE PRESS / POST OFFICE BOX 2321 / SANTA FE, NM 87504-2321 /USA
(505) 988-4418 / ORDERS ONLY (800) 243-5644 / FAX (505) 988-1025

IMPERIAL YELLOW

Eucalyptus Grove
1970

*T*he telephone answering machine was blinking all morning, but I worked to ignore it as I painted the last touches of color and long black lines on the canvas clamped onto my easel, one of the twenty nearly finished paintings in my studio. I wondered what my old friend, Simon Grunewald, gone years now, would have thought of my current work, the layers of meaning I sought to include. I used the techniques that I, the watchful boy in his studio, saw him include in his canvases. Of course, he never painted objects, only ideas, but the practice was the same for any painting. A vermilion dash where one least expects it pulled the eye deeper into the composition and involved the viewer without asking his permission.

I still used the suggestions from another friend from my formative years, Latraviata Johns, a stately English painter with years of attentive work at the easel. She told me that surprise, mystery or an appealing darkness could lift a painting well out of the ordinary. I could summon her voice in my mind today, clipped and high with an imbedded amusement, when I mixed a shade of deep brownish-black or plum purple for that very purpose. *Darker, sweetness, or it will not work.*

The opening night for my solo exhibit was on Friday, two days away, so whatever I painted must be minor, small touches here and there. The show was virtually complete, related pieces for a local gallery at the prime midsummer slot. The gallery staff had sold most of the paintings already from photographs mailed out in advance to collectors. Much to the annoyance of the gallery people, I kept the canvases sequestered in my studio until the last minute, discovering a corner that could be improved on this one and a change of hue on that one.

Some of my artist friends believed that you are never actually finished with a canvas, that you merely stopped working on it. For me the pressures to give it up were mounting as the hours before the exhibit clicked away. All the pictures needed more work, a red line to delineate the edge of a table or a wash of muted yellow to mask over the too bright spot in an upper corner. After three hours of this fine tuning, I gave in to the blinking light.

The message was from my cousin Mary, at her office. "Give me a call, Donovan; important." Her name was on my list beside the phone with a private number in the brokerage office in downtown Los Angeles.

"Mary here," she answered.

"It's Donovan. You always sound so impressive and so corporate with your office voice. I hope the urgent news is that you are coming on Friday after all, as you ought."

"Not a chance, much as I want. Sunday night is a command performance for all of us in Laguna. Anna won't divulge the reason for our gathering, but I would come if I were you."

"Why now, in mid-summer? Anna always has the meetings in December."

"Something that won't wait."

"Okay. I'll book a flight for Saturday morning. It should arrive by mid-afternoon. You'll be missing some wonderful new paintings, my love, but I assure you, I wouldn't be there myself if I could."

"I hate to miss it, you know. I'll be waiting outside the arrivals gate. We can have the evening together and then I'll drive us down to Laguna on Sunday morning."

Anna was our grandmother, eighty-nine, who lived on her own in a eucalyptus grove above Laguna Beach; on her own except for Delores, her paid companion. The command performances were just that, required-attendance events that the invited miss at their peril. I doubted that my ideas were vital to the success of the family finances, but Anna sought them anyway.

I have made a living at painting for the last twenty years, and by comparison to some of my painter friends, a good living, but the comfortable extras of my life, a grand house, swimming pool, foreign automobiles with cloth tops, gardens and European trips would be scarce or nonexistent without Anna's check. I felt ill-at-ease with the family wealth and tried to keep the extent of it secret from my friends and fellow painters.

Anna dished out our family checks twice a year, the same way she served her family dinners, platters clustered closely in front of her while she spooned out portions to each of us, presumably based upon our current favor.

She fully approved of my being a painter, but worried about my money sense. "You especially, Donovan, need to plan ahead. Just because you're the handsome one of the Merrills, doesn't mean you don't need to budget."

Anna had survived two husbands and a lover. We, her grandchildren, were what remained of the family, her own four children now dead. Thirty years ago I became a close part of Anna's world when a series of events one summer changed the lives of the whole family.

Blue Puzzle
1938

The morning started like any other, with a midsummer fog pressing down on the waters of Balboa Bay. Donovan and his brothers, Gareth, older by three years and Whiting, younger by three, stood ankle deep in the shoreside waters in a row, eldest to youngest, waiting for the call from inside that would push them, yelling and laughing, into the chilly bay. Some Nordic ancestor had passed on the cold water gene, the one that made a sixty-one degree swim feel like a comfortable eighty-two, to surface in these boys thirty generations later.

"You first, Donovan," Gareth said, shoving him on the back of his shoulders. Donovan gave into the push and dived under the still, early morning waters, surfacing twenty feet from shore. With that the other two followed suit, but not with the skill of Donovan, by far the best swimmer in the family. He stayed ahead of his brothers as they swam out to the sailing boats, still unseen in the fog, moored in the middle of the bay. This was the ritual of their mornings, before their mother or Leonore, her helper, cooked breakfast and their father finally emerged late from the cottage bedroom, on vacation time.

Whiting yelled to Donovan, "Don't forget. We've got to be back by nine. Don't swim too far." Whiting was the brother who paid attention to deadlines and ultimatums, the one who felt order must be maintained, and who passed on instructions from on high.

They continued the swim out to the boats, a hundred yards away and just now becoming visible in the fog. The outlines of the summer cottages on shore disappeared behind them in the dome of pearlescent white.

Donovan stayed ahead of his brothers, stopping only to rest for a few seconds at the buoy holding the line for the first boat. When the other two had almost reached him, he was off again with splashes toward the silhouette of the next boat out in the bay. Their father, Jameson, had taught them that this was the easy way to swim across from Balboa Island to Newport on the other side, to divide and conquer. Breaking a long distance swim into a series of sprints appealed to the boys and they often did the whole sequence twice a day. Donovan could swim it on his own, against the express instructions of his parents.

"Let's go back, Donovan. We'll be late," called Whiting. But Donovan disappeared into the fog. Gareth and Whiting turned around for the swim back to shore. The whole family was expected at the marina in about thirty minutes, for the start of their sailing trip to Catalina Island. They would join the Honeycutt family, with their three daughters on the eighty-foot sloop *Honeytime* for the long day trip to Catalina. There were four cabins, one each for the parents and one each for the Merrill and Honeycutt offspring. The women cooked meals in the galley, sat in the sun on deck and the men and boys tended the lines, charts, sails and matters of navigation.

This trip had evolved into a tradition between the two families, with three previous summers to establish it. They sailed out against the wind and it was always a long day of tacking back and forth. The *Honeytime* would spend the night, or perhaps two nights if things went well, moored in Avalon Harbor, and then set out on a return trip, a fast-moving sail back to Balboa with the prevailing winds at their back. The round-trip to Catalina had become the highlight of the summer for both families.

Donovan continued his swim without his brothers from boat to boat in the fog. There was a rocky stretch of shore when he reached the Newport side, so he turned around and rested an extra long spell at the first buoy on the return. The heavily fogged morning swims were his favorite, the room of silence following him out and back. If he swam ahead of his brothers, this was the only time he was truly alone. Not in the constant company of brothers and family. Alone. Quiet. Happy.

At last, the Balboa Island shore appeared in the mist. He had drifted down-shore so must swim parallel to the island for a while to emerge at the same location. It was important always to depart and return at the same place, Donovan thought. He could see his father, dressed in white trousers, a blue shirt and red bandana kerchief, waiting on the beach with a towel.

"Donovan, you're in deep trouble. We're already almost an hour late for the Honeycutts and you know how important an early start is."

"I'm sorry, Dad."

"Here, dry off. Your mother has decided that you should

be punished by not going to Catalina. You can stay with Leonore at the cottage."

"Okay." It was not really a punishment for Donovan in his secret mind. The Honeycutt girls, each a foot taller than the corresponding Merrill boy, were impatient and ill-tempered, and *Honeytime* cabins smelled of cleaning fluid and damp. Since the trip was popular with everyone else, Donovan never talked about his own strong dislike to his family.

"And we've told Leonore that you cannot swim in the Bay or even go to the beach until we get back. That's four full days in the cottage."

Now that was a punishment. Leonore did not like him very much, but he could put up with that. No swimming in Balboa Bay was going to hurt. His mother had a keen sense of justice and she could concoct with sweet irony the perfect penalty when things went awry.

Donovan and his father walked back to the cottage where the rest of the family stood by the car, impatient to be on their way. Whiting looked very proud in his white trousers, blue shirt, and kerchief matching his father's outfit in diminished version. Gareth, already seated in the back, did not seem to care one way or another. His mother, without a word, shook an angry finger at him and stepped into the front seat.

With Donovan captured and no more to do, they were into off to the marina. Leonore stood on the cottage porch waiting for Donovan.

"In a pickle again, Donovan?" she said.

"I guess so."

"You make everybody late, you must pay. Come in and I'll cook your breakfast."

"Can we have pancakes today?"

"They would not be in the spirit of punishment. However, we do have a new jig-saw puzzle that your father brought down. A thousand pieces. Since you are forbidden to swim, we should finish it in two or three days." Leonore came from Germany, so she still used Old World words like "forbidden."

With that, his horrible days began. After a breakfast of scrambled eggs and orange juice Donovan went into the room he shared with his brothers. He had never just sat in his room, before. He was not going to like this. He tried to read for a while, but he lost interest and lay on his bed thinking.

Late in the morning, Leonore, after cleaning the cottage and washing the dishes, set up the puzzle on the breakfast table in the kitchen. It was a puzzle with the image of a Canton Blue and White platter, a circular scene of a country nobleman and his many concubines, standing or sitting around a many-roomed house and its porches, willow trees and fishponds in the foreground with sharp mountains and fluffy clouds behind. Since the whole puzzle was all the same blue color, it was going to be hard. Leonore turned the pieces to color side up.

Leonore asked him, "So why does it take so long over to Catalina and so quick to come back? I will never understand that." Leonore spoke perfect English, but she still pronounced her "Ws" like "Vs" and it always made Donovan smile.

"It's called tacking," he replied. "Back and forth at an angle when you go into the wind."

"Into the wind? However can you sail into the wind? Why do you laugh?"

"It's too complicated to explain. You're getting all the blue heads and hats in your pile. That's not right."

"And you've piled up all the clouds and flying birds. Stop complaining. I picked the heads first."

"Maybe we shouldn't pick anything and hoard it. That's the way Gareth plays."

"It's the right way. Gareth is right."

They worked all morning to delineate the outside border of the plate, a repetition of small waves with fishes. After stopping for lunch, Donovan went to his room for a nap. The pattern of their days was now set: a few hours with the puzzle, a meal, and a nap, then more hours with the puzzle and another meal. The center of the puzzle went slowly, even with each of them hoarding a pile of like-patterned pieces.

At night when the light was not good for puzzles, Leonore read out loud. A couple of months without the radio was good for the boys, Donovan's mother had said, making them pay attention to books more, to what mattered in the world. Donovan liked to hear Leonore read as she sat in an amorphous chair with a heavily ruffled slipcover of brownish roses and faded stems. A floor lamp with a yellowed parchment shade cast a cone of warm light around Leonore. She read well, with a change of voice for the different characters even though they all sounded somewhat German. She always skipped through much of the long wordy parts without dialog.

Leonore was a very thin woman, with closely cut dark hair. Donovan thought she did not really look at all like a woman, almost like a slim man dressed up as a woman. She wore pale dresses without sleeves in a faint pattern of flowers, the fabric washed almost to oblivion. Donovan felt her ribs and backbone when he had to hug her before going to bed and she smelled slightly of vinegar.

But her voice was soft and the story compelling, so Donovan always liked the hours before bedtime when she read. His mother had chosen a pile of books at the library before they left Pasadena, a special vacation arrangement from the downtown branch. Dickens was everybody's favorite. Leonore had read Tale of Two Cities twice in their years at the cottage. Hawthorne and Melville put everybody to sleep, so they were vetoed, and they had all read Mark Twain in school. That night Leonore started an Agatha Christie murder mystery. Donovan's mother disapproved of children's books like the Hardy Boys or Nancy Drew, but English mysteries and Mary Roberts Rinehart were allowed.

On their third night alone together, Leonore was reading the part about the arrival of an anonymous hate letter, pasted together from magazine headlines. Leonore could imitate Miss Marple's voice with an English accent, so that Donovan pictured the old woman's thin lips pouring out righteous outrage. The High Street in St. Mary Mead must have been a dangerous place.

There was a knock at the door. It startled Donovan. Leonore put down the book and went to the door.

It was Donovan's grandfather McBeale and his son Eugene, Jr. They never had come down to Balboa Island before, so why now in the evening after it was dark?

Grandfather McBeale said, "We did not know who we would find here. Why are you here and not on the boat?"

"It was decided that Donovan stay here as a punishment," Leonore replied. She switched on another light.

"Donovan, sit down, because we have bad news," his grandfather said. He leaned over and put his hand up to his eyes. He wiped his eyes on a handkerchief and blew his nose. Donovan wondered what could be so bad that his grandfather, a man, would cry tears.

"The *Honeytime* never arrived at Avalon Bay. Since they filed a mooring permit by phone last week, the harbormaster called me this afternoon. It was important to follow up on no-shows, he said."

"What does this mean? Have they gone somewhere else?" Leonore asked.

"We don't think so."

Eugene, Jr. spoke up. "The harbormaster said that there were late afternoon squalls off Catalina on the day they were supposed to arrive. The day was clear before that, but apparently your family and the Honeycutts got a late start. They ran right into the storm when they should have already been in the harbor. He told us that the *Honeytime* must have capsized with all aboard. The Coast Guard has given up the search."

Leonore lowered her glasses and looked strongly at Donovan, who did not understand what had happened.

He said, "But we went through a storm last year and it wasn't all that bad. We got to wear those yellow slickers and lower the sails."

Eugene, Jr. said, "It could have been a rogue wave in the middle of the squall. A wave like that can turn a boat upside down and sink it in a matter of seconds."

Grandfather McBeale, who had stopped crying, took off his glasses and wiped them, said, "I always told Jameson that it was too dangerous to sail in the channel with the whole family, but he wouldn't listen. We'll wait to see if there's any more news, but I think that they were all lost at sea."

Donovan looked over at Leonore and she watched him with her glasses down on her nose. Did that mean she thought he was to blame because he made them all late? He could not return her gaze, so lowered his eyes to the floor. How could a storm be his fault?

"Let's get some sleep and tomorrow we'll drive you back to Pasadena. Is their car at the marina?" Eugene, Jr., said.

Donovan nodded.

"We'll go by there on the way back and I can jump the starter." He and Grandfather McBeale went into the parents' bedroom to lie down.

Donovan walked slowly to the bedroom he had shared with his brothers. A bunk bed for him and Whiting, and a single one for Gareth. It could not be possible that his long swim had caused all their deaths as Leonore seemed to believe. She always said he was to blame for everything.

Thoughts of treading water between giant waves and the faces of his brothers swirled around as he fell asleep. He dreamed that they were on a slow carousel twirling around deep into blue waters, all his family and the Honeycutt girls holding on to painted horses as it circled down, rotating a grim path until it was too black so see. A long corkscrew of bubbles followed up to the surface.

Bosom of the Family

The trip to Pasadena the next day took three hours with Grandfather McBeale, Leonore and Donovan in one car and Eugene, Jr. following behind in the cross-wired family sedan with all the family's belongings.

The three of them in the front car rode most of the way in silence, but Donovan's head was full of noisy scenarios. What if Leonore told everybody that Donovan had killed his family? What if the police came to investigate and he would have to lie about it? Donovan knew that so far Grandfather McBeale did not know of Leonore's suspicions about who should be blamed. Maybe she would not talk.

Leonore asked, "What will happen now?"

"There will be an investigation, I am sure. Maybe some other boat saw them, saw the accident. We will have a service at the church where Donovan's other grandfather is pastor."

"What about Donovan?"

"The family will meet and decide. Too soon to say."

Leonore turned to Donovan in the back seat. He was looking down at his hands in his lap, motionless.

Grandfather McBeale drove to the north side of Pasadena, where the residents ignored their front yards and the houses needed paint. He stopped the car in front of Leonore's white stucco apartment house, an overgrown pair of arborvitae crowding each door. She turned around in the car to look at Donovan again in the back seat and said, "Donovan, here's the book we were reading. You'll have to finish it on your own. And the blue puzzle. Take care, *liebchen*. I will come by to see you when you get settled. It was not your fault, the weather." She handed the book and the puzzle box over to him and walked all the way to her door before she turned around to wave as they drove off.

Donovan suddenly felt cold; he knew that Leonore was the last member of his family, even if she was only a hired member, and now she was gone, too. He was alone. He had often thought about being alone when he swam the waters of the bay, his brothers taunting him. It was different, somehow empty and unrewarding, now that they were really gone. He felt guilty about thinking such thoughts.

Grandfather McBeale drove them by the Merrill house on Madison Avenue, the house where they all lived before the Balboa Island vacation. Donovan's mother purchased the house with an inheritance from her Cousin Jennie: three thousand dollars. Grandfather had a key and opened the front door. The house smelled musty, forgotten, with a hint of the bacon that Leonore cooked weeks ago on their last breakfast before Balboa. It was already lifeless, as if abandoned a decade before.

"Donovan, please go up and pack up some of your clothes in this suitcase. You are coming to our house for a while. Don't take too long," Grandfather McBeale said.

Donovan put some shirts, trousers, another pair of shoes and his two favorite books into the one piece of luggage that his grandfather gave him. As he turned to go, he remembered to go back for his crystal radio and headphones, for nights when he could not sleep.

He looked around the house and asked his grandfather, "What will happen to our house? Can't I just live here? I know how to lock all the doors and how to jiggle the water heater when it doesn't work. I always walk to school by myself, anyway."

"You're too young to be on your own, Donovan."

"But what will happen to our house?"

"I expect we'll sell it and put the proceeds into an annuity for you, until you come of age. Eugene, Jr. will handle all that since he works for an insurance company."

"When do I come of age?"

"When you are twenty-one."

"Can't I decide what to do? I'm tall for nine years." Donovan tended to stoop a bit, so others did not think of him as tall.

"I'm sorry, no. You're much too young to make such decisions, and besides the courts would not allow it. Come along, son."

At the McBeale house on the other side of town, Grandmother McBeale had been crying, her eyes swollen so much that she had taken off her glasses. She looked strange, different without her glasses. She hugged Donovan, but she did not want to talk, so Donovan was sent straight upstairs to the spare room.

He had always liked staying in the spare room with its high, four-poster bed and sheets with the smell of lavender. But this time it was different. The room seemed chilly, the bed too high, uncomfortable and the curtains now kept out the warm light.

Each of his brothers and the McBeale cousins customarily had a few days every year with their grandparents, equality of treatment being important in the family. Grandmother McBeale kept a list on the back of the pantry door with each name and the date and length of the last visit.

The McBeales had arrived in California with money from generations of lumber enterprise. While other families prospered in the balmy air, the McBeales were running out of money from bad deals and family members who dipped into the till. Some got more than others; Grandfather McBeale had watched while his brothers and sisters depleted the family resources. Donovan only heard the whispers of the troubles at family dinners.

After he sat on the bed for a while, Donovan heard voices downstairs. He tip-toed to the top of the stairs where he could not be seen and listened.

It was Eugene, Jr. talking. "We can't take him, you know, Papa. We've just built the house with a room for each of the children, and I can't ask them to share."

Grandfather McBeale said, "I know, Eugene, but we're notably crowded here, too."

"You've got the spare room. He could stay there."

Grandmother McBeale, who had recovered from her spasm of tears, said, "We can't have him staying here for the next ten years. My family from Minnesota visit California every winter and they would have nowhere else to stay. It's just impossible."

Grandfather McBeale said, "I can never forgive Jameson

for what he did to our daughter and the boys. And now he's put his orphan on us. Just when we are finally settled again."

Donovan did not want to listen anymore. He returned to the spare room and climbed up on the bed, trying not to think about being an orphan. What exactly was an orphan? He started to read the Agatha Christie book, but it wasn't the same without Leonore's accent for Miss Marple. His heart was not in it and he soon dozed off.

He woke when the doorbell downstairs rang. Hearing voices again, he crept back to the top of the stairs. At first the conversation was muffled, then he recognized his Grandmother Merrill's voice. They were talking about the accident.

She said, "Is Donovan here with you?"

"Yes, but he can't stay for very long. You know how it is," Grandmother McBeale said.

"May, I don't know at all how it is. What a ludicrous thing to say. There will always be room for a grandchild with us. He will stay until he's ready to go to college, or as long as he wants."

Grandfather McBeale said, "Anna, that is a kind offer. Of course, you must look after Donovan. You've solved our problem."

"Ask Donovan to pack his things," she said.

Grandfather McBeale said, "First, I have to say something, Anna, to get if off my chest. It's been eating away at me all day. I cannot forgive your son or his memory for endangering his whole family and our beloved daughter. It was reckless to go sailing with them all. Something bad was eventually bound to happen."

Grandmother Merrill said, "What a thing to say. Unhappiness lurks out there for everyone, Eugene, like a storm on the horizon. We've lost our beloved son. Our firstborn, Jameson, and our firstborn grandson, Gareth. The pride of two generations is at the bottom of the sea."

"But Jameson was the cause of it all. Had he acted differently, more prudently, they would all be alive."

"You will not put this misfortune on Jameson's dead shoulders, Eugene. To blame someone for God's will is unkind and foolish. I'm beginning to believe you have always been both."

Donovan remembered the families in Dickens who were cast out onto the wet streets of London, nowhere warm and dry to go. He wondered if when it was discovered that his long swim was the cause, would he have a place to stay with either his Grandmother Merrill or the McBeales? Was this a secret he would have to carry inside forever?

"Donovan, please come down here," his grandfather called up the stairs. Donovan slowly descended, stopping a few steps from the bottom.

Grandmother Merrill said, "Hello, Donovan, my dear. You've grown so much taller. You will be coming to live with me and your Grandfather Merrill. Please pack up your belongings and take them right out to the automobile."

He ran back up the stairs and packed in a few minutes. He smoothed out the nap wrinkles and plumped the pillows. Grandmother McBeale required the grandchildren to plump the pillows and leave the bed with a smooth spread for the next grandchild's visit. They were all standing at the bottom of the stairs as he came down. Grandmother Merrill had not taken off her long coat or her large hat with black feathers; she stood with her purse between two hands.

Grandfather McBeale said, "Let's not make this a thing between us, Anna. Donovan is welcome in both our houses, as you know."

"But not for so very long in the new McBeale house, it would appear," she said.

Grandfather McBeale said, "We'll come visit you often, Donovan." Grandmother McBeale started to cry again and took off her glasses. Donovan could feel the sharpness of her garnet brooch on his cheek as she hugged him, and Grandfather McBeale shook his hand gravely.

Jacaranda Blossoms

Donovan lifted his suitcase and the puzzle box into the trunk. Grandmother Merrill's automobile was a grey sedan with four doors, seats with a prickly fabric and a chrome sailing ship as an ornament for the hood. She sat behind the wheel as one on uneasy terms with machinery, her back erect, and motioned for him to take the seat beside her. She started the car and let it idle for a while.

"Donovan, don't let Eugene make you feel unwanted. He can be a pig sometimes, but May is blameless, just a helpless captive. I love you very much."

"Thank you, grandmother."

"'Grandmother' makes me sound as if I were high on a granite column. You must call me Anna from now on. Gareth and Whiting will stay innocent in our memories, as we grow older. It was not your fault, you know."

"Thank you, Anna." He did not know any other boys his age who called their grandmother by her first name.

She drove down the long avenue lined with palm trees, so tall that Donovan could see only the reticulated trunks passing by. She drove slowly, with gloved hands firmly on the wheel. She looked straight ahead, even when she talked to Donovan. Anna and the automobile were not friends, but they had made a necessary, tenuous relationship.

"Li Fong is cleaning the detritus from the sewing room for you at the rectory. It is a small, but sunny room. I always hated sewing, Donovan, because my mother told me I would never get married without mastering the hemstitch. Now your coming has released me. Be careful for fallen pins and needles, since I must have dropped a couple of hundred there over the years."

"Okay."

"I prefer 'yes, Anna' to 'Okay.'"

"Yes, Anna."

"Thank you, that sounds better. There is a good elementary school walking distance from the rectory. John James Audubon Elementary School. As I remember, the principal is a pompous twit, but you won't have to see him often. We will enroll you as soon as possible."

"Yes, Anna."

They came to an intersection, where Anna lowered her window with the chrome crank and put her arm out signaling a left turn. She was still looking straight ahead, and Donovan knew she did not see a van approaching quickly from the right.

"Watch out, Anna."

She braked sharply to avoid a collision. He hoped she was not upset by his calling out.

"Why does a bread truck travel so fast? You were right to warn me. As a girl, I always understood horses better than cars." Donovan also thought she seemed to know what he was thinking. They continued their very slow pace down the road, faster cars honking as they overtook and passed them.

One man shook a fist at them as he went by; Anna shook back her gloved version. As they proceeded majestically to San Miguel, a town adjoining Pasadena to the south, Anna looked neither left nor right, slowly rocking the steering wheel back and forth to correct their path forward.

The palm trees turned into orange groves, dense and shiny green. The ground between the trees had been freshly turned and it smelled of warmth and fertility. It was mid-afternoon and thunderclouds had built up over the San Gabriel Mountains that ringed the north side of the valley. At last, they reached their turn-off. The brown sign with carved golden letters announced Church of the Holy Spirit, The Right Rev. James Dark Merrill, DD. A graveled drive with large pepper trees on each side led a thousand feet back from the road, revealing the yellow stucco and grey stone church.

The rectory hid behind hedges and tall shrubs, and Anna parked the car at a sharp angle in the driveway. A low building with brown shingles, it had a pitched roof with heavy, overhanging timbers. Several high-back bamboo chairs sat in the shade of the porch, green pots of succulents and cacti crowded on the floor. The house looked dark and cool inside.

"Come in, dear," she said, opening the door so Donovan could pass with his outsized suitcase, the puzzle pieces making a jiggling sound as he walked. They went through the sitting room, which smelled of citrus oil and dusty fabric, and down a hallway to the sewing room. The daybed was parallel to the wall, with Anna's table for sewing up against the windows.

Anna left him to unpack in the veneer cherry chifforobe. At one side of the wardrobe hung Anna's mandarin robes that she sometimes wore for family dinners, floor length silk robes embroidered with dragons. He felt the thick brocade and remembered when Grandfather Merrill said how good Anna looked in the robes, so straight-backed that she was almost Chinese herself.

Donovan finished moving in, putting his books and radio in a drawer of the bedside table. Then he walked down the hall, pausing at the kitchen door.

Anna saw him and said, "Do you remember meeting Li Fong? She is to a kitchen what Einstein is to time."

"Hello, Li Fong." Donovan shook her hand with a firm grip, a lesson from his father. Li Fong did not look at him. Her hand was cold and moist and limp. He wondered if Chinese people were not taught to make a proper handclasp; or did Li Fong dislike his intrusion into the rectory?

Anna said, "Li Fong is teaching me Chinese. I know the words for vegetables and kitchen utensils." She held up a long-handled spoon. "Did you know that this is a *shaozi*? She hasn't yet told me the important words, though, for things like revolution, explosion or women's suffrage, but she will. If you want to spend some time in the kitchen, she will teach you too."

"Thank you, but can I go outside now?"

"*May* I go outside now."

"Please?" Anna nodded and beckoned him away. He walked out of the kitchen and through the front door. Several gardens surrounded the rectory, a kitchen garden for Anna, with herbs and vegetables, and a larger flower garden that the cook's husband, Ah Fong, tended. He could hear Ah Fong clipping the inside of the tall hedge as he walked around past Anna's angled car and down the drive.

The church cemetery adjoined the church, through rusticated stone columns and a pair of iron gates with the date 1874. A sign announced that the cemetery was open only during the day. Donovan walked quickly past the cottage where the sexton lived.

But at that moment the door flew open and the sexton called out, "Young man, come back here."

Donovan retraced his steps. The sexton was a fat man with thinning brown hair; he wore a white shirt buttoned at the collar without a tie, black armbands midway up both his sleeves. Donovan knew he could outrun him if he had to, but waited for what he would say.

"This is a private cemetery, not a play ground."

"I know. My grandfather is the pastor here."

"So you are one of Dr. Merrill's grandsons? Are your brothers the ones that drowned? We read about it in the newspaper."

"Yes sir."

"Well, the Merrill plot is on the left just ahead and we'll bury them there when they're found."

"They haven't been found."

"They will be, unless the sharks eat them. My name is Mr. Erasmus. You can go in this time, but head right to your family plot and don't walk around. You must always knock at my door and ask me when you want to go into my cemetery."

"I thought it was my grandfather's cemetery."

"No, it is my cemetery. Church and burying-ground are

separate and independent. I am the sexton and the director here. You must ask my permission. By my reckoning, young boys and gravestones don't belong together. So, even though you are Dr. Merrill's grandson, don't come back very often."

"I will ask Grandfather."

"Do as you please. Dr. Merrill is a saint in my books, and I doubt very much he will take the side of a snotty young boy."

Donovan walked on down the avenue, pleased to be away from Mr. Erasmus, who smelled of liquor. The cemetery was large, covered with trees, shrub roses and stone monuments. He passed a red granite Greek temple with the name Jarman and a large black obelisk engraved with the name Pilson. A round-topped stone was engraved with the name Wallwood and underneath in italics, *Far Better Now*.

The avenue was lined with jacaranda trees in bloom, the violet-colored blossoms fallen to the ground along the avenue, over the mausoleums and all across the Merrill plot. It was a small, twenty by twenty plot with no monuments, only stone markers flat with the ground. There was a Theodore Merrill, aged 2, a Helena Merrill, aged 1, and on a single stone, a Henry Harrison Merrill aged 95 and his beloved wife, Cora aged 90, *Together in Paradise*. Donovan did not know who any of them were.

He walked farther along the avenue where his mother one Sunday had shown him the McBeale section. It had a white marble plinth with a large hand pointing to heaven. The four sides were engraved with a repeating frieze of *McBeale - McBeale - McBeale*. This was a larger plot than the Merrill plot, and he found a stone for Jacob, one for Robert (Roby) McBeale and a curving headstone for Agnes McBeale.

Donovan's mother told him last year that, "If the Merrill

plot is full, you can always go to sleep with the McBeale's over here. It's the law in California. Remember that. There's plenty of room over here." He wondered at the time how he was supposed speak up for himself if he was dead.

He would come back to explore farther into the cemetery, he thought, but now Anna might be wondering where he was. He ran back past Mr. Erasmus's cottage without stopping and around the bend to the rectory.

Ah Fong was standing in the driveway, clipping the outside of the eugenia hedge. He saw Donovan and stopped. "You are Donovan? Very sorry for your family. So sad."

Donovan said, "Thank you." He did not feel sad. He did not feel anything. Donovan wondered if he should feel more strongly the loss of his brothers. Was he a bad brother for not crying more?

"I am Ah Fong."

"I remember. You take care of the garden here?"

"Twenty years now." He was tall with narrow shoulders, and he wore blue cotton pants with a matching blue overshirt. The lenses on his glasses were perfectly round and thick.

Donovan said, "Can I help you sometime? I like to work in the garden. I know how to prune roses. I used to mow the lawn for my parents in Pasadena, but I didn't like raking it up."

"I mow and I prune at the Merrill rectory. It would be wrong to ask a young boy to do my work. Good gardening is very serious."

"Okay. Yes, Ah Fong." He remembered Anna's correction.

"But you can watch. I mow tomorrow morning and you can sit on the porch and teach me better English."

"But you already know English."

"Better English."

Donovan walked back through the garden to the house. Anna was sitting in one of the bamboo chairs on the porch, reading. "Have you found your moorings?"

"Yes. I'm going to teach Ah Fong English tomorrow. Better English. I like him more than Mr. Erasmus. "

"You mustn't mind Mr. Erasmus. He has never had time for boys. Cemetery work is very serious."

Donovan wondered if everything was serious at the rectory. "He said it was his cemetery and I mustn't come too often."

"So it is, even though we have the full right to be buried there. Did you go by the Merrill plot?"

"Yes. I didn't recognize any of the family names."

"The two infants were your father's brother and sister. They were never strong and passed over one winter when we had storms, the same year that your great grandfather and mother died. Spanish flu got them all."

"Mother said one time that there's plenty of room in the McBeale plot if the Merrill plot is filled."

"Such grim choices. Come talk to me while I cook your grandfather's dinner." She got up and went into the kitchen.

"I thought Li Fong cooked the dinner," Donovan said as he followed her.

"No, I always cook the evening meal. Li Fong takes care of us the rest of the day, and then she goes home to her own family at night. Besides, I keep my best recipes secret. All of China might know about my beaten biscuits." Donovan watched as she whipped a bowl of eggs with a long fork.

Lilies that Fester
1970

*I*could trace my delight in houses and towns that were crumbling, in disrepair, paintless, shutters angling from the windows to my boyhood in the 1930s Pasadena. Eastern moneyed families, deprived of their extra, discretionary resources, abandoned their California winter houses to the fates. Gardens became overgrown, summer houses and pavilions were choked by ornamental vines, and the main houses grew steadily more decrepit.

Dozens of mansions along Orange Grove and Oak Knoll were left forgotten, front gates locked, an open invitation to a curious juvenile. A mere few were maintained in prime condition, Japanese gardeners trimming the hedges around full swimming pools, rose bushes dead-headed and lawns seeded and mown, as if the owners were arriving on the next train. The unhappiness of the outside world, the Dust Bowl, the Depression and bread lines ceased to exist on these manicured grounds.

It was irresistible for exploratory young boys. To slip over a wall encrusted with fig vine and swim a few laps in the green-tiled pool before the gardeners with pith helmets chased them out, brandishing hedge clippers over their heads, chopping, chopping, chopping was a delicious excitement. I could run faster than the old Japanese men, who seemed to savor the unsuccessful chase, looking forward to the next sessions. The houses were an easy access, elegant locks on the French doors now giving up their tenacity to young fingers. Empty ballrooms looked out on leaf clogged terraces, water stains enlarging on the plastered walls, the faux bamboo chairs in gilded stacks and the silk draperies rotting in the California sun.

It was a sweet paradox to grow up in a place that was rotting and falling down, but it offered an adventure for me and my brothers to clamber over walls into forgotten gardens and creep along the disintegrating loggias.

I chose the Beaux Arts in 1950 Paris for my art school just because it appeared decrepit and old-fashioned, the official catalog cover with a photograph of its water-stained entrance foyer. Anna encouraged me, never questioning the appropriateness of my choice. Simon was still alive then, working doggedly at his modernist canvases in the Laguna studio.

"What do you think of the Beaux Arts?" I asked him as he worked, as ever sitting before the easel with a long brush.

"It was stodgy and academic when I went to school in Berlin. The faculty had no truck with modernism, and even their own Impressionists were viewed with suspicion. Of course, the French, quick to change sides, are very proud now of their turn-of-the-century artists."

"What would I learn there?"

"Classical technique, life drawing, and plaster casts. You

know much of that already, Donovan. Art Students League in New York would be a better choice."

"I like the idea of Paris and Anna does, too. New York scares me, but not Europe."

"You will become an artist wherever you go, son. We have already talked about that."

"I know. I just wanted to get your take on it."

"Why don't you just start painting here in Laguna? At one of the studios here?"

"You always say that."

"I mean it. Close the studio door. That's the first rule."

"I'll think about it, Simon."

I did not take Simon's advice and I took little other advice either. That would be the last time I was with Simon, who died during my years in Europe. Anna asked me not to come back for the funeral. There would be a time for a private ceremony later.

Curriculum in Paris was strictly traditional. Life drawing was mandatory, the techniques of painting were taught in all their variety. An old professor still knew the secrets to grinding pigments from minerals and melding them into thin oils, his course mandatory. I never felt there was enough studio time, the few easels at the school in constant demand for the more promising graduate students. To earn a diploma, students were asked for three full years of work, but foreigners, who were generally dismissed as unimportant in the future of French art, could earn a *diplome de l'etrangére* in two. Before graduation day, Anna kindly wrote to ask if a Provençal summer or a sojourn in Rome would serve as a polish for my studies.

I took her up on her suggestions, doing both in succession

with the check she sent in response. I painted a few dozen canvases in the countryside around Grasse, leasing a Cushman motor scooter for the summer and heading out each morning before sunrise. The room I rented from Madame Duplessix above the market included a breakfast and a simple night meal. Madame was full of solicitude during the start of the summer, sweet almond cakes and a glass of Cassis at bedside every night.

"Bon jour, my young painter," she said one morning, "you will be very famous one day, I know. There will be a *plaque historique* by my front door." She had spent extra time on her hair and the room filled with a perfume of flowers.

"I hope so, Madame. I hope so."

"Come, I have fresh figs and *café au lait* downstairs. On the terrace."

"Oh, I told Gerard I would have breakfast with him."

"Gerard? That Corsican waiter next door?"

"Yes. We've become friends."

"He has the bad reputation, and he is a Corsican, *n'est-pas?*"

"We have a good time, laugh a lot."

"Happily, the fig season is long." Madame seemed to have plans that did not match my own. She closed the door with a bit more gusto than before.

Gerard and I spent all our spare time together, swimming in the sea, hiking along the corniche and exploring the inland hills for private picnic sites. He was short and dark, exuding a sultry, peasant musk as he held onto my waist on the back of the Cushman.

At the end of August, Madame felt my impending

departure was good riddance, that I should be happier with my own kind, where I do not disappoint those who care. The Cassis and cakes ceased to appear on the night table. Gerard promised to visit me in Rome and I wondered if I ought to stay on in that yellow-ochre paradise, everything perfect save Madame's disapproval.

After a last swim with Gerard on the pebbled beach, we lunched across from the train station. He said, "You should stay here with me. There is a larger room upstairs at my hotel, large enough for you to paint."

"I would like that, but I've already booked for Rome."

"You will not find a body like mine among the Romans."

"I know, Gerard."

"I make you happy, no?"

"Very happy and I will miss you."

"Then, stay."

It was a game with Gerard to win at everything. He always swam farther out and hiked higher up the hill. If I stayed, a more attractive American would catch his eye. It was better to go before that happened.

I took the train to Rome and found, by asking at an early morning café, a full artist's studio for rent behind the Pantheon, four floors up and without hot water. It was curiously dark for a studio since the large window faced the side wall of the monument, dark gray with lichen and bird nests, perfect light for a series of *grisaille*, Piranesi-like renderings of Rome's antiquities.

There was a centuries-old art supply store in the nearby Piazza Riboli, a single room paneled in pear-wood with the selections cached away behind cupboard doors or in one of the many drawers. An attached ladder on wheels gave access to the items near the ceiling. Customers were not allowed to browse but must present the Signore with an exact written list, items which he then fetched with maddening languor. It took me several weeks to amass enough Italian to actually buy the supplies, because Signore was heartless with misspellings. Slowly I learned the right words for a Bright No. 3 Bristle Brush and a tube of cadmium yellow, *per favore*.

I loved my occluded Roman studio with its underwater, pearlescent light. Gerard came to stay for the planned week in November, just as the rains started. He hated Rome from the outset, asked me to come back to the crystal ambience of Grasse. From the first day he disapproved of the food, the wine, the people, the smell, the unFrenchness of it all.

"What can you expect from a country with nine governments in two months?" he said, as he combed his shiny hair in my small lavatory mirror.

"I think they are just finding their way. The war was hard on Rome and, for that matter, France is not exactly a sea of stability now."

"The war was hard on everybody, but the French accept setbacks with more style. We do not whine like Italians."

"Maybe we should just relax and enjoy ourselves. Get dressed and we'll go down to the *circolo* for supper."

"I can't bathe. The water here does not get hot." He crossed his arms.

"We can heat some up on the gas ring. I can wash your back with the sponge and clean those fetching armpits."

He would not be placated. "The Romans smell bad every time we go out."

"And the French don't?"

It was obviously not going well. He returned to Grasse two days early, still unbathed, and both of us unfulfilled. Rome that winter was inundated with rain, relieved by the rare day of sun. When it did peek out, the Romans nearby set tables and chairs up on the street, while I rushed out to do sketches of the Pantheon and the city views down the adjoining streets. Neighbors claimed that this was most unusual, a sunny Roman winter could usually be counted upon, my chest cold would disappear before Easter.

As January turned into February, I became homesick for the warmth of California, Anna and my hillside home in Laguna, which in my mind was a fabled paradise of gold. The Italian Line took me from Genoa to Manhattan; then a five day train trip across the long stretches of Mid-America and I was home.

I should have been overjoyed to be back. It did not seem right, however, with Anna busy with her properties and everybody else was too occupied to discuss at length the wonders of Europe, the art I had seen there, to listen to the many artistic expressions in other languages that I learned there. The Korean War was in full tilt and men my age were wanted for the front lines. I had no wish to become a soldier, but there was no alternative for a man not officially continuing his school days. If you left university, you must expect to be drafted into the Army within months.

As I seriously considered an enlistment in the navy to avoid the man-eating machine of the front-line infantry, one of my lungs collapsed. The dampness of Rome had lingered, bringing on pneumonia and a month in the hospital. None of the services wanted a man with a weakness in the chest.

Convalescence took a full half-year, Anna looking after every comfort and convincing me that patience was the only road in bronchial affairs. In a way, the military had appeared to be an answer of sorts, a place I might find my compass.

Anna's investments had grown under her nurture; she established a generous allowance for each of her grandchildren, a monthly check she wrote out herself in her beautiful handwriting. She filled in the amount exactly: Three hundred dollars and no cents. It was obvious by now that she could not give me the answers I needed, busy with her hillside matters. Laguna did not want me, Korea did not want me, and I did not want any more of Paris or Rome.

I bought a car and headed east, ultimately destined for the ferment of New York, a studio above a warehouse in an artistic quarter. If the art world was there, I wanted to be a part of it even if the city did scare me.

"Anna, I want to go to New York," I told her one night after dinner. We were seated on the west-facing porch watching the sunset over the water, having small cups of Mexican coffee.

"To do what?" she asked.

"To carry on with my painting. It's too comfortable here, too much like a hothouse."

"It may be a myth that art grows large in adversity."

"Laguna is too easy for me. You deserve it, but I think I need to try somewhere else."

"I know you need to tilt with the world. I will miss you. You are my North Star."

"I will miss you, too. But you understand, don't you?"

She put her warm hand over on mine and patted it slowly.

A week later, I headed out across the desert, the car packed with clothes and supplies. I drove through the day to the Grand Canyon and spent the night at the large, rim-side hotel built of dark-brown logs.

A few days later I arrived in Santa Fe, a pinon-incensed town against the mountains. It was like a stop on the Silk Road, a forgotten village in the Himalayan foothills, where refugees from the urban world hid away. On the first night I met a crowd of artists at the main hotel, the bar thick with smoke and talk of why the bohemian life mattered. That was 1956 and Canyon Road was a dirt trail for burros, the few galleries showed local work around the Plaza.

Alex, a tall, graceful man with the white mustache said, "If New York calls, you must answer. But why not try it here for a while?"

"How long have you been here?" I asked.

"Since the war. The family wanted me out of Philadelphia. My mother said she could not bear to look at me anymore. A few meetings with the family attorney and I can live a life here without worry, if not one of Lucullan ease. I've bought some houses as they become available and I rent them to my friends."

"I take it that you have one available?"

"Smart boy. You'll go far."

I rented his house by the month, because I did not want to feel ensnared in a long lease, New York beckoning. That first adobe cottage had three rooms, one of which was a studio with a high ceiling and a window facing east. I think now that the morning light over the mountains, clear and filled with promise, was what trapped me. A new painting every day, the absolution of sins.

Except for the occasional visit, I did not go on to New York. It does not now seem possible or logical that I have spent the last fourteen years in Santa Fe. At first working in a gallery, then painting in the mornings and working at odd jobs in the afternoons and then, at last, without much to-do and with no proper announcement, I plunged into the role of becoming a full-time painter. A creeping evolution into art rather than a revolution with fireworks and banners.

I know now that it was a valuable and necessary terrace, another level to be mastered before going on to the next. I met the other painters in town, attended parties throughout the year and painted every day, long mornings of intense activity and a few desultory hours in the afternoons.

I exhibited work in the same gallery as Carole Francis, then a fledgling painter. Her work was popular with collectors, she having two exhibits each year. Her pictures were colorful and accessible, loosely painted landscapes of the Hispanic farms and fields of Northern New Mexico. I knew better than to tell her, but she reminded me of a younger version of Anna, her long light hair often coiled up with combs. She was tall and patrician, her movements graceful without pretense, a personal style unique among the other painters in town.

My own paintings took more time to be appreciated and the first exhibits went by without a single sale. I invited Carole out for a dinner to celebrate my sale of a small painting. After we were seated in the dining room with checkered table clothes and the ubiquitous Chianti bottles with candles, I said, "Is it bad luck to celebrate a sale?"

"Not at all, Donovan. But more to celebrate the fact that you do not seem to be falling off the path so often."

"You mean I'm becoming a painter?"

"Becoming the person who will become the painter. I think it's a longer process than anyone knows."

Fondue was the specialty of that restaurant, so we dipped our chunks into the bubbling cheese. I said, "But you're already there. You are a painter."

"I think so. When you realize that you can make a living painting, something you love to do, and the guilt subsides at being so lucky, you're there. You do not have to worry about sales, who will like your work, you are just concerned with getting it right."

"I do worry about sales and, also, whether or not people will consider my work serious, important enough to collect. I want to make sales. It's on my mind as I paint."

"When that departs, you're there. Let me have that cube of Parma ham."

Like a small mountain spring at its source, a trickle of my confidence began, growing bolder as it cascaded. There were only one or two sales a month to start, then five a month, and during the next summer, a dozen paintings disappeared in one week. The following year collectors returned to buy a second and third painting, and Anna's check often stayed unopened on the desk for a week after its arrival.

I did, as Carole foretold, stop the worry about sales. The time at the easel was spent thinking about the exact color for that shadow, the dynamics of composition and did the painting please me.

Living became comfortable in Santa Fe with its curious attraction for painters, writers, and malcontents of all waters. Anna visited me once, taking the train from Pasadena to Lamy.

At the time I was renting a larger house from Alex, one with a studio, a proper guest room and an overgrown garden alongside the gurgling waters of the Acequia Madre. My painter friends loved meeting Anna, who captured them with stories of Laguna in its hey-day, painters frolicking along the beaches in the warm winter fogs.

She pulled me aside during one party to tell me how much she approved of Carole and was there any hope that we would get together.

"I doubt it, Anna," I answered.

"My spouses made me as unhappy as they did happy. I can't honestly advocate marriage for anybody else."

"Carole is my best friend, and always will be."

Anna said, "She might be sad to those exact words."

I explained that we were as together as much as we would ever be, why nothing of a committed nature was possible. Anna took it all well, no pressures for me to continue the Merrill dynasty, to make babies for long summer visits to her hillside. She did not come again to Santa Fe, and now she seldom leaves Laguna at all.

Under the Pepper Tree
1938

Grandfather Merrill, The Pastor of Church of the Holy Spirit, was a distant figure for Donovan, as unapproachable as God himself. The parishioners considered him a very holy person, a good, simple man of the faith, but Donovan saw him as the occupant of the library, not to be disturbed when he was writing his sermons, which seemed to be every afternoon of the week. He gave long prayers before each meal at the rectory, spoke mostly to Anna and sometimes smiled absently when he looked at Donovan. It was an automatic smile, however, and Donovan imagined that he was really thinking of holy topics. On weekends he was intensely busy with church matters: marriages and baptisms on Saturday, early and late services on Sunday mornings and private counseling on Sunday afternoons.

On the Monday after Donovan arrived to live at the rectory, Anna walked with him to the nearby elementary school. Classes had already started at the schools in San Miguel, although the hot days of August were not over. They sat in the principal's outer office and Donovan could hear the murmur of classes up and down the halls. After a wait of fifteen minutes, they were ushered in by the secretary.

The principal, Mr. Cutter, welcomed Anna. "Mrs. Merrill, we are honored to have you visit Audubon Elementary. What may I do for you?"

"This is my grandson, Donovan Merrill. He is nine years old. I would like to see him enrolled here in the third grade. His records will be forwarded in time from Pasadena, and he will be living with Dr. Merrill and me at the rectory."

"Fine. Since the O'Brian twins moved back to San Francisco, there is space for him in Miss Mulock's class. I am sure he will be happy there."

Mr. Cutter asked Anna to wait while he escorted Donovan to Miss Mulock's room. Class was under way when they walked in. Donovan was introduced and asked to take a seat by the windows.

Miss Mulock, who wore no lipstick or rouge, said, "Class, please welcome Donovan Merrill."

"Welcome Donovan Merrill," they parroted in unison.

She continued, "We are learning about fractions today, Donovan. Have you learned about them already?"

"No."

"Well, you'll catch up quickly I am sure."

In the weeks following, Donovan caught up with the rest in Miss Mulock's class. If the studies in the classroom were easy for him, making friends with other students was not.

He was a bit taller than the others and he tended to shy away from the established groups. Most of the students from his grade introduced themselves, but after their first talk, they did not invite him back to sit or play. He often had lunch by himself, an apple and a ham-and-cheese sandwich from Li Fong.

He noticed the other students who were not included in groups. There were several black boys and girls, who kept to themselves on the edge of the playground. A few Hispanics made their own group on the far side of the grounds, eating lunches with tortillas and beans, and a Chinese group stood together near the school door. A blonde boy with a pale complexion sat by himself every day with his own, red lunch box.

Donovan, in the second week, sat down beside him. "Can I sit with you?"

"You can't have any of my lunch."

"I have my own. See here."

They ate in silence for a while. Then the boy said, "Most of the other students just want to have part of my mother's chocolate cookies. She makes good cookies."

"I've got my own cookie." Donovan noticed that David's lunch consisted entirely of cookies, some speckled, some chocolate and others dusted with powdered sugar.

"My name is David. David Messenger."

"I'm Donovan Merrill."

After this first attempt, they ate every lunch together. The tables were taken by the older or high-profile younger students, so they sat on the ground under a pepper tree at the side of the grounds. One day, David asked Donovan where he lived.

"With my grandmother, Anna, and my grandfather at the church rectory."

"The one on Roses Road?"

"Yes. Do you want to explore the cemetery sometime?"

"I have already, but the caretaker is very nosy. You have to look out for him."

"How did you get by him? He's always at the cottage window."

"I came back a second time and climbed over the wall at the back of the cemetery. There's a tree outside that you can climb up and drop down on the cemetery side of the wall."

Donovan said, "Let's do it again this week-end. I saw some mausoleums I want to look into and there are some family vaults with open doors.".

David promised to come by the rectory on Saturday afternoon and they would walk around the outside to his tree and climb over. That evening while Anna was preparing dinner, he told her about his new friend at school.

"I'm glad you have a friend. When may I meet your David?'

"This weekend. He's going to come by and we going to walk around San Miguel." Donovan avoided details.

"Good. I'll give you both iced tea when you're tuckered."

"David is a hiker. He also wants me to go with him in the San Gabriel Mountains sometime. He has been all the way up San Gregonio Peak."

"We'll have to talk about that. For a while, I don't want you to go too far. Get used to life around the rectory before venturing out farther. Please ask me before you go into the San Gabriels."

"That's all right. I don't want to go that far myself."

"Your grandfather is leaving for San Francisco tomorrow. The diocese is meeting for a week up there, so we'll be on our own here. A visiting minister from Oregon, Mr. Folsom, will be giving the Sunday service in his stead."

Donovan went to his room right after dinner. He put on the ear-phones and adjusted his crystal radio. First it was music broadcast from somewhere in Texas, then he moved the pointer to the other side of the small, shiny hill on the crystal and heard news of the world. Hitler raced ahead into Europe, with shrill and fruitless denunciations from neighboring prime ministers. The Japanese were at war with China and the government of Ethiopia had fallen. Donovan did not understand how a government could fall.

A Metallic Groan

Anna drove them to the train station in Pasadena. Grandfather Merrill sat next to her on the front seat and Donovan took a place with the luggage in the rear. Donovan thought that Anna drove a bit better with her husband instead of just her grandson. Maybe it was like when Donovan was asked to swim for guests, to see how fast he could swim for a boy of his age, he always swam better than on his own.

Grandfather Merrill turned around and said, "Donovan, you will look after our Anna while I'm gone, please?"

"Yes, sir."

"And tonight you will meet our dear friends, Partridge Sanborn and his companion, Frieda. Partridge has sold his family business, the jewelry store. I had hoped to be here at Anna's celebration dinner for him, but diocese matters come first."

Anna said, "Partridge and Frieda said to wish you God-speed."

"Donovan, you must be a good host in my stead. Perhaps

52

you should even offer Partridge a toast to his success," Grandfather Merrill said.

The date palms crowding the Pasadena train station were full of strident blackbirds as Donovan carried the pigskin suitcases. The porters at the train station were quick to recognize Grandfather Merrill's position as a man of God and rushed to help Donovan. After Grandfather Merrill boarded and waved from his window, they waited until the west-bound train was out of sight down the tracks, then Anna drove them back to the rectory.

"Donovan, I will be busy cooking with Li Fong in the kitchen most of the day, so you will have to entertain yourself," she said.

"It's Saturday and my friend, David, is coming by. We are going for a walk around the park in San Miguel." He thought it best to omit mention of the foray into Mr. Erasmus's cemetery.

"Bring your friend into the kitchen so that I may meet him before you go."

"I will, Anna."

He waited on the front porch for David, who ambled up the walk only a few minutes late. He did not look directly at Donovan, but played with the tendrils of the vine growing on the post. "Morning."

"Morning. Anna, my grandmother, wants to meet you."

They walked through the sitting room to the kitchen and the two women were talking in Chinese. Donovan introduced, as he had been taught, Anna and Li Fong to David. Anna chopped onions with a cleaver, the strong aroma filling the kitchen.

"David Messenger? Your family must be the Messengers who live over on El Molino Street. How is your mother?" She finished chopping the onions and started to reduce similarly the stalks of celery to small cubes.

"Fine. She's at home today, not at the office."

"I've forgotten where your mother works."

"At the *Tribune*. She writes the cooking column."

"Paulette's Kitchen? I read it out loud to Li Fong every week; some of the words are hard to turn into Chinese, though. Your mother must be a wonderful cook."

"Yes, mam. She just wrote a cookbook."

"I saw the title, so clever: *Easy Cooking for Tired Women*. I would love to meet her, so we'll have her to tea. Li Fong makes exquisite rice cakes with honey and lavender." Li Fong smiled as she peeled the potatoes.

Anna continued, "Donovan, I think David is a good friend for you. He has a strong face and anybody with that much blond hair must have a sunny disposition. And the two of you mustn't bother Mr. Erasmus. He is very touchy about boys wanting to come into his cemetery grounds."

They were anxious to escape, so they awkwardly backed out of the kitchen and ran outside. Without words they continued to run out to the road away from church and cemetery.

Donovan said, "If we climb over the back wall, we aren't really bothering Mr. Erasmus at all, are we?"

"I guess not."

"If we just came through the front gate, that would be bothering him, wouldn't it?"

"Yes. Of course, we'll be super quiet so as not to disturb him," David said, warming to the broken logic of Donovan's questions.

The boys circled around the far side of the walled cemetery, walking through the adjoining orange orchard, across several overgrown backyards. Finally they came to the tree David had described. It grew in the back garden of a large house, a forgotten avocado tree, perhaps started from seed, with many trunks, several of which arched up and over the cemetery wall. It proved to be no obstacle for two nine-year-olds, who shinnied up one of the trunks, then crawled along a branch, dropping to the ground across the wall.

They were a long way from the front gate and the dangers posed by Mr. Erasmus. This was the oldest part of the cemetery, with large trees and tall shrubs to hide behind. Rose bushes, planted decades ago, made domes of color with looping branches bending all the way to the ground. Sixty foot conifers lent a dark gravitas to the corners. Although it was less than a century old, the church-yard for Donovan appeared ancient and primordial, hallowed ground locked away from time.

They ran to the closest monument, an obelisk on a high base, and fell flat into the grass. Donovan peered around the base in the direction of the front gate and the possibility of a poised Mr. Erasmus. They could barely make out the front gate and cottage through the many bushes and low-branched trees.

"David, over there is the vault with the open door. Follow me." He ran in a crouching position the hundred feet to the vault. In a few seconds, David did the same. They fell flat in the grass next to it and peered once again towards the front gate. It was all clear. No evidence of Mr. Erasmus.

The bronze door to the vault was ajar about a foot and the leaded windows were thick with dust. It was dark inside and Donovan wondered if he would smell the dead people inside, if death had a tropical smell like gardenias.

"Do you want to look in?" David asked.

"I think so. We'll just glance in and then we'll run over there behind that tree."

"Do you want me to do it?"

"No. I'm ready."

Donovan thought he heard a noise. He held out an arm to stop David and they waited, stock still, listening for almost a minute. Then Donovan walked to the door on his toes and tried to push the door farther inwards, but it did not move.

Donovan then gave it a hard push and the heavy bronze opened with a metallic groan and a terrible, low fluttering sound came from the darkness within. David and Donovan both gave a yell and ran as fast as they could away, dropping into the high grass by a row of curved-top gravestones. As they turned around to look, two pigeons flew out. Donovan could hear his heart beating.

"It was only the birds," he said.

"I know, but it could have been something else. You were right to run."

"I think Mr. Erasmus heard us. Look there." He pointed to the gate.

Mr. Erasmus walked cautiously along the avenue with an alert cock to his head and a heavy stick in his hand. The boys stayed completely still in the high grasses. He came slowly their way, looking left and right, but not straying off the roadway onto the grass. Donovan thought they could outrun Mr. Erasmus at the last minute, if they were discovered. Chances were that Mr. Erasmus would not even see them so far away if they did not show themselves.

"Don't move," he whispered to David. Mr. Erasmus

continued his sweep toward them along the avenue closer and closer, occasionally brandishing his stick. "I know you're there and you'll be sorry when I find you," he called.

Donovan, his heart thumping, tried to lie even flatter in the grasses as Mr. Erasmus continued. He reached over to David, who was face down, and whispered to him not to move. Then, from the open windows of the sexton's cottage came the rings from a telephone. Mr. Erasmus brought down his stick and turned around. "I'll be back," he said over his shoulder as he retraced his steps.

The boys raced back to the avocado tree, but the overhanging branches were too high for them to return that way. They walked along beside the wall, and climbed over with the aid of the same many-branched shrub that David had used on his earlier foray. Both of them got scratches on their arms and faces as they clambered up and over the wall. Returning the way that they had come, David left Donovan on the driveway to the church.

"Let's do it again, next week," Donovan said.

"We'll go right into the vault and see what's there," David said as he ran in the direction of his own house, jumping up to touch the bottoms of low-hanging branches as he went.

At the rectory, Donovan walked silently past the kitchen door to his room and washed his scratches in the adjoining bathroom. The sleeves of his shirt would hide those on his arm, but there was a very obvious slash on his cheek. He avoided Anna until that evening, when Mr. Sanborn and Frieda were about to arrive.

She took a second look at him as he came into the sitting room. "What is that?" she asked.

"A scratch from a bush. It doesn't hurt at all."

"So there wasn't enough open space at the park that you had to hide in the bushes? Rose bushes by the looks of it."

"It seemed like a good place to hide and we didn't see the thorns."

"I recall that there are a great number of shrub roses in Mr. Erasmus's cemetery, where I asked you not to go."

"No, Anna, you asked me not to bother Mr. Erasmus."

"So I did. For heaven's sake, don't risk his displeasure again. Go put some Cuticura salve on it and come back. I think I hear Partridge's car in the drive."

Donovan did as he was told, a long streak of the salve. It smelled of camphor and eucalyptus. Since Anna could see right into his mind, he resolved that it would be foolish to lie to her again. He could hear the talk in the sitting room as he walked back along the hall.

"Frieda and Partridge, this is our Donovan."

"How do you do?" He walked up to each of them and shook their hands.

"What a splendid boy you are, Donovan. You've already lost at least one battle here, it appears," Mr. Sanborn said, touching his cheek.

"It was a rose bush."

"When I was your age, roses were my archenemies. I spent entire summers with scratches on arms and scabs on knees." Mr. Sanborn was a short, slight man with a kindly bend to his frame. Donovan thought he ought to work in a library, stamping the return dates and restacking the books, instead of owning a jewelry store.

Anna made them cocktails, which she called Old Fashions,

complete with orange slices and Maraschino cherries. Despite Prohibition, the kitchen cabinets of the rectory always held a bottle of good whisky. Anna gave Donovan a glass of iced water and made one for herself. Mr. Sanborn and Anna did most of the talking, both turning to look at Donovan or Frieda now and then.

Mr. Sanborn said, "Donovan, your grandmother is the best cook in San Miguel. We've had many superb meals here. I have always been entranced by the fact that a lovely, modest rector's wife had such a fine hand with spices and peppers. Chinese sauces and garlic in an Anglican parsonage, so welcome the way Anna uses them. If something happened to Frieda I would just have to kidnap Anna away from the rectory. James wouldn't mind, I'm sure."

"He might," Anna said with a smile.

Frieda, as if to justify her non-cooking existence, said, "You see, I write during the day, so there's no time for the kitchen." Everybody nodded in solemn accord.

Mr. Sanborn said, "There are many good restaurants in San Miguel, my dear, so you mustn't fret about it. We manage very well."

Anna interceded, "It is much more important to have lovely poems in the world than another roast chicken."

Mr. Sanborn beamed with pride. "If we can't find a publisher for her new poems, I'm going to print them myself. Do you know how we met, Donovan? I saw her writing on the top deck of the *Île de France*, the world cruise in the winter of nineteen thirty-two. Just off the Straits of Malacca, I took my daily stroll around the boat deck and there she was sitting at a table on the lee of the wind, writing in her journal, hair blowing every which way. She was so engrossed that she did not even see me when I sat down in the next chair. I knew right then that this was a serious lady."

Anna said to Donovan, "Frieda's home is Berlin, but there are political problems there right now, so she can't go home."

Donovan thought Frieda did not like being talked about, as her mouth pursed a bit. When she turned to look at him, the thick-lensed glasses enlarged her eyes like a frightened animal. She fingered the large brooch pinned over her heart, an asymmetrical, golden spider with eight diamonds where feet ought to be and a large ruby in the center. When the conversation between Anna and Mr. Sanborn came to a lull, she said, "Anna, look what Partridge gave me. The ruby came from a temple in India."

"What a lovely brooch. Partridge has the best taste."

He said, "My mother taught me, or rather insisted upon, that the only proper gift from a gentleman to a lady was a pair of opera glasses or a finely wrought fan. Anything of a more personal nature, like gloves or a pocketbook, was quite incorrect. Well, Frieda now has a dresser drawer full of fans and glasses, so I thought it was time to give her something personal, even though mother might have clucked. This is the Twentieth Century after all."

"I love it," Frieda said.

"I wanted to share the bounty I received from the sale of the store, and," looking at Donovan and speaking behind his hand in a loud whisper, "after our dinner I have a surprise for Anna."

She heard and said, "Partridge, you know you mustn't give me jewelry. That would bring up a loud clucking sound from your mother's tomb."

"We'll see."

They walked into the dining room where Anna had set the table with green and yellow plates on a pale green linen cloth. Already on the table was a bowl of chopped salad and glasses with water. After they were seated, she brought platters of sliced roast chicken, browned potatoes and French green beans from the kitchen. Donovan knew that this was her best meal, the menu she saved for special occasions.

Anna served them in turn from the platters, composing a plate styled expressly for each. For Mr. Sanborn there was mostly chicken, no potatoes and a pile of green beans, and the plate for Donovan had mostly potatoes with several spoons of gravy. Frieda took a bite of Anna's peppery chicken, winced and hid her mouth behind a napkin.

After the dessert of a Charlotte Russe that Anna spooned out into glass bowls at the table, Mr. Sanborn said he had an announcement.

"A few weeks ago I was reading the Sunday *Los Angeles Times*. The real estate for sale section. I ran upon this small ad which I have here." He reached into his inside coat pocket and pulled out a folded pile of papers. Putting on his reading glasses, he picked out a newspaper clipping with torn edges, "This is what it said: 'Laguna Beach Sea View Lot, perfect for the house above the sea. Utilities nearby, good road for access' then there's the price and a telephone number."

He paused and took a spoonful of his Charlotte Russe. "I was able to close the deal entirely by mail and we received the deed yesterday. It clearly says Anna Bronson Merrill, comma, owner."

"Partridge, I couldn't possibly accept."

"Of course you can. I wanted the ones I love the most to share in my sale. I've found something else for James, an old English bible in a fully operational pigskin cover with lovely gold stampings. Late Seventeenth Century, I believe."

"These gifts are so expensive, Partridge, Anna said. "You should put away the money into something safe, for your retirement."

"There's plenty more to put aside. Frieda's brooch cost much more than either of your gifts, so I've gotten things in the right order." Frieda narrowed her eyes a bit, trying to figure what the prices for those two other gifts must be. Her hand went up again to caress the ruby.

"I will talk to James when he returns. You remembered my mentioning a house by the sea a while ago, Partridge. Thank you."

"Yes. We were discussing what you would do with the baptism monies that James gives to you, and you said 'build a house where I can see the sea.'"

"Thank you, so much, but I will still have to think about accepting such a generous gift. It was only the wildest dream when I said that about the house, the sort of idea you hold on to for years and then eventually forget. However, I believe there is almost enough money to build a house right now, a very small one. I shall repay you, if I decide to keep your gift." Anna was noticeably warming to the idea of her house by the sea.

"I do not wish to be repaid. What is the use of extra money if not to share?"

Mr. Sanborn left the deed in an envelope on the dining table when he and Frieda departed. Donovan watched as Anna put it away in a kitchen drawer when they cleared the dishes.

While Anna washed the dishes and Donovan dried them, she said, "Laguna Beach. I have always loved it there."

"I know where it is. Just down the coast from Balboa Island."

"Years ago we visited an artist friend from James's university days. His house was right above the surf on a high, rocky cliff. He painted the sea every day, even on foggy mornings and stormy afternoons. Doesn't that sound like a good way to spend your life? Painting what you see in nature, walking around the hills?"

"Is he still there?"

"I don't think so. He talked of moving to France because he believed that America was too hard a place for an artist to live and make a living. He sold the house to another painter. We haven't been back to Laguna since."

"Would you build your house there this winter?"

"Yes, if you want to do something, do it right now. I think all the time about your father and your brothers, and their passing so suddenly. How quickly bad things can happen."

"What exactly is baptism money?"

"Your grandfather gives me the money that parishioners pay him for the sacramental ceremonies. Funerals, weddings and baptisms. It's always in cash. It belongs by long tradition, going back to the earliest days in England, to the wife of the Anglican pastor. It is for her personal use, not for churchly affairs. Wives of vicars bought sheep or cattle, small holdings in the village, silver and linen for the house. I always call it the Baptism Money because that is the happiest of the ceremonies, certainly happier than funerals and probably, all things considered, marriages."

"How much is there?"

"Let's count it out. That's what the house will cost." She brought down the row of green glazed ginger jars. Taking off their lids, she poured out the baptism money onto the kitchen table. Six jars full. It made an impressive pile, from which she counted out the bills and Donovan stacked up the coins: a few silver dollars, many fifty cent pieces, quarters down to pennies.

After ten minutes of counting, Anna wrote out a long list of each denomination, and added them up with a short pencil. The total was just over three thousand dollars.

"This should build a handsome house. Shingled, I think, with hinged casement windows I can open up right to the view. A small kitchen, two bedrooms, and if there is enough left over, a porch to sit and watch the sunsets."

"How long will it take to build?" Donovan asked. "Can we go there next summer?"

"We will plan on it."

In Time for Handel
1970

ight years ago, I met Tomas de la Pena at a cocktail party in Santa Fe. He was introduced as a writer from Mexico City but what I saw was the most handsome man I had ever seen. Tobacco brown eyes with black hair, smooth, slightly olive-tan skin, and an athlete's bearing. He was shy at first, perhaps because I came on so strong, but within a week we were living together in my small, rented house. It was a tentative coming together at first, two men searching out the qualities in each other, opening sensual pathways.

It was obvious we needed more space, and we decided to build an adobe house together. Friends had built houses by themselves, laying the adobe blocks, hoisting the vigas up for a roof and plastering the walls. It was the amateur's dream, to build a house made of earth, thick walls to cool the summer and keep in the warmth on winter nights.

I had purchased a piece of land that spring, a lot with an existing swimming pool, Olympic in size, from an old woman who used to swim there regularly on summer days. She swam the waters between the islands in her Hawaiian girlhood, braved the English Channel, and was a member of the 1928 Olympic swimming team. She was dispirited by the onset of bad health and the impossibility of ever using her vast water feature again. She wanted someone she knew and liked to have her extravagant pool, so priced it attractively for me.

The only proviso to the sale was my promise to build a long, high wall between the pool and her house, so that she could not see and be reminded of life's punishments, the dry remainder of her days. A contractor friend completed the wall within a month of my owning the property and I pondered what sort of house to build alongside my sixty meter lanes.

I filled the pool with water in May, hoses running full tilt for four days to fill it. The private well proved up to the task, never once faltering. At first, I thought to build a one room cottage, a *garconnière*, amused by the irony of a tiny house next to such a huge tank of water. During the winters, I could live modestly in the single room, heating it only with the corner fireplace, and then have my friends over for Neronian naval engagements in the summer, barges and banners aplenty. But Tomas came along and everything took a different turn.

A larger house was definitely in order. We scratched the outlines of rooms in the dirt, enlarging the main salon because it looked too small on the ground. Then we added the other rooms to this side and that, bathrooms and closets where they ought to be, hallways between, and long porches on either side. It still felt too small, so we expanded everything by thirty percent, moving the lines out in the dirt. At last the plan seemed right when we walked through it like a labyrinth, turning imaginary corners and opening doors yet to be hung.

I hired the contractor friend again to put in the concrete

footings and ordered twenty-thousand adobe bricks for ten cents each, laid in. This was a time before the need for city permits and building inspectors, citizens being trusted to build safely what they needed.

A week into our earnest but awkward adobe laying we realized what an immense task we had set out for ourselves. We struggled to lay three hundred adobes a day with a stout helper to mix the mud. Tomas calculated that if we labored every day, even on week-ends, that we might be finished on Easter Sunday, nine months away, just in time to hear Handel and collect the eggs. I hired a family of adoberos who gently pushed us out of the way and laid up our walls while we watched in the cool shade of adjoining pinons, thinking about window openings, ceiling heights and the paint colors.

By the first snow, the roof was on and the final coat of outside stucco finished. It was only when we put a few chairs in the main sitting room, the blizzard swirling about outside, fires aflame in the fireplaces, could we see the surprisingly vast scale of our plan. The fear that the rooms would be too small and pinched proved groundless. Quite the opposite, our thirty percent enlargement made the house huge.

The next year we built the practical parts, a studio for me, a study for Tomas and a garage for the cars. The pool still dominated the structures, however, like the arcaded water at Hadrian's villa. We both felt that it was our house, a joint effort, decisions about plaster and finish made after lengthy discussion. Tomas always preferred the spare, almost Zen solutions to my more plumy choices, his bone white versus my eggplant purple. In the end, he usually got his way, and that made less important the disparity between Tomas's small family income and the larger one provided me by Anna.

The scale of the large sitting room that centered the house surpassed any of the furnishings I already owned, so I looked for church pieces, oaken cassones and sideboards accustomed to holding heavy monstrances and rows of bronze candlesticks. I found a twelve-foot long chest of drawers long enough to hold vestments flat.

A shop in Albuquerque provided four ceremonial chairs with high backs and elaborate gilded finials. At the far end, I put my Regence game table, large enough to bring out the jig-saw puzzle from my Balboa Island summers, the Chinese courtyard garden with concubines. Tomas put the puzzle away into a cupboard several times, but I brought it back out each time and it now has its own, permanent place in our house, compelling in its incompletion.

At first, Tomas took to the indolent life, swimming and sunning. I do believe some people should remain ornamental and not feel obligated to toil, and Tomas was one of those. Since my income was a gift, it never bothered me to share it. But, in the curious way that life provides, I had an ingrained work ethic, in those years spending six to seven hours in my studio. Painting provided the center to my life, the studio was the place I went for completion and enlargement every day. Surely Puritan ancestors had a hand in it, judgmental in their tall, dark hats and buckled shoes.

Although Anna's largesse allowed me to be disinterested in the selling of my work, indifferent to market pressures and gallery advice, the paintings sold well from the beginning, after a short, lurching start. Collectors came by my studio and often mistook my lack of interest in the pricing of my work as a subtle way to bargain, to push the prices higher. They went higher yet and my paintings disappeared almost as fast as I could paint them.

The popularity of my canvases became a fact that I could count upon, and as I grew more involved with the complexity of the work, I spent the time to insert layers of meaning in each piece. I wondered if Anna's money had not been there, would I have pushed myself to add the tiers of fulsomeness and density that characterize my current work? Was I proving to myself that I was not just another dilettante artist with a trust fund, a species so prevalent in Santa Fe? The painter responds to pressures from within as surely as those from without.

As I was going through this maturation process, Tomas seemed to stand still. He wrote a collection of short stories about his family, piquant tales of an innocent among those of high position, a wide-eyed narrator beckoned into the dark-paneled chambers of Mexican power.

On winter nights, he read me the stories as they were written and we stayed up late talking about ways to tweak their curiosity and poignancy. Tomas was very happy while he wrote the stories and I was relieved that he had found himself in writing. The collection was published first in New York, then, translated into Spanish, in Mexico City.

The book sold better in Mexico, giving him a reputation for being a young rebel. The Mexican establishment endured being made sport of, as long as it came from an insider. His face on the cover was not an accidental choice. In the wake of that, several North American magazines asked for stories in the same vein. A Hollywood producer paid Tomas for an option on his stories, a sum that made it easy for him to more than meet his living expenses. I was immensely proud of him and took every opportunity to tell him so.

He started the novel in our fourth year together, working desultorily on it during the winter and giving in to the delights of the pool and its sunny surround in the summer. As the writing faltered, he told me that he believed that he was a fraud, not deserving the acclaim from his stories.

I was sitting on the edge of the pool when he stopped his laps and said, "My stories were not really art, merely family eavesdropping."

"But you've taken them and made them greater. Art is often about taking the commonplace and ennobling it."

"Writing is art only when it is made up from nothing."

"That's nonsense."

"A true writer takes a pile of sticks, rubs them together and makes fire. Like you make a painting."

"You've done that, made fire."

"I was given the sticks and they were already on fire, so it does not count."

Nothing would convince him otherwise. It became clear to me that Tomas had an innately low opinion of himself, something hammered into him from a family expecting larger results than he could deliver. If he could succeed at writing more than his story collection, a well-received novel, then his status would surely go up in both his own and his family's unforgiving value system. But that was not happening.

White Brocade
1938

It was Thursday morning of James Merrill's week away in San Francisco. Donovan liked having Anna to himself at mealtime, because she asked him questions and told him stories of the old San Miguel. It was not like this with the three of them together when Anna and James talked between themselves most of the meal. They spoke an almost private language, often leaving Donovan totally confused.

Li Fong served Anna and Donovan their breakfast at the table in the kitchen, sun streaming in from the garden and a slight breeze making the bamboo grove rustle and creak. Eggs and bacon, toast, marmalade, and orange juice. She said something to Anna in Chinese.

Anna switched to English, "I will talk to him when we're done here." She looked at Donovan, "She says that Ah Fong must speak with me."

They walked into the garden after breakfast and found Ah Fong planting rows of small purple cabbage in the vegetable garden. He stood up when he saw them coming and made an almost imperceptible bow to them both. Donovan knew that

Anna had asked him to stop the old practice of the ceremonial bow, to let it stay in the Old World, but it was ingrained in his smallest cells, not a notion that could be dropped.

"Good morning. Li Fong says you have something to say to me."

"Yes, Miss Merrill. Good morning. My eldest brother now stays with us. His name is Wo Fong and he is new from China."

"Is he a master gardener like you?"

"Not a gardener, like me, but a high clerk from the Nanking constabulary. A most important man in Nanking. Everybody says that he speaks perfect English from his years at missionary school."

"I would like to meet him."

"Good. May I bring him by this afternoon?"

"Yes. I'll serve tea to you both at four o'clock. You will join Mrs. Messenger, the famous cookbook writer."

"Not tea for me, please, only for Wo Fong. Since our father dies, he is head of the Fong family."

"We will make rice cakes. And, Ah Fong, I think a gardener is just as important as a clerk, if not more important. We could probably live without files and reports, but where would we be without vegetables and flowers?"

"Thank you, Miss Merrill. May I still not come myself?"

Anna assented. Donovan had just enough time to walk to school. He usually tarried about with David when school was over, but this day he came directly back to the rectory, eager to meet the high official from Nanking and David's mother. Anna had set up the bamboo chairs on the porch for tea, a tray of cups and saucers, silver spoons, napkins, lemon wedges and tea cakes in readiness for her guests. A footed dish of pickled kumquats sailed high above the rest of the tray. Donovan knew that this was a more elaborate spread than she would prepare for her family, or even fancier than for the ladies from the altar guild.

Anna came out of the house when Donovan walked up to the porch. She was wearing one of the mandarin silk robes, a white brocade with a yellow dragon. She had arranged her hair up with mother-of-pearl combs and yellow sandals with white silk stockings.

In response to Donovan's look, she said, "To honor our guest. I have few occasions to wear it, and it seemed appropriate today."

Punctually at four, Wo Fong appeared at the garden gate. He wore a black robe of silk satin with elaborate frogs for closures from his chest to the ground and a black circular hat. He was taller than his brother, without a trace of Ah Fong's servility. Hands hidden in his sleeves, he walked with deliberate, small steps.

"Mrs. Merrill, how nice of you to ask me here."

"Anna, please."

"Anna, then. What a beautiful silken robe. It must be from the palace collection. The yellow dragon is reserved for only the most important, titled people."

"I saw it at a Chinese mercantile in San Francisco and it spoke to me."

"Ah. And you listened."

Tea proceeded when Li Fong brought the white porcelain tea-pot. She nodded ceremonially to her brother-in-law, without looking directly at him. He gave no sign of recognition back. Anna served the rice cakes with lavender and the tea with lemon wedges.

"Our other guest is late, and since the tea is hot, we must start without her. My tea is a cross between an English tea and a Chinese tea."

"A joy for a homesick man."

Anna included Donovan, giving him a plate with a rice cake, candied dates and one pickled kumquat. She and Wo Fong talked about the world situation in the Far East, and the difficulties of coming to the West. As Wo Fong spoke, Donovan thought about Leonore, since he talked with the same accent that she had tried to summon for Miss Marple. Wo Fong said that there might be a position for him as a deputy clerk in the city hall offices in San Miguel, quite similar to his work in China.

"There are so many families from China here in San Miguel and other communities in Southern California. The city needs someone who can converse with them, understand their needs."

"You speak such good English, as if you studied in England itself."

"The missionary schools were excellent when I was a boy. The English family from Somerset taught us to speak correctly or we were punished severely. Just like in England, itself, they told me; boys must sit in the corner until they got it right."

"Tell me about your own family," she said.

"We come from a village outside of Nanking, in the country where they grow peaches and plums. Family orchards surround our village, and most of us worked on the land. There is one house of the Fongs said to be two thousand years old, a courtyard with fifty rooms surrounding. Half of them are now in disrepair, roof-tiles fallen on the ground, much the same as the family itself. A few of us were given scholarships to the imperial school in Nanking, what was left of it, and afterwards, we worked in the government bureaus. The Japanese committed horrible massacres in Nanking last year."

"How did you get away?"

"Three of us, all Fong cousins, walked away secretly at night, along the back roads to a safe place by the river. We hired a boat to take us down-river, again only at night, to Shanghai. The city was in turmoil, but it was easier to hide there. The English church people in the city center remembered us from their trips to the village. They smuggled us aboard the same ship that was bringing the missionaries home, away from the war."

"I understand it is very difficult to gain entry in the United States."

"A little known provision allowed us to come in. I knew that Fongs are merchants in San Francisco and families of merchants were exempted from the Seclusion Law."

"I'm so glad."

"The other Fongs here have farms and nurseries, along the coast south from here. They came here before the Seclusion, mostly uncles and male cousins. Some, like your Ah Fong have found employ as domestics, although the family history is for much higher position. Do not misunderstand, Ah Fong is very happy to be with you."

"He tells me that you are related to the important Fongs in Hawaii, the family with nine daughters."

"It is so. Henry Ah Fong has had great success."

Donovan noticed that Anna reached over and patted

Wo Fong's arm often when she talked. Wo Fong flinched the first time she touched him, but settled down as she repeated her gestures. On several occasions she left her hand on his arm for half a minute or so. Donovan remembered that she touched everyone a great deal, patting and squeezing arms to make a point. Was Anna flirting with Wo Fong? Maybe the Chinese did not customarily pat each other so much.

The doorbell rang; it was Mrs. Messenger, with many apologies for her tardiness. She was blonde, full-bodied and lithe. She wore a small hat and was dressed in a long-lapelled blue suit and high-heeled shoes of a matching color with open toes.

"Please Mrs. Messenger, come and sit with us. This is a friend, Wo Fong. The tea is still hot and we have rice cakes left," Anna said, giving her a cup and a plate.

Mrs. Messenger took a bite from the rice cake. "I love Chinese cooking. We get so many letters about it and I must learn more. This is delicious."

"Li Fong is our cook. Maybe I could arrange for you to discuss with her the recipes."

"I would love that. Mr. Fong, are you new to San Miguel?"

Wo Fong caught Mrs. Messenger up on the details of his arrival and his hopes for high position at the city hall. She asked many questions about his new employment, and the elevated standing of the Fongs back in China. He, in polite return, heard about her position as a columnist at the paper. As the tea drew to a close, Anna said, "You must both come to dinner when James gets back from San Francisco. We have friends who would enjoy meeting you."

Wo Fong said, "I prefer, Mrs. Merrill, to come back only for tea. We always have the night meal with our own family, doors closed. In China, tea time is for friends and associates."

"We'll do that, then."

"And, if I know beforehand, I can bring some fresh vegetables from the Fong farms. We have eggplants, bok choi, long beans and mustards."

"Fresh vegetables from the coast. I will ask Ah Fong to pass the invitation along." Anna was clearly charmed with Wo Fong.

"Until then, I bid you goodbye," he said. "And a particular *au revoir* to you, Mrs. Messenger." He bowed deeply to them each in turn. Anna and Donovan stood up and watched him walk down the front walkway to the gate with very small steps. It seemed he would never reach the gate and go out.

"A very interesting man, don't you think?" Mrs. Messenger said.

They sat down again and Anna said, "I admire you, Mrs. Messenger, for having a career, being independent."

"It was not all lemonade and cookies, I can tell you."

"What then?"

"When I graduated from Stanford in nineteen twenty-nine, I took a year off and traveled through France. All the girls of my class were doing it. When I got back, the Market had crashed and nobody wanted to hire a woman, no matter how good her college degree was."

"What did you do?"

"I married and kept house for two years. David came along, a sweet baby."

"He's become a handsome boy."

"Some say he takes after his father, a tennis pro who up and left us one day. All alone, no money. I hope David doesn't take after William."

"Did you start the cooking column then?"

"Yes. I knew the editor at the *Tribune* and he owed my father some favors. I was always a good cook, it came naturally, and Stanford honed my writing skills, so I started the column. The rest you know."

Mrs. Messenger stood up to take her leave. "You were a dear to include me, Mrs. Merrill. I so enjoyed meeting your other guest." Donovan watched her walk down the drive, with her swinging gait.

He turned back to Anna, "Wo Fong smiled a lot. I think he liked you."

"He was being polite. Upper class Chinese are the picture of politeness, even when they disapprove."

"Do you think he disapproved of us?"

"I shouldn't think so. He was taken aback by my robe, though. You heard him say that it was from the Imperial family and every Chinese would know. He might think that I don't deserve to wear it. Only for very important, titled people, he said."

"Grandfather Merrill says you look more Chinese than the Chinese themselves when you wear it."

Donovan was troubled by Anna's obvious attraction to Wo Fong. How could she be taken in by such an unattractive man, not the sort Donovan could find any reason to admire. Perhaps it was all a joke, an adult joke he did not understand.

Dance Without Veils

David and Donovan had an unspoken sense of quid pro quo in their adventures. If Donovan hosted a day at the cemetery vault and its helter-skelter conclusion, David felt bound to find an escapade to match. He told Donovan that he should come over to the Messenger house that night, that he had something to show him.

"I don't know if I can. I'll have to ask."

"Late. After everybody has gone to bed."

"You mean, just sneak out and come over?"

"Yes. Come around to the back door."

So Donovan mentioned nothing of this to Anna at dinner that night. When they finished washing and drying the dishes, he said he was going to his room to go to bed early. Anna kissed him goodnight.

At first, he listened in the dark to his crystal radio, moving the pointer around to stations over the world. He could not understand most of the languages, but he knew that one broadcast was certainly South American from the music.

Another was from somewhere in Europe because he heard the words Paris and Berlin.

He waited for about an hour until he heard the door to Anna's room click shut. The window in his room opened right out to the garden and it was an easy drop to the ground. David's house was one block away, but everything seemed dark and strange in the streetlights, a world apart. There were several cars parked in the driveway of the Messenger house, which he skirted when he went around to the back. He sat down at the kitchen door, the concrete steps crowded with pots of succulents and leggy geraniums.

In a few minutes, the back door opened. "Shh...follow me," David said. He led Donovan around to the front of the house. The high, arched windows of the sitting room were covered with draperies, but little shafts of light showed through here and there. David looked at one, then another and finally found an opening large enough so they both could see into the brightly-lit sitting room.

David's mother, Paulette, was dancing naked. A Victrola played and two businessmen in suits, with their hats on the sofa beside them, watched as she cavorted about the room, fondling her large breasts in front of them, teasing them with a wiggle of the hips. "I Got Plenty of Nothing." She dipped low with legs spread to show them what was there, shaking back and forth, and one of the men clapped his hands, laughing. The two boys watched this strange episode for about five minutes without a word.

"What do you think?" David asked, when they pulled away from the window.

"I've never seen a naked lady before."

"She does it all the time. Almost every week."

"You're really lucky."

"I can't sleep much when the music starts, so I come out here and watch."

"Why does she do it?"

"The men pay her money for it. She says the newspaper doesn't pay her all that much. We usually go out for dinner the next night."

"I'll see you tomorrow. Thanks a lot."

Donovan ran all the way home and pulled himself up through the casement window to his room. The world seemed to be a stranger place than he had imagined.

The next day at breakfast, Anna said, "Well, your grandfather gets back tomorrow. I'll be cooking a roast to welcome him home. Just the family, though."

Donovan cancelled the next exploration of the cemetery with David, fearing too much activity might get discovered. It would be better to wait, he told David. At dinner that night, Grandfather Merrill was full of tales about the diocesan meeting. He told Anna about mutual friends, the bishop of this, the rector of that, new rules from the governing board. Donovan wondered when Anna would tell him about the gift of the Laguna Beach property, but there were many more liturgical tales before she found the opportunity.

At last, she said, "The dinner with Partridge and Frieda went well, don't you think, Donovan?"

He nodded, as her question did not require his answer. Grandfather Merrill intervened, "How are they both? Did the sale of his store go without a hitch?"

"They are fine and apparently the sale did go through

because he gave Frieda the most handsome brooch, a golden spider with diamonds and a large ruby from India. He said he is holding back a surprise for you as well, which I mustn't divulge."

"He is a most generous man. The vestry could not get along without him and every year he makes such a large contribution to the permanent fund."

Anna paused, "I told Donovan that events in our lives seem to be rushing together, crowding toward us. There is a sense of so little time." Why was she talking about this, when the divulging of Laguna Beach awaited?

Grandfather Merrill logged easily into any conversation about eternity. "That clock is always there. Earthly life is transitory, the reward long and beautiful for Christians of the faith. What brings on these thoughts, my dear?"

"Actually Partridge did. He wanted to celebrate his good fortune from the sale of his business with gifts to his dear ones. He gave me the deed to a small lot in Laguna Beach. Above the sea."

"How extraordinary. What did you say to him?"

Anna went to the kitchen to replenish the gravy boat and the supply of carrots. "At first, I said I could not keep it, that I would have to talk to you. He was insistent and told us he would be deeply offended if I turned it down. So I accepted."

"I think that was wise."

Anna said, "After Partridge and Frieda left, Donovan and I counted out the baptism money. I thought now I finally have a place to use it, before I've become a very old lady who cannot think of such a project. It's just over three thousand dollars, by the way."

"You have many years before you are an old lady."

"James, sometimes I wonder if you didn't marry the wrong sister. Emmeline was so sweet and spiritual and she would have been totally fulfilled here at the rectory."

"But, dear, I love you. Emmeline is an agreeable sister, full of simple piety, but she has no fire. You are the catch of the Bronson clan."

"Well, the sister full of fire feels that time is crushing in. Do it now is the message, or the bath chair and walking cane will be here."

"A house in Laguna is a wonderful idea. I wouldn't have thought of it myself, but Partridge is a perceptive man. It will be an adventure for you and Donovan."

Grandfather Merrill heard and understood the message underneath Anna's tale. Something was stirring in the previously still waters and it would be unwise to disregard it. He stood up and kissed Anna on the forehead, "It's a lovely gift from Partridge. Of course, you must proceed with building a house there as soon as possible. We'll drive down there next week and start the process."

"James, I think Donovan and I should take the street car down there. It's an easy trip; the Red Cars go all the way to Newport. You will need the automobile here during the week."

"I think we should drive. This is an important turn of events."

"No, I insist. Your flock has missed you during your conclave, so another week away from them is not wise. Donovan will look after me, be my escort, my companion."

Grandfather Merrill finally agreed and Donovan felt the

excitement mount at his promotion to a companion for his grandmother, not just another grandchild. Anna said he could miss a bit of school since he was such a good student. She would write the principal a letter, and they would leave on Monday morning.

Dripping Wine Glass
1970

Tomas put together a lunch in the shade of the portal facing the garden, two plates of raw vegetables, lettuces, sliced hardboiled eggs, a stack of white tuna, capers, sliced peppers, and cottage cheese. Our summer lunches together were a favorite time for me, usually in the cool calm of our kitchen portal, different from the larger groups that tended to dominate our evenings.

I thought of Harold Nicholson and Vita Sackville West at lunch, safely away from the garden helpers, on their Erechtheum at Sissinghurst. The carafe of white wine was dripping from the humidity, rare in the dry air of Santa Fe. I immediately wondered if storms were building up, each day more threatening, to culminate in a downpour for my opening night. Summer rain in the Sangre de Cristos was always a benison, but it could upstage and discompose an art event, finery dampened and indoors so crowded that backs pushed into the paintings. I felt that storms awaited my opening night.

Filling my glass from the carafe, Tomas said, "So it's done? Another show. You should feel proud of yourself."

"Just relieved. If you have a few good paintings, even just one or two, it's all worth it."

"So easy for you." Here it was again, Tomas's misguided belief that accomplishment for me was like falling off a log. Mere existence was hard for him, easy for me. I worked effortlessly to succeed, he struggled, only to fail.

"It may seem that way, but it was hard work, Tomas."

"What did Mary want?"

I explained the plans for the trip to Laguna in a few days. Tomas usually enjoyed going to California, so these family conclaves were not a chore. Anna was delighted with Tomas, she having predicted that I would marry a Mexican beauty with obsidian eyes, "a sweet, pliant thing," she said. The fact that Tomas was a man, not a woman, did not seem to matter to Anna. I would be hard pressed, however, to ever describe Tomas as 'pliant.'

Anna was so different from Grandmother McBeale. She was always in rebellion, searching for freedom from the decisions of men. At eighty-nine, it could be said that Anna had achieved true independence. I could not think of any man or woman, for that matter, who could tell her what to do.

Grandmother McBeale, however, was imbedded in the patriarchal McBeale family, where men made all the choices and the women would not think of raising a question. Grandfather McBeale brought his siblings into a series of bad business decisions, willful and foolish, that resulted in the total loss of the many millions they had inherited. At a time when California was expanding, exultant, full of opportunity, everybody making millions on real estate, he managed to lose money on everything he turned his hand to. The McBeales sold their houses, moving into cottages.

Anna, like a duchess in her own county, made Tomas feel welcome from the beginning. She paid attention to Tomas's every word on our visits, often ignoring me completely. I understood how important that was, how unlike other families I knew.

At the lunch table, Tomas said, "I like your cousin Mary. She says you are her favorite family member, after Anna. What was she like as a child?"

"Not the ball-busting executive you see today. She was a serious child, almost somber, and never the favorite. Her sister, Annabelle, same age as me, was the beautiful oldest girl, blonde ringlets and the ability to make the older men notice."

"Did you know Mary as a child?"

"Not really. I battled with Annabelle when Mary was an infant, both of us about ten. When her mother died, Mary came to live with Anna in the years I went off to Europe. She got the second round of life in Laguna. Anna worked her wonders on Mary, the healing power of unquestioned love."

"Wasn't she interested in art?"

"No. It was obvious that she belonged in another world, not the amorphous, shifting pursuit of art. She was led softly away from the easel."

"How did she become so adept at money?" Tomas asked.

"Anna gave her that strong woman thing, that she could do anything a man could, even if it wasn't art. I think she introduced her to the president of the Laguna bank and it immediately took. She found her place working with people rather than alone, like Simon and me, in the studio. The ability with money must have been built in."

"I feel close to her because in my family I was different, too. They wanted me to be like them, intellectuals. Mexico was in ferment then, and they said that the writers and teachers would lead the way. I was first in soccer and tennis, but sports were treated like an affliction by the aunts and uncles. The mind was the thing. When I told them that I did not want to write or be a professor, they washed their hands of me."

"But you turned out all right. An intellectual and a writer despite them."

"I guess so."

Tomas was not an intellectual, but he was tender on the subject so it was better to include him among them. He fought with how to write the novel about his youth, about growing up in his over-qualified family, all of them leaders in the liberal opposition to the ruling group.

The family lived in an ancient house in the center of the city, nearly a hundred rooms opening into a succession of leafy courtyards, maiden great-aunts and indolent cousins in residence, all with the same long faces from Andalucia. It was a small city unto itself, the liberal, free-thinking, younger members of the de la Penas in constant disagreement with the older, entrenched uncles. Every meal at the thirty-foot long table in the main dining room was encircled with debate as noisy as a provincial legislature. From the snippets that Tomas told me, it was a story full of surprise and danger, but the novel languished in a rough draft. Tomas was unable to put a finish on it.

Whether it's a painting or a book, I have a notion that the middle stretches are the most difficult. Artistic beginnings are filled with promise and joy, the first lines suggesting much to follow. I could start a new painting every day, filled with the anticipation of beautiful things to come, the sketchy lines and early forms promising brilliance.

Then, the going got sluggish through the middle portion, the heart of the matter. I strained to keep the distinct tone that I started, a twist or secret touch that would make it all sparkle. Simon was saying the same thing when he told me that art was a juggling act, that you must keep the golden balls in the air long enough to fool the eye. Then, when this long trip through the middle darkness is done, the finale is often as easy as the start. The finishing strokes are a coda to the prelude, reinforcing the joy of the original idea.

Tomas did not have the innate ability or experience to get through those midpoint badlands, to push through to the culmination. He tried to make a writing schedule, to work the same hours at his book that I did in the studio, but the day called out to him to go running, go for a swim, or prune the apple trees. Anything active over something thoughtful.

I saw that Tomas's great beauty, a joy for me, was a curse for him. We tried to craft a relationship of equals, because both of us believed in that equality, but it kept dissolving into one of my being the post and his being the vine, albeit a vine with floridly beautiful flowers and alluring, exotic leaves. It was as if his astounding good looks made anything else impossible, beauty stealing all hope.

"How's the book coming?" I asked.

"I hit a wall last week and can't get beyond it."

"Do you want to talk about it? You know that sometimes helps."

"No, I want to let it stew."

"Maybe the trip to Laguna will help. We need only stay a few days with Anna, then we can go out on our own. We can drive up the coast to San Francisco."

In Questa Reggia
1938

On Monday morning, Anna found a small wicker suitcase for Donovan and she packed a larger version for herself. Grandfather Merrill in the front passenger seat and Ah Fong at the wheel drove them to the street-car stop at the San Gabriel Mission. They waited in the auto until it arrived, the crackle of overhead electricity louder and louder as it approached. "Take care of yourself, my dear." They boarded and waved to Grandfather Merrill and Ah Fong in a jerky departure down the rails, sparks falling from the wire above.

The Red Car stopped often and the seats filled up before they had gone a half hour. Anna let Donovan sit next to the window and they watched as houses and buildings went by, interspersed with small farms and citrus groves. Just before they came into Los Angeles itself, they passed through a dark tunnel, the city a glowing reward at the far end.

They transferred to the beach line in a circle of tracks with waiting cars. Donovan carried both wicker cases and they searched for the transfer car, finding the one with the Newport/

Beaches sign. A short wait and they were off with a lurch.

Anna said, "We'll be there just before sunset. If I remember correctly, October is a beautiful time on the coast. No fog to speak of, warm evenings."

"I like the fog. I can get lost in it."

"It will come back in the spring and summer."

They went past the farming communities between Los Angeles and Laguna. Chinese and Japanese farms with rows of vegetables, fields of deep green alfalfa, larger spreads with lines of berries and citrus, olives, peaches, plums. The bounty of California spread on both sides of the tracks, lines of eucalyptus trees to mark boundaries and break the spring winds. They stopped at each of the beach towns on their way south, Mira Mar, Bay City, Anaheim Landing, Sunset Beach, and Huntington Beach, with long expanses between the towns where only the ice-plant covered the dunes which bordered the surf.

At Newport the trolley line came to an end in a large circle of date palms, full of noisy purple grackles and seabirds, and the conductor switched the seats to face back towards Los Angeles. Two taxis waited for fares, so Anna waved at the first one to pull forward.

"We need to go to Laguna Beach, please."

The driver said, "I'll have to drive back without a fare. That's twenty miles and will cost three dollars."

"So much? Well, we've got to get there."

"Where in Laguna?"

"The main hotel, what is it called?"

"El Delirio Hotel. Right on the beach?"

"Yes. That's the one."

They drove to the ferry landing for the twenty minute trip over to Balboa Island, space for only three cars down the middle of the ferry. They got out of the taxi as they crossed and Donovan could see where he last swam across from side to side on a day that seemed a lifetime away. Dolphins in formation followed the ferry across. He was going to point out to Anna the beach where the Merrill family swam, but got taken up in a rush of emotional crosscurrents. Sadness and happiness together. It was better not to talk. Anna put her arm around the young boy and they watched in silence as the ferry pulled in.

The taxi drove them across the island to a small bridge, over the salt-water canal then down the coast road past a large lagoon and the boat channel from Balboa Bay out to the sea. The vista of the roiling open sea brought up memories of what happened there the last summer. Would this view always uncover the buried chunks of sadness? At last, the taxi went up the hill to Corona del Mar, a small beach community and the final stretch into the cliffs above Laguna Beach. It was sunset as they pulled up to the hulking, gray concrete El Delirio.

Anna paid the driver and Donovan carried the bags into the hotel. She asked for two rooms with an adjoining door, so the clerk searched through the list until he found them. He escorted them to the elevator, opened the ironwork door with a filigree design of fishes, sea-horses and seaweed, and took them up to the top floor. Their rooms each had a small balcony facing west over the beach into the sunset. Anna opened the door between the two rooms.

"Thank you, ma'am," the clerk said when Anna tipped him a quarter. "The dining room is open until nine o'clock. Shall I make a reservation for you?"

"Yes, please. A table for two in about an hour."

She and Donovan sat down in the wooden chairs on the balcony of her room, watching the red sun go behind a band of storm clouds right on the horizon. At last a sliver of red shone brightly under the clouds and in a few minutes descended slowly under the horizon.

"I think we're going to like it here, Donovan."

"Yes, Anna. How will we find your lot?"

"I'll ask for a map tonight and we'll walk there first thing in the morning. Right after breakfast. Laguna is small."

"I can't wait."

The dining room was nearly empty when they arrived, an off-season night. The room had a coffered ceiling with painted marine motifs in each section, and small lamps with orange shades sat in the centers of the white clothed tables. The only other guests were a group of three gathered around a circular table in the corner and a couple that sat in the far other corner. The waiter seated Anna and Donovan near the group.

As they read the menus, the old man at the next table called across to them, "Welcome to Laguna Beach. Are you staying long?"

Anna smiled and said, "Thank you. We don't know how long."

"She's going to build a house here," Donovan said.

"How exciting. Where?" the old man asked.

"I don't know precisely," Anna replied. "The property is on Waterbird Lane."

"I know it; that plot was for sale all last summer. So you are the one who bought it? Please, won't you join us? The dining room is so empty this time of year and we have extra chairs at our table. We live here in Laguna."

Donovan thought Anna would surely say no, but she said yes. Everybody stood up and rearranged the chairs for them at the larger table.

"I'm Simon Grunewald and this is my son, Portman. Our lady friend is Latraviata Johns. She and I are artists, scratching out a living here. Portman helps me out in my studio, a blessing every day."

"I'm Anna Merrill, and this is my grandson, Donovan. You're so fortunate to live here. And to be artists," Anna said.

"I prefer to call myself a painter," Latraviata said.

"So touchy you are, my dear," Simon said. "You make art, artists make art. What's the difference?"

She replied, "Painter is the more exact term. It refers to what I do: one who puts paint on a canvas. And the word 'artist' should refer to how well I do that. It's bad form, maybe bad luck, for painters to call themselves artists."

"I stand corrected. She is English and therefore a lover of those fine points of diction invisible to anyone else. So we both make paintings and drawings, a part of our small artistic community, Mrs. Merrill."

"Anna, please."

"Anna, let us order some dinners for you and Donovan, then we can talk more. The seafood ought to be good here, but it is not. White cardboard with lumpy cream sauce. I suggest the chicken or the lamb."

Simon had a shock of white hair, longer than most men wore it, and an impressive nose around which were crowded in close proximity his kind eyes and thin mouth. He was a small man, and wore a linen suit with a vest and a black tie. Anna thought he resembled a musician, or perhaps a conductor of symphonies, more than a painter. What did Hayden look like without his powdered wig? Or perhaps Brahms if he had lived longer?

Latraviata looked every bit of her English self, lanky and regal, once a beauty with skin like pink alabaster, now starting to wrinkle in the California sun. Her eyes were a bright blue and her long hair, still golden, although a muted, silvery gold, peeked out from under her canary yellow turban.

She said, "Neither Simon nor I can cook at all. Not so much as a cutlet or a poached egg. We meet here at least twice a week to have a meal, however lacking it is in quality. Sometimes we are a much larger group of locals, but we are the inner, hard core."

"I love to cook and will have all of you over when the house is finished," Anna said.

"Mr. Sanborn says that Anna is the best cook in Southern California," Donovan said proudly.

Anna said, "He is, of course, a thoroughly impartial judge."

"I feel sure that your Mr. Sanborn is absolutely right and Laguna is seeing the dawn of its gastronomical future," Latraviata said.

When asked why she chose to build a house here, Anna told the story of Mr. Sanborn's gift and the baptism money. It sounded like a fable the way she told it, Donovan thought, fate and worthiness conspiring to open up vistas and new settings for chosen favorites. They had at long last arrived in their secret kingdom above the surf, innocents on a track among the worldly.

"You are very adventuresome, so unusual for a minister's wife. Why are you striking out just now? Whatever made you yearn for more than cozy nights in the parsonage?" Latraviata asked as she adjusted her turban.

"I told Donovan that I felt that a time had come, like a page turning for a new chapter. Events arose to make this happen, and I could either turn away or I could embrace the idea. I had so many dreams about cross-roads, diverging paths, and of course the sea."

Simon said, "So here you are and we can now look forward to home-cooked fried snapper and roast lamb."

"My best meal is a roast chicken with rosemary, roast potatoes and, if I can find them, fresh green beans in a parsley sauce. It will be my first dinner here and you are all invited."

"Do you have someone to build your house?" he asked.

"No, we haven't really seen the land yet. I hope to talk to some builders in the next few days."

"I have the answer. Let me bring Esperanzo by. He is a master builder from Mexico with a large family of workers. Esperanzo Mendoza. He built my studio and several of our friends' houses."

Anna listened as the talk turned to painting, the prices of oil colors and the scarcity of galleries available to them in town. Although she had nothing to add to the conversation, she knew it was right for her to be in the middle of these creative people.

Latraviata said, "We must make it an early evening here. Studios await us in the morning, so we can't allow late, bibulous dinners to muddy our thoughts. After you finish with Simon's builder-friends tomorrow, you and Donovan please come by for tea. I am at the end of the road over there, Abalone Cove.

The small but wild peninsula I call home."

"I think I know the former owner. Bartlett?"

"Yes indeed. I bought his Abalone Cove five years ago. Please do come by."

"We shall."

The evening drew to a close and Simon promised to bring Esperanzo Mendoza by the Waterbird Lane lot tomorrow. It had been a long day, so Donovan and Anna postponed their walk around the town center and went right to bed and to sleep. Donovan could hear her snoring in the next room, a soft bubbling sound, not unlike the rhythm of the waves on the beach below.

A Good Rock

Donovan woke early and Anna was still asleep. He dressed quietly and ran down the stairs, avoiding the clanking elevator. A door in the lobby was marked Beach Access, so he raced down the flight of scored-concrete steps right onto the sand in front of the hotel. There was no fog, only a slight hovering layer of mist on the water. The waves were subdued, splashing on the shore with a gentle roll.

He walked along to the north end of the cove where the surf broke onto a cluster of rocks. Waves rippled across the tidal pools. Crabs scurried away and colonies of sea anemones waved their arms like fat chrysanthemums in the shallow, clear water. He heard music from the cliff above, coming from an open studio window at the very tip of the headland. Latraviata was already at work, thick Russian chords falling down to the sand. The locked gate at the beach end of her staircase was simply marked Entry To Abalone Cove Is Not Possible.

He ran back down the beach all the way to the hotel. He looked into the dining room first, and Anna was there, surrounded by breakfast dishes.

"I saw you from the balcony. Do you like it here?" she asked, patting the chair next to her.

"I think so. There was nobody on the beach and I heard loud music coming from Latraviata's studio."

"Miss Johns, until she gives you permission to call her Latraviata. They have Irish oatmeal here and sliced oranges, which I've already ordered for you."

After breakfast, Anna put on a large sun hat, carried a rolled parasol, and they set out to find No.11 Waterbird Lane. The clerk at the front desk had drawn a circle around where he thought it was on the map, a walk of some fifteen minutes. It was uphill to the lot and they both breathed heavily when they found the sign. There were the same words as the *Los Angeles Times* ad: For Sale, Sea View Lot, with a SOLD banner pasted across. It was a long way from the sea.

"I think Sea View Lot may be stretching things a bit," Anna said.

"But, look, I can see a piece of the ocean over there, between those trees."

"When someone describes a sea view lot, I expect a proper vista of white-foaming surf and long stretches of sandy beach. No matter, though, I just worry that Mr. Sanborn paid too much."

"And look at that big rock along the side of the lot. I can climb it like a mountain."

"Well, it's our land and it's where we're going to build."

The sun was getting stronger and Anna put up her parasol, small bamboo struts holding taut the yellow paper. Anna's face was washed in a golden hue, her white hair restored to blonde. As they went over to sit on the rock, to

Donovan she had changed to a young woman.

She said, "The longer am I here, the better it feels. Even though you can barely see the water, it's protected from wind by this small escarpment. And there's plenty of room in front of the outcropping to build a house."

A car pulled up; it was Simon Grunewald with Esperanzo Mendoza following in his truck closely behind. They got out and walked over to the rock.

"This is Esperanzo Mendoza. Mrs. Merrill," Simon said.

"Mr. Mendoza," Anna said.

He took off his hat, then shook her hand.

He said, "This is a fine site. A level piece with a good rock for the garden."

He walked slowly around the whole property, ninety feet wide by a hundred and fifty feet long. The developer lots in Laguna were small and crowded together, but this one, perhaps a hold-over from an earlier survey, was larger than most. He stooped over to pick up a handful of the soil, stomped down on the ground around the rock. Simon said he must get back to his studio and departed.

"We can build you a good house here, Mrs. Merrill." Donovan wondered why Anna did not tell Mr. Mendoza to call her Anna.

"So, Mr. Mendoza, do we need to draw a plan or may I just tell you what I want?"

"You tell me. I have a son who is a carpenter and two cousins who know all there is about stone."

"I've spent some time thinking about it. I want a house of wood with a stone footing, shingles on the walls and roof. The windows that hinge on the side and open out, casements, I believe, so the whole house will feel the breeze."

Mr. Mendoza made quick notes on a pad and said, "I know a man who can make them. Any size we need."

She continued, "Two bedrooms, one bathroom with a large tub, a sitting room with a place for a dining table, a fireplace, and a small kitchen with a view of the sea. What do you call them, Dutch doors, which open at the top for breezes but a closed bottom to keep the strolling animals and neighboring children out."

"I understand."

"And the house cannot cost more than two thousand, eight hundred dollars." She told Mr. Mendoza the story of the baptism and marriage money, omitting the mention of funerals. "That is all I have to spend."

"Yes."

"If there is some money left when you finish, I would like a porch facing west so we can watch the sunsets. And I see the house all in dark brown and green. Woodland colors to make it cozy for foggy mornings when we light the eucalyptus logs in the fireplace."

"I will build it for you. You must pay me five hundred dollars now. The rest when it is done. We will start next week."

"How long will it take? It is the middle of October now."

"With some clear weather, four months and a little more. Let's say, the last day of February."

"Very good, Mr. Mendoza. I have the money here." Donovan held her parasol as she counted out from her pocketbook the five hundred dollars in small bills, smoothing them down as she counted. She searched around in the purse for another rubber band and encircled the pile with a snap.

Donovan was amazed that spending so much money was that easy. He thought that papers and plans needed to be signed and filed away at city offices, permissions and variances granted.

Anna took Mr. Mendoza's hand again and said, "I have every faith in you, Mr. Mendoza. I will be back on the first of March."

"Thank you, Mrs. Merrill. It will be a good house."

He offered to drive them to the hotel, but Anna said they would walk since it was all downhill. She looked back at the property for a moment, then she took Donovan's arm and they walked briskly toward the hotel, her parasol glowing.

"Do you know what Esperanzo means?" Donovan asked.

"It must mean 'the hopeful one' or 'the man with hope.' What a good name for a builder of houses."

They ate a late lunch at the hotel and each took a nap with French doors open to the sound of the sea. It was a still afternoon and the sun streamed into their rooms, heating the floor between the open curtains.

Donovan woke with a jerk, perspiration dripping on his neck. He put on his bathing trunks, took a towel from the bathroom and ran down the stairs to the beach. The water was cold, but Donovan swam strongly out through the surf to the still water beyond. He looked back to the whole cove and the hotel, where Anna was on her balcony waving to him.

He could not hold away the image of Gareth and Whiting in his mind, how they could have been swimming beside him, taunting him to go out farther. Why did the cold water bring up memories, scenes from the family before the Balboa summer? After ten minutes of treading water, looking back to shore, he wondered if Anna could see into his mind from afar when she motioned for him to come back in.

He swam to shore and dried off. Up at the rooms, he excitedly told her about the water and the beach. She said, "You're a good swimmer, but I wouldn't push your ability too far. It's only a few months since your family went, so you must take care, my dear. I can't have you leaving me, too. Mrs. Johns has invited us to tea, so get dressed and we'll walk over there. I am anxious to see Bartlett's old house and studio again."

They walked around by the road to the front entrance to Latraviata's house. The long front garden was overgrown with banana trees, heliconias and semi-tropical shrubs, a narrow winding path a hundred feet long giving access through to the front doorway. The door was open and, again, they could hear loud music pouring out from the studio.

"Hello," called Anna, and they walked cautiously in. No sign of Latraviata, so they went through the dark rooms to the studio at the far, ocean-end of the house. From the door, they looked into her work space. She was at the easel, sitting on a high-backed stool with her paintbrush perpendicular to the canvas. It was a large canvas, a scene of Laguna hills with eucalyptus trees, thin lines of clouds visible on the horizon.

She turned and saw them. "Let me switch the music off. I love the Russians so much, they get my blood going in the morning, keep it up all day." It was an electric record player in a blonde wood cabinet, the latest innovation. As Donovan watched, she pulled up the curving arm, which held the needle in a small ivory replica of a human hand, perfect down to the red fingernails, with a scratching noise, and the music ended.

"Welcome to my studio. This is where the deed is done. I'm finishing up this piece for a Los Angeles bank, a commission for their downtown offices."

Anna said, "What a good place to work. Doesn't the view distract you, though? Windows looking out to the horizon on all sides?"

"No. I just turn the other way. When I get going on a studio piece, I don't even hear the door bell or the telephone. Only Rachmaninoff and the brush on the canvas. So let's have tea. Come with me."

She led them back through the house to the cool kitchen with unwashed dishes piled high in the sink. Filling the tea-kettle with water, she rinsed out a round, brown teapot in the sink, the type Anna called a Proper English Teapot. With the soiled tea-cups and saucers retrieved from under the dinner plates, she rinsed, dried them and arranged them on the tray.

Anna, immediately at home in a kitchen, put on an apron and finished the washing up while Latraviata assembled the tray of tea paraphernalia.

The painter said, "Tomorrow, I would like to have the two of you, the Grunewalds and some others to dinner. It will celebrate my completion of the bank commission. There's a woman in town who can cook for me and we'll have it out on the terrace above the sea, if it's not too windy."

Anna said, "You should let me cook for you. I would love to do it."

"That's not fair, as you are supposed to be one of the guests."

Anna heard in the other woman's voice the slight sound

of her relenting and said, "No, it's settled. Donovan and I will do the shopping tomorrow morning and I'll cook the dinner. After that, I'll sit down on the terrace to be one of the guests."

"Splendid. How lucky we are here to be getting you as a neighbor, Anna."

"Miss Johns, may I walk down the steps to the sea?" Donovan asked.

Latraviata granted the awaited first name permission and said yes to his question. Donovan smiled back to Anna.

"Thank you, Latraviata." He went quickly outside to the savor of pronouncing her name, again and again. Her terrace was two hundred feet above the rocky sea below, and the staircase started with steps cut into the stone cliff to a landing with a roofed pergola, then a wooden stair took up the cause, angling back and forth down the cliff. Another landing, just above the surf, was wet with the ocean spray, and the final dozen steps descended to the closed gate that Donovan saw from the beach. It was three hundred and six steps down, Donovan counted.

Up above, Anna and Latraviata had their English tea, in the newly washed cups and saucers, a waste bowl, a pitcher of heated milk and assorted biscuits from tins.

"It's wrong to envy, but I think I do envy your life here. Living above the surf and working in your beautiful studio," Anna said.

"I love it, too. Each day I remind myself how I hated the gray afternoons of England and the constricted life I had to live there."

"Were you married?"

She nodded. "I am still. He is a good man, actually, but entirely bland like rice pudding without the raisins. It wasn't his fault, really, as he was bred to be boring. The Johns are a lovely, landed family with large houses in Kent, gardens and servants. They trace back to the Conquest. They husband their animals and the land, their fortune, breed more little Johns for continuance, but nothing more. What passes for art in their houses are the portraits of ancestors by forgotten painters of slight ability. Thin, tall lady in a blue dress with delphiniums behind on the stairs next to a fat lady, round pink cheeks with wolf-hounds on a leash. On and on as you go up. Most of my friends considered me a lucky woman and my marriage a good match, however."

"That would be difficult for a woman of talent like you, being caught in a trap."

"I hated it there: too cozy, too smugly right. We are separated but not divorced. I know he was almost delighted for me to go away, since my aversion to country life made everybody around me unhappy as well. Compared to his sister, I was a termagant; now he has the time to play with his cows and inspect the wheat-fields." She poured them a half a cup of tea from the brown pot and filled the cup with warm milk. She looked up at Anna with a question if the tea arrangement was correct.

Anna nodded her consent at the milky brew, "I understand. How did you decide it was time to go? What happened that one day?"

"Nothing, really. Two weeks of constant rain finally stopped; it was morning and I looked out my window at the sun and warmth, birds at last drying off, shaking their feathers enough to sing. I knew I wanted more light, both physically and emotionally. So I went down to Derrick's study and told him that, although I loved him profoundly, I was leaving."

"Did he object?"

"Heavens no, and he wouldn't think to ask me why. He did wonder where I was going. I told him Provence or Morocco or California, I hadn't decided yet."

"He was not unhappy?"

"Unhappy? Perhaps. I saw a flash of hurt in his eyes, but he recovered quickly. Americans might find it difficult to understand the layers of the English class system, the powers that some have and the obligations that constrict others. Although Derrick Johns was from a good, Norman family with wealth, position and land, my family was immeasurably finer with its beginnings in the ancient trunk of England. The Johns plodded along with their rents and harvests, but the Oswalds, my family, made their way through fifty generations by their wits and their abilities. They had a little land, but longstanding connections to the throne, titles if they chose and wealth from many sources. They were writers, scholars, artists, poets, and composers who could dance a courtly step and weave among the corridors of power for their own gain. A Johns would never think to question the decision of an Oswald."

"Were you in love with Derrick in the beginning?"

"I must have been. It was all arranged and I was too young to question. Then it became more and more apparent that it would never be enough just to be a country wife of high rank. Derrick loved me completely, so I must truly be a thankless wretch. He asked me to write when I got settled, which I do. He keeps my bank account replenished when it gets too low and I write him longer letters on holidays. It's all very civilized, as only the English truly understand. I sent him a new painting for the manor house this last summer, told him where to hang it."

"How did you know you would succeed as a painter? Had you studied art?

"As a girl, yes, but only in the most rudimentary way. My dear father took me for many hours to the museums of London and they were the happiest of my youth. I just knew, deep down, I could do it."

"Did you come right to California?"

"Yes. Carmel at first, but it was too chilly up there. Southern California was better and I came here the next year, bought Bartlett's house and studio the first week. I told the estate agents to send the bill to Derrick, which he paid without comment. I struggled with my work for a year in the studio. It got imperceptibly better the next year and the third I felt a blossoming, green leaves and promising buds along the branches."

"It's clear you are now in full bloom. As I said before, I am envious."

"Do I sense in your questions an unhappiness with your own life?"

Anna was uncomfortable with the light thrown back on her, but knew that Latraviata's candor demanded the same from her. "I think unhappiness is the wrong word. I love James and my life in San Miguel, but something else beckons. At first I convinced myself that I needed to show Donovan the interesting things in the world, but I knew it was a lie. I am looking for something for myself. I think the right word might be restless."

"Yes. You must consider me a friend, Anna."

"I already do."

Donovan came into the room with an excited description of the stairway, shore birds and boats at sea. Anna said they had overstayed their welcome and they would see Latraviata tomorrow.

"By the way, what menu should we have for your guests?"

"It's seems only right that the cook should choose. There will be seven or eight guests." She rummaged around in a drawer, pulled out a handful of five and ten dollar bills that she gave to Anna. Through the banana trees and palms of the front garden, she accompanied them to the front gate and watched, waving, as they went down the lane to the town center.

When they returned to their rooms at El Delirio, Anna told Donovan that he was on his own for a couple of hours, because she must write a letter to James. She pulled out a page of the hotel stationery.

My Dearest, What an exciting few days. Donovan and I found my land at 11 Waterbird Lane and, if a bit off the track, it was all that could be expected. I arranged with a most capable builder to start as soon as possible and paid him a deposit. We have made friends here already, artists in the town who have taken us up like forgotten waifs.

You will like them, I know. Donovan swims in the sea, a strong swimmer it appears. I have met a woman painter and we have become dear friends, like girlhood chums. We will be back at the rectory on Friday night, so please ask Li Fong to arrange for the evening meal. I miss my quiet life in San Miguel but what a joy to have new horizons. Every year now we can have an interlude by the sea, away from your churchly pressures. Your loving wife, Anna.

110

She wondered as she wrote if he would take to her new friends, so unlike the members of the vestry and the altar guild. This seaside town and its artistic denizens might as well be in Patagonia or Tibet.

Unhappy Children
1970

This would be my sixth solo exhibition, three of them at the same gallery in Santa Fe and three in other western cities. The paintings that I had been working on for the past year would be on display for everybody to view and judge. Most of the opening-nighters will be festive and pleasant, effusive about my new work, but there will always be a few acquaintances across the room with the body language of disapproval. It never gets easy.

Perhaps, if you were a painter with a complex, full ego, sure you were the best in the world, a Picasso or an O'Keeffe, it would have been a grand occasion, full of joy and adulation. But for me, it was a time to endure, a necessity in the scheme of things, looking often at my watch for the seven-thirty end to the event. I consistently felt that I needed four or five more days, or even several weeks to finish the work, and here I was serving an uncooked meal.

Solo exhibits have their own merit, however much I came down on them. True collectors walked by with supporting comment, friends encircle you and the odd person makes an unexpected, telling observation. If you never exposed your work to strangers, none of that would happen. Of course, the real reason galleries press painters into one-person shows has nothing to do with such abstract notions. It's money. A one-man show sells more paintings, whatever the emotional pressures that might put upon their artist. Dance harder, sing louder.

By this, the sixth show, I realized that there could be other, deeper benefits. One was the harvest effect. If man as a species had a long run as a hunter-gatherer, he also had many eons growing plants for his food, and both of these endeavors required an episode with a beginning, a middle and an end. The farmer planted, tended and harvested, culminating with a season of autumnal completion. The painter works for a period, then lets go. End of episode. Fulfillment. Look forward to another year.

Another benefit was the simple pulling together of your recent work into a new space, not your own studio. The gallery staff looked at my pictures with different, experienced eyes and decided where each should hang, how this one related more closely with that one, or contrasted with another. Instead of spread haphazardly around your work space, stacked against the walls or upon each other, the paintings now showed themselves in new ways. It was immediately clear where you had won and where you had come near failure. Clear in a way that could never happen in your studio.

Carole Francis came by during the closing minutes of the reception. "Donovan, it's almost over. I know you're relieved. Again."

"I'm ready to sit down and have a drink."

Carole was now a distinguished Santa Fe artist, recognized by the whole community as one of the town's treasures. Her exhibits sold out in the first minutes and commissions from all over the world kept her busy in the other months. I held a measure of guilt about Carole's single status after all these years. She enfolded Tomas in her love, but made it very clear that her love for me was as strong as ever. She often said that there would be a time for the two of us, which usually prompted me to change the subject.

She said, "I'll be at Tomas's party a little late. Another opening to attend."

"I may be late, myself."

"Don't make Tomas mad."

He had organized a seated dinner for fifty. It was, in his mind, the only proper way to mark the occasion. He was good at organizing social events, but I would have preferred to wait a day or two. It was Carole who observed that painters' companions--wives, husbands, lovers, brothers, sisters--who should by all rights share in the joy of an artist's exhibit, often went into a deep funk at the opening reception. That their companion was now the center of attention, the momentary focus of the art community, somehow endangered them, made their own worth precarious. They frequently did very strange things, like dyeing their hair a new color, getting an odd sickness that required trips to the emergency room, wrecking the car or setting the kitchen on fire. Tomas's version of this was to plan a dinner party that I expressly did not want and from which no amount of reason could dissuade him.

The Ludlow Gallery was adept at clearing out opening night receptions when their time was over. Lights were dimmed, then five minutes later, shut off completely. The grumbling remnants, plastic glasses of white wine in hand, oozed out the door and the place was finally empty, except for me and the staff. I asked them to turn the lights on again, that I wanted to look at the paintings alone. They left me to lock up.

This exhibit was for twenty paintings, a considerably fewer number than in past years. Since the price of my work had grown gradually higher as the paintings became easier to sell, the gallery was not annoyed at this smaller number. They produced a slick-papered, full color catalogue with essays extolling my brilliance and full page reproduction of all except the last two paintings, which I had worked on right to the end. Go down fighting, Simon used to say, the Excalibur of Art still in your hand. Never give up.

The paintings for this show were an homage of Anna, still-life paintings of the objects I remember from her houses. I knew she would not attend, replete in her hillside house, but I wanted to paint them nonetheless. I had seen a photograph of a table crowded with the objects and fabrics that Matisse used again and again in his work, photographed in a book about his art. He was quoted, "The object is an actor: an object can play a different role in ten different paintings."

So I did the same thing, photographing all the objects I had used in my paintings clustered together on a sideboard, like a boat full of refugees from a tropical island or all the children from a summer camp, unhappy in the sun. Here was the cast, without costume or makeup, waiting to perform. We used the photograph on the back of the announcement for the exhibit.

Some of the pieces I had owned for many years, memories imbedded deep in their surface. Most were of Chinese origin--yellow porcelain bowls and platters, weathered figurines, bronze fragments, stone bits that I had collected, odd pieces of fabric. I found at an ephemera shop two steamship stickers from

Shanghai to the US, half in English, half in Chinese and pages from a Mandarin edition of Jane Austen, which I crumpled for something sharp against the smooth porcelain.

As I painted them, my thoughts returned to Anna's curious attraction to Wo Fong. Her interest in him had bothered me deeply as a boy because I did not understand it. He was not attractive in any physical way, but he must have represented an exotic escape from the long days at the rectory. He was still an enigma for me.

If Laguna was a community of different and new dances for Anna and me, we joined right in. I'm very glad we did, rather than pulling back in alarm. Those years made a solid footing for what I was to become, a foundation for the importance of art, painting and a productive life.

But there was something more about Anna and things Chinese. She had, I think, a sensual attraction to Chinese men of rank. Rank was the operative word. They needed to have power. A very strange attribute in an Episcopal minister's wife to have sexual longings for Sino-males. She would deny it vehemently, I know, but as I remember the episode of her patting Wo Fong's arm, I knew it was so.

It was good to let the paintings go. The harvest was over.

The telephone rang and it was Tomas.

"When are you coming? Everybody's here and dinner is ready to be served."

"Sorry. Time just got away from me."

"I can't start the serving without you."

"Please do. Start serving everybody. I'll be right there, I promise."

Braised in Milk
1938

At one o'clock in the afternoon, Anna and Donovan were at the local market where they introduced themselves to the owner, Mr. Featherstone. "I'm Anna Merrill and this is my grandson, Donovan."

"You are new to Laguna? Welcome," Mr. Featherstone, the grocer, said.

"Anna's building a house on the hill," Donovan said.

She said, "Yes, soon to be bonafide residents. We are cooking tonight for Mrs. Latraviata Johns, a celebration dinner. What sort of roasts do you have?"

"A lovely leg of lamb, a sirloin tip roast, and pork loins of various weights. We know that Mrs. Johns doesn't cook, so it is a treat to have stock from our store finally in her house."

"The pork loin roast, please. Cut it large enough for eight, if you will, and roll it tightly with four loops of strings. Linen strings, if you have them." Mr. Featherstone was happy to provide for a real cook.

The fall crop of artichokes was in, displayed in a pyramid in the produce section. Anna counted out eight of those, potatoes, carrots, capers, milk, flour, sugar, coffee. It was better to assume that Latraviata's house was totally bare, Anna thought. Salt, pepper, spices, butter, waxed paper, and everything for the meal. The dinner appeared whole in her mind as she shopped, platters served on the terrace.

It was too heavy a load for them to carry, so the Featherstone son promised to deliver it at Latraviata's in half an hour. They walked slowly out to the promontory, the truck pulling up behind them just as they arrived at the front gate.

Latraviata was occupied in the studio, so Anna and Donovan unloaded the groceries into the kitchen. Anna asked Donovan to wash and dry all the dishes already stacked in the sink while she browned the roast in butter, turning it over several times in a cast-iron pan. She would braise the pork roast in a bath of milk, a slow Italian recipe that cooked the pork to a tender and juicy end, with the milk transformed to nut brown clusters of gravy.

She cut the tops off the artichokes and leveled the leaf ends with scissors. The carrots and potatoes were washed, peeled, and cut into pieces, ready for boiling. From the sugar, coffee, eggs, cream, and flour she assembled an Austrian coffee charlotte in three levels, dark on the bottom to light on top, which would bake in a pan of water after the roast came out. She made the sugar cookies to accompany the pudding, and they baked alongside the roast, giving a sweet overtone to the aromas of roasting pork.

Latraviata did not appear in the kitchen until five o'clock, assured by a childhood of privilege, staff always in the kitchen, that her party was being prepared with the best of hands. Pots were steaming on the stove top, and the oven gave out its wafting of a finished roast. She had invited everybody for five-thirty, while it was still light on her seaside terrace. She laid forks, spoons, knives, plates, and glasses on the table, with a patterned cloth from India that she produced from a bottom drawer, and the promise of a still evening on the seaside terrace made itself true. As the finishing touch, she cut tropical blossoms from her front thicket and floated them in a deep platter of water.

"Anna, my dear. It is more of a miracle for me to see a meal appear out of nowhere than to see a painting evolve. I realize it isn't exactly from nowhere, but you are a genius."

"It comes easily for me. I love to do it. I believe everything is now in readiness. The Austrian charlotte will come out while we're at table."

"I see sugar cookies with a fork finish, as well."

The first to arrive were Simon Grunewald and Portman. Simon kissed Latraviata on the cheek and shook Anna's hands enthusiastically, patting Donovan on the head. Portman shook everybody's hand as well, pumping the arm with much bravado.

Latraviata produced a bottle of a sweetly bitter Tuscan wine, which she poured into small, footed glasses. For Donovan, she watered it down to a light pink. They walked to the front of the terrace, a coral-orange sky coming up as if ordered.

Two women arrived next and they were introduced as Agnes and Mary Louise, a fellow painter and her companion, a writer. Latraviata brought Agnes over to Anna, while Mary Louise spoke to the others.

"Agnes, this is a dear friend who is moving here soon. Anna Merrill."

Anna said, "A summer resident only, I think. You are all

so lucky to be here the year around."

Agnes, who had close-cropped hair and strong hands, said, "Winter can be stormy, but I get my best work done during our tempests. Rain and wind pelting the studio, dark clouds all day. December and January can be practically Wagnerian, but I love it here then. Mary Louise re-reads Proust or the Russians every winter, sometimes out loud to me while I am at the easel. Are you a painter, too?"

"No, although I share your appreciation of unsettled weather."

Latraviata said, "Agnes paints the most compelling scenes from the Bible, large tableaux to pique the faithful. The last time I was in her studio she was working on a vast view of the Dead Sea, with multitudes of animals and fishermen eyeing each warily on the shore. A triumph of Christian skepticism, I thought."

"I would love to see your work, "Anna said.

"You must come by tomorrow. Mary Louise and I can offer you a lunch, nothing fancy."

Before Anna could accept or decline, Latraviata said, "We have Anna to thank for our celebration dinner tonight. I have just seen it all laid out in the kitchen and succulent delights await."

"At last a good cook in Laguna. So many wonderful artists who cannot melt butter without burning it. You are most welcome, Anna," said Agnes.

They sat down at the round table, Anna and Latraviata reserving the chairs near the doors for themselves. They brought the platters of food, the tender pork slices in the rich brown gravy that the milk had become, steaming bowls of potatoes and carrots, a platter of green salad, each with spoons and forks for serving. Anna returned with a plate of artichokes surrounded by small bowls of melted butter.

Simon winked and said, "I'll just take this old, overcooked end piece," forking the first slice onto his plate as if he were performing a valuable disposal service for the other guests.

"Get that fake martyr's tone out of your voice, Simon. It's only right that our eminent septuagenarian should have the coveted end piece," Latraviata said, pulling the cork from a bottle of wine with a twist. She had connections with the wine merchants across the Mexican border, who kept her cupboard full.

"What a treat," Agnes said.

Simon said, "I think Anna's arrival signals a new Epicurean age in Laguna. Gone are the dry meats and tasteless vegetables of El Delirio. No more imitation strawberry Junket and thin fish soups. Let's drink to our new palmy days."

The evening went on with spirited conversation, energized by the food and wines. After the pudding and cookies, when a slight breeze made the terrace too cool, Anna served the coffee inside. Latraviata's sitting room was a bohemian jungle of furniture, paintings, houseplants on stands and statues on plinths. Even when she turned on every lamp, all with dark amber parchment shades, the room was barely lit. A stronger light might have revealed the spider webs, bird droppings, dust and scattered evidence of an owner without a shred of interest in housework, but the illusion of elegance was unquestioned in her gloomy, grimy salon.

By ten the guests were gone and Anna and Latraviata had washed all the dishes.

"It was so much fun. Donovan and I must be off on the early car from Newport. James would be totally bereft if I were not in my pew this Sunday."

"My dear, I will think about you and your restless plight. Of course, you and Donovan must stay here your next trip. I have two rarely used spare rooms down that hall, from which I promise to shake out the spiders before you arrive."

"Thank you, but rooms at El Delirio keep us from being a bother."

"Absolutely no..."

Anna interrupted her. "Being asked is almost as good as actually staying."

"Very well. When will you return?"

"Mr. Mendoza promises to have the house finished by the first of March."

"Not sooner? How tragic for us to be doomed to the El Delirio. Not a single edible meal until Spring, but there it is. You must travel safely."

"Please tell Agnes I will come by her studio the next trip."

The two women hugged and Anna woke Donovan who was sleeping on the sitting room sofa. They went out through the tropical thicket.

As they approached the hotel, Anna said, "Did you have a good time?"

"Yes. Simon wants me to work in his studio next summer."

"Next summer? I don't think we'll be here all summer."

"He wants me to stretch canvases and keep his brushes clean, if we stay the whole summer."

"You could learn a great deal." It was better not to argue about possibilities.

"I'm sleepy," Donovan said.

"Yes. Get some good sleep, because we have a long trip back tomorrow. I'll wake you early."

Behind Magnolias

Whatever else came from their week in Laguna Beach, Donovan's standing among his classmates at Audubon School was vastly improved. David, proud to divulge inside information early, had spread the word that Donovan was helping his grandmother plan a new house on the cliffs above the beach. She had taken him out of school with only a short note to the principal, not waiting for a proper answer with permission.

Miss Mulock did not lose the opportunity to seek reprisal for her being left out of the process. "Donovan, will you tell us about your stolen week in Laguna?"

Donovan was mortified to be called forward this way. "It was good, thank you."

"More details, please."

"I met some artists. Painters, who do nothing but paint all day long."

"What sort of paintings did you see?"

Miss Mulock continued to press Donovan for a description of what was an exotic locale to her group, prying into the smallest particulars. Donovan reluctantly produced answers about the town, its denizens and their visit. His reticence set just the right tone with the other classmates, a pride-filled report would have had the opposite result. That week Donovan became an accepted personage, no longer a faceless fellow student.

At lunch, Donovan asked David, "Why did you tell?"

"She asked me where you were, and I thought it was all right."

"Well, it wasn't."

For the first time other students came up to talk to them at lunch under their pepper tree. Several walked by to just say hello, not breaking their stride as they talked. Marjorie Eastover, a tall, pretty girl who was not part of any popular group, sat down beside them. Donovan knew she lived in a three-story, white-shingled house on two lots. He saw her there on his way home one day. The front had a green lawn, the house itself hiding behind a row of magnolia trees. There was a sign near the street that said, Dr. Portius Eastover, Radiotics.

"Hello, Donovan," she said. "I've been to Laguna Beach, too. Last summer my father took us there for a month. He rented us a house on a cliff above the sea. It was really foggy, every day."

"I saw you when I was walking home."

"I saw you, too. Maybe we can walk home together."

Marjorie strolled away from them, and David said, "I don't like her." Donovan knew it was because she had intervened between the two of them. It was better not to object too much, he thought. In his school back in Pasadena, old friends almost invariably did not like his new friends.

After classes that afternoon, David made a point of asking

if he could walk with him. It was obvious that he needed to pay more attention to Donovan, lest Marjorie move in. They did not say anything as they passed the Eastover house, but Donovan could see someone behind the magnolias at the upstairs window. They continued on to the church driveway, where David said goodbye.

After dinner, Anna's finely tuned warning system told her that the McBeale grandparents were on their way for a surprise visit. She started a pot of coffee and brought cups and saucers down from the shelves. Grandfather Merrill said he had God's Work to do in his study and would not be available. Anna and Donovan were washing and drying the dishes when the doorbell rang.

They sat in a circle in the chairs of the sitting room. Grandfather McBeale said, "Your grandmother and I are concerned for you, Donovan. Are things going well?"

He said, looking at Anna, "Yes. I made an A in school."

Anna said, "He's a bright boy and can do anything he sets his mind to."

"We heard that you took him out of school for a trip to Laguna."

"Yes. He didn't miss anything of importance, because he made an A anyway. There is much to learn in a trip to a strange, new place."

"Well, as long as it doesn't happen too often. The reason for our visit is to tell you that Eugene, Jr. has sold the Pasadena house and invested the money in an annuity with his company. It will pay for Donovan's college and perhaps more. Donovan just needs to sign these papers."

"Is that a safe investment?" Anna asked. "My father lost

a great deal in the panic of eighteen ninety-two and always afterward he said that annuities were 'rat food'."

"Eugene, Jr. works for the company itself and says it is rock solid. They invest the money for you, then pay out the dividends when they are needed."

She poured the McBeales each a cup of coffee while Donovan slowly wrote his signature on each page. Without asking, Anna stirred in a dollop of thick cream and a spoonful of sugar. She said as she passed the cups, "Donovan has told me he wants to go to art school, so we must look for the best place. I am sure that Eugene Jr.'s annuity will pay the tuition for the Art Student's League in New York or perhaps even a school in Europe."

"But his parents always planned on his going to law school."

"No, I think that was intended for Gareth, the firstborn. Donovan is an artist, and if he chooses what is in his heart, he will be a success."

"Well, now that Gareth is gone, Donovan moves into that firstborn place. We had always planned to have a grandson come to the McBeale firm."

"It doesn't work that way, Eugene. Donovan can never become a firstborn, and because of that, he was given other talents. Just look at his thumb, a sure sign of artistic ability. He will become a great painter, but he would be a commonplace, unmotivated lawyer."

They all three stopped talk and looked over at Donovan, hoping to see outward evidence of his greatness or commonplaceness, nodules of the future, in this unhappy boy with scuffed shoes and denim trousers. As he secretly felt his thumb for lumps indicative of talent, Donovan saw from their expressions that the McBeales did not believe Anna.

Grandfather McBeale said, "Well, we have time to discuss all of this further." His years handling difficult probate cases provided a firm belief in the compromise, difficult opponents who eventually gave up their issues of discord when whipped down by endless opposition. While he stood up and adjusted his coat, Grandmother McBeale quickly gulped her cup of coffee and stood up as well. With pleasantries all around, they were gone.

Donovan said to Anna, "Don't you like Grandfather McBeale?"

"We can't always like all of our family, but we can love them."

"Would you love me more if I was a firstborn, like Dad and Gareth?"

Anna did not reply, but leaned down to kiss Donovan on the top of his head. It was time for bed, she said, and love did not come in sizes. If you loved somebody, you loved somebody.

No Cavalry Boots

After several weeks of waiting, Marjorie Eastover at last succeeded in getting Donovan alone on their walk home. She saw an opening when David was away momentarily during lunch and closed in. She sat down next to Donovan and said, "Why don't we walk home together this afternoon? I want to show you father's office."

"His office? Why?"

"Because he has all these books with strange pictures, people without clothes."

"Okay."

"He's away in Los Angeles every Wednesday. So we'll have it to ourselves. Mother never leaves the kitchen."

When David came back, they stopped talking. The bell signaling the end of the lunch recess rang. At the end of classes, David had arranged to meet his mother at the newspaper offices, so he walked off in another direction. Donovan waited for Marjorie, and they strolled north.

At the sign for her father's office, Donovan asked, "What are radiotics?"

"Father made that word up. Static electricity is supposed to cure things, so it needed to have a scientific-sounding name. He invented the radiotic machines, too. They are all made for him in Cleveland."

"Can he just make up a name? Is that right?"

"Of course. America is a free place, he says, you can do anything you want. We even changed our name."

"What was it before?"

"Estovich. It's Russian and father wanted us to sound more American, so he changed it to Eastover."

Donovan looked around, without success, for evidence of Russia as they walked into the front hall of the Eastover house. There were no samovars, cavalry boots or Cossack swords sitting about as he had imagined and there were no exotic spices or musky aromas from the steppes. Although the outside of the house was painted white, the inside walls were a dark maroon and a long, matching runner went down the whole length of the hallway. Dr. Eastover's office was off to the right, behind a pair of French doors with the panes painted white.

Marjorie opened the door and led them in. There was an examining table in the middle of the room, machines that looked like large vacuum cleaners against one wall, and a roll-top desk against the other. A row of hooks held a line of doctor's white coats, with a stethoscope and head mirror hanging at the end. "The books are over here." She pulled a medical text down from the shelf and showed Donovan a picture of a naked syphilis patient.

"Oh my. Are there more?" he asked.

They went through all the illustrations in the book, without comment. Finally, Donovan asked, "Are there any with people that aren't sick?"

"No, silly, that's what these books are for. Books about naked, sick people."

"You're really lucky to have these."

"I know."

Marjorie put the book back on the shelf and the visit was over. She walked to the door and opened it for Donovan. "Next time, I can show you how the machines work."

Donovan promised to show her the cemetery in return for this disclosure, but they did not set an exact date.

November in Southern California was a blessed time, warm, clear sunshine during the days, with a hint of coolness at night. Gardens took a pause before winter, but roses still bloomed and rain showers started to green the surrounding hills. The abundance of a California spring was yet to come, but the sense of waiting in paradise permeated the days as the light grew increasingly golden, nights longer.

The visit to the Laguna artists percolated in Donovan's mind and he tried to draw and paint with the supplies that Anna had provided. At first he just drew with a pencil the objects around the house, vases, bowls, books and the like. Then he sat on the front porch and drew the bamboo stalks that surrounded the entire house. He filled several notebooks with bamboo sketches and they grew increasingly skillful as he went along.

Anna sat for him one day on the front porch, in her Chinese robe with a deep yellow fan in her hand. Donovan started a large drawing of her seated in the high-backed chair. After thirty minutes, she asked if she could see.

He turned the sketchbook around so she could see. He said, "It's not quite right yet."

"A good start, though. You've quite caught my hair and the fan."

"Do you think so?"

"Absolutely yes. We'll do this again, my dear. I can see you as a painter when you grow up, painting clouds again and again, wonderful colors. Blues and violets, ochres, and deep impressive, stormy colors."

It became a pattern for them in the hour right after school. Anna had iced tea with peppermint leaves prepared and was already seated on the porch, with the supplies on a table. Donovan immediately started a sketch and, if things went well, they could spend an hour together. His sketchbooks filled up, so he drew on the back sides of all the pages.

In the times when she was busy with rectory duties, he gathered together the objects to make a still life. He thought they were progressing better than the portraits of Anna, so he was eager to continue in that vein. It was a Saturday afternoon, and he went around the rectory collecting items for his composition. He discovered some lemons in the kitchen, a brass plate, a yellow bowl and a white linen towel, arranging them in a corner of his room with a shaft of afternoon light.

For an hour, while the light was still raking across, he sketched in the details. The brass plate reflected the yellow of the bowl, and the lemons were a slightly different shade. He noticed how the colors of the objects were picked up in the white cloth, especially in its folds.

Anna's voice startled him, "Oh, my gracious. You've taken the yellow bowl from the sitting room."

"Is that wrong, Anna?"

"I would hate to see it broken. It has no great value, though."

Anna sat down on his bed. "Your grandfather and I got

that in San Francisco on our honeymoon. I saw it in a window of an antiques shop, not in Chinatown but up on St. Francis Square. It was so beautiful, that I asked James if we could go in and look."

Donovan said, "I didn't know."

Anna continued, "We went in and I asked about it. The owner said he had just purchased the entire estate of an old, single man and this was one of several yellow bowls. He thought they were Japanese or Korean, he did not know which. They had their own storage cases, round boxes covered with dark blue silk, and rosewood stands. I told him we were on our honeymoon, and this is what I wanted to celebrate our visit."

"So he sold it to you?"

"Actually, he gave it us. It was the largest of the three bowls. He saw your grandfather's clerical collar and said he would earn merit in heaven to help a man of god and his wife. He would raise the price on the other two to cover it."

"I will put it back. I'm sorry."

"No. Finish your painting, but be very careful. I feel that since it was given to us, it has a special place in our house. Don't bang it down or the like. I love looking at it, the elegant way the sides curve outward then go flat at the top."

After she left, Donovan felt ill at ease with the bowl in his room, so he quickly put it back in its curve-legged stand in the sitting room. He could paint another bowl, the white one that he found on the kitchen counter. He knew that Anna loved the objects in her house like no one else in the family; each piece treasured for some memory.

Strictures, Schemes
1970

*T*omas would be upset with me, since I did not leave the gallery as I promised. I needed some more time to look at my paintings. Only twenty minutes, or so. It couldn't wait until tomorrow, because all the energy from the opening night would have evaporated. Now they were full of energy, radiating back what so many people looking at them had generated. I theorized that there was a quality that the mythic paintings of the world have, among many others, a radiance from having been idolized, like the radium dial on a watch after a spell in the sun. *Guernica, Mona Lisa, Primavera, Dejeuner sur l'Herbes* and the *Nympheas* all exude this air of well-being, quite apart from their artistic value, from having been admired, adored, and on display for generations.

Albeit a provincial, small event, my opening reception had imbued the canvases with a version of this stature that I wanted to observe, perhaps to experience them in some non-physical way without other people around to distract. I pulled a chair from the adjoining office and sat down in their midst.

I could easily see the passages that were successful,

ventures and experiments I had pushed myself to include in the paintings. The new light source, from the left, was a good idea, making me pay closer attention to the mechanics of lighting. The luster on the lighted side of the objects was extra-embellished, particularly where they sat next to a dark shadow.

Another stricture I had put upon myself was obvious to me, but perhaps not to others. I wanted no object to touch another object, or even to overlap visually. They should stand as isolated bits, incapable of communication except with the wash of light over them onto a neighbor. Islands, not peninsulas. A loosely spaced crowd, each member suspicious of getting too close to a neighbor.

For me, this constraint gave the paintings a loneliness that belied the friendly colors of the blue-and-white porcelain, the white-white-white backgrounds of starched clean linens, and the sunniness of the yellow objects. Here were all these happy items, but I nevertheless sensed a certain lurking anxiety as well.

In most of the paintings, I included several pieces from the jig-saw puzzle that I have carried around for so many years, yet to complete. I made sure that no piece touched another piece. I included at least one of those that Leonore hoarded, the heads of the concubines, and a touch of cloudy sky from the ones that I sequestered in my pile. Were these the cloudy skies that Anna had foretold?

The third requirement was a consistent, small line of fire red around the dark side of every major object, as if a devilish light source stroked them with a crimson glow. I remember Latraviata at her easel doing exactly this with her landscapes, limning a crimson line around the dark side of her clouds or groves of trees. "Persimmon red from sultry nights in harem gardens," she had said. Gardens in a harem were images that did not resonate effectively with me, but I understood what persimmon red was.

On the yellow bowls, I used a single-haired brush to follow the sumptuous ogee curve on the dark side. I called it a Chinese Red, a yellowed red with a touch of green, a hot, ochre red with no blue in it. The blue and white objects, soup tureens with recollections of family dinners, candlesticks and jelly bowls, all needed a wider line

The telephone rang but I ignored it. It would be Tomas.

Scale was the last element in my new paintings that I wanted to study. I had an idea that when objects in a canvas are slightly larger than their actual size, say about ten or fifteen percent larger, that they somehow appealed more strongly to the modern eye. This idea occurred to me when I was painting a motif where I had accidentally scaled everything that much smaller than actual, reduced by fifteen to twenty percent. I could not rid that motif of the quality of being pinched, penurious, not quite right.

If our hidden mind tells us that objects slightly too small are somehow dry and parched, wouldn't that same mind say the objects only a small percentage larger than life size are generous, well-seated and ebullient? Not a single person at the opening night mentioned the scale to me, but many commented how enthusiastic and impassioned my new paintings were.

Most were exactly square canvases, 40 inches by 40 inches. This is definitely an inert size, neither making a statement for itself nor taking away anything. I had painted two canvases in a slightly off-square size, 40 inches wide by 41 inches high. They appeared square to all but the highly tutored eye. Those were curiously the favorites of the show.

So a stasis was created by being pulled two ways at once. The lonely placement of the objects and the devilish red lines fought against the slightly larger scale and off-square rectangle, to reach an equilibrium. Like a richly fought battle that finally brings you back to home, wounded but content.

I also wondered how much my choice of subject matter dated from the day that Anna asked me to be careful of her yellow bowl. Were these paintings an adult response to a childhood embarrassment? Probably so.

But it was time to truly let the paintings go. The gallery staff had sold most before the reception or during it, so this would be the last time I could see them all together. Sometimes I wondered if my designs and plans were the product of an overactive mind, a neurotic mind, instead of the considered elements of what made painting good. Did they offer an enrichment that avoided calling attention to itself? All the constraints and parameters appeared to be worth the effort. I could see that I was, at least, on the right track. I turned off the lights and went out the side door to the gallery, the one that locked automatically. Tomas's party awaited.

Uprooted Plum
1939

Donovan liked little in the Anglican services at The Church of the Holy Spirit besides the deep, oaken quality of his Grandfather Merrill's voice. Particularly at the end of the services, down it went, lower and lower. It was a baritone rock, kindly and mossy, tumbling majestically down an uneven slope, "Life everlasting, for ever and ever, world without end. Amen." The rest of the service went entirely over Donovan's head, hymns, prayers, sermons, collection plates while he thought of other things, schoolwork, family vaults and radiotics, but that final vocal descent once again brought him sharply into a full appreciation of his grandfather's ability.

Although he tried to love his Grandfather Merrill, he felt a gulf between them. It was different from the apartness he sensed with Grandfather McBeale, who Donovan saw as somebody he could disagree with, make fun of and talk about to other people. This holy grandfather lived on a dais in the well-guarded world of his own, between heaven and earth, impervious to his grandson.

One stormy day that winter they were alone together

in the church, with the wind whistling around the corners. Grandfather Merrill had asked him to help in changing the white-on-black hymn numbers on celluloid rectangles in the sign of the church. This was normally the responsibility of the altar guild, dedicated ladies who arranged flowers and polished brass, but the storm caused scheduling disruptions and threw this task back on the pastor himself.

He was up on a step ladder, Donovan below with the compartmented, pine box with the numbers. "Give me two, seven, and nine, please, Donovan."

"Yes, sir."

"And one, three, and six finishes it. A lively Scottish hymn as I recall. Shepherds on the high hills with rosy sunset light."

"May I ask you a question, Grandfather?"

"Certainly."

"How can somebody sitteth of the right hand of God? I don't understand."

"It's a symbolic gesture of becoming at one with our Lord."

"And the Holy Spirit. What does he look like?"

Grandfather Merrill came down the ladder before answering. "Again, he is a symbolic manifestation of the mystery of God. He probably doesn't have a face since he is a metaphor for the mysticism of God. Have you learned in school what a metaphor is?"

"No."

"It is a figure of speech where one word stands in for another, as in the phrase a mighty fortress is our god."

"Wouldn't it be easier to just say things right out like they really are?"

"Minds better than ours decided that this was the better way."

"If there really is a God, why are there so many symbols?"

His grandfather closed the ladder with an annoyed snap and said "The words 'if there really is' evidence a bitter, suspicious mind in one so young. Does a nine year old boy have the right to question thousands of years of practice and teaching of divinity schools the world over?"

"But Grandfather, I'm ten now."

"Nevertheless, your skepticism is unusual and unattractive in someone your age, ten to be sure, but if this is all an elaborate scheme to get out of Sunday School, it won't work. You will attend every Sunday, without fail. Understood?"

"Yes, sir."

Donovan tried to form another question that would not make his grandfather angry, but the choirmaster intervened with pressing issues about the music for that coming Sunday. It was just as well, because he knew whatever he said would cause more anger from his grandfather. They took the numbers box and the folded ladder away into the vestry. Donovan's short excursion into Trinitarianism came to an unresolved close with a howl of wind around the corners of the church.

The winter storms went on for days, over Christmas week and beyond. Black clouds and rain swept in from the Pacific. Dangerous surf pounded the shores and winds were strong enough to uproot many of the venerable eucalyptus trees along the borders of citrus groves in San Miguel, some falling on houses with children sleeping and others crushing slow-moving automobiles like beetles. The local newspapers headlined the storms and their victims, one photograph of a great fallen trunk with flattened headlights peering out from under.

A week later, the storms continued their relentless press in from the sea. At breakfast Anna announced to both Donovan and Grandfather Merrill, "I had a troubling dream last night. It was our unfinished house in Laguna, looking vulnerable and small. Great waves washed up so high that they tore down the chimney. I saw the broken fireplace heading out to sea like so many pieces of flotsam, almost racing away from land. James, you were on one piece, a shaft of light coming down upon you and Donovan and I were in the dark on another. I woke with a start."

Grandfather Merrill said, "I am sure you are anxious about the house, and your uneasiness came back in a dream."

"I thought it might be an omen. The fireplace, after all, is the heart of the house," she said.

"True omens in dreams are very rare. Perhaps it was just an undigested bit of roast."

"Then this morning, I started to worry about Latraviata, who lives right on the water."

Donovan said, "But her house is way above the sea on her cliff. Three hundred and six steps."

Grandfather Merrill said, "The paper reported that the entire length of the shipping pier at Newport was washed away. Witnesses said it disappeared in minutes, crumpled into kindling. You may be right to worry."

"I will be anxious until I hear otherwise from somebody in Laguna."

That Sunday, Grandfather Merrill gave special prayers for those lost in storms and the sermon was about a peaceful mind in troubled times. Donovan went into his usual trance, thinking personal thoughts about artists and medical illustrations, until his grandfather's final prayers of the service, cascading sonorously down to a baritone "For ever and ever" turning into a vibrating bass, "Amen."

In the Monday mail, Anna received a letter from Simon Grunewald. She read it aloud to Donovan:

My dear Anna. I know that you are anxious about your house and for the safety of your new friends in this winter tempest. Since the telephone lines are still down, Esperanzo Mendoza has asked me to write you that your house is safe. The stone footings his boys put in held firm in the downhill wash of water and they had just finished the roof when the first storm arrived, so it is dry inside. They are so pleased to be building a house for the wife of a holy man, that they have named it Santacasita.

All is well there, as they can now work inside in the bad weather. Latraviata's studio survived the onslaught and winds almost intact, but the wooden portions of her grand stairway are on their way to China. Some of her windows were broken, but Esperanzo's family took time out to repair them. It was a fearful line of storms, unlike any we have seen before, blowing away my favorite plum tree, stripped right out of the ground, roots and all, and away in a single gust. No more green gage happiness in July. Everybody else in Laguna is well, if sodden. Your dear friend, Simon.

"My dream was nearly right, but it was Latraviata's house, not mine," Anna said.

"Should we go down there, do you think?" Donovan asked.

142

"No. Everything sounds under control now. I do like the idea of the house having the name Santacasita. It rings well, doesn't it?"

"What does it mean?"

"Sainted house, or blessed little house, I think. But in Spanish, it sounds more graceful."

Anna asked Donovan to invite David to join them on Saturday, and they would take the Red Car into Los Angeles. She would be shopping for the furnishings for Santacasita, and it seemed appropriate, since the Mendozas came from Mexico, that she buy Mexican items from Olvera Street.

"I thought the two of you might enjoy Olvera Street. David is your best friend, and it is good to include him in family activities."

"I will ask him. I think he's mad at me, though."

"Why ever?"

"Because we met a girl at the school named Marjorie Eastover. She lives right down there on Granada Street, and she didn't ask David to see her father's office. Only me."

"That wasn't nice of her. Then, we definitely must include David for Saturday."

By the time Saturday arrived, David had accepted Anna's invitation. Ah Fong drove them all to the Mission stop to catch the Red Car early in the morning.

The trip into the city took about an hour, at first starting and stopping through each suburban town, then racing into the last few miles through the hills, the wheels clacking on the tracks, and then decelerating through the final tunnel. They were at Olvera Street by ten o'clock, where a street full of shops awaited Anna on the slope up to the church.

"If you get tired of my shopping, you boys can play in the park there, but don't go too far afield. We'll start here at the shops on the right, go all the way up to the cathedral, then I'll do the shops on the left. We should gather here at La Posada if we get separated. Just at noon, I think."

The first shop was filled with shelves of pottery and glassware. Anna chose bright green plates and dishes and glasses in a bubbly pale green. Some platters, pitchers, a tureen and a stack of mixing bowls, all in shades of green and white. The choices for dinnerware were done. Anna checked those off her list and told the owner, "Can you ship these to Laguna? They go to Eleven Waterbird Lane, but people might know it as Santacasita."

"No problem, Senora. We will make a strong crate, pack them carefully in damp sawdust, and they will safely be there in three weeks."

"Splendid."

The next sold all the goods for her kitchen, roasters and frying pans, covered stew pots, terra cotta soufflé dishes, three different sauce pans and a small high-sided pan for clarifying butter. Wooden spoons, steel spoons, knives, a bread knife, spatulas, forks, strainers, a sifter and a nest of funnels. She also bought a very plain service of steel flatware with bone handles, and a pale yellow breadbox. This shop-owner also would be delighted to send these on to Santacasita.

Anna had put aside the money at home that she must pay Mr. Mendoza and the remainder sum she had in her purse. She bought sheets and pillowcases at the linen shop, with instructions for curtains to be made from white cotton panels for the casement windows. "A very deep hem on the bottom and a tunnel for the hanging rod on the top, no embroidery whatsoever. About this long"...(The merchant measured the distance between her hands with a tape.)..."since it won't matter if they hang down too far." The towels and washcloths she chose were from Oaxaca, rough, country terry cloth, pure white. She delighted in the discovery of a pile of soft cotton dish towels, hemmed painstakingly by hand, from Mexico City, hidden behind stacks of brightly dyed coarser versions. These were quality, hand-sewn items for the finest house, the owner said approvingly.

The furniture for the house she bought at several different shops. Four single beds with painted headboards, apples and doves in festoons. Chairs and bedside tables at a shop specializing in the carved wood items from Chiapas, jungle-cut hardwoods that were waxed and polished. A dining table and chairs, lamps made from brass candlesticks with parchment shades and circular grass placemats. The owner said, "Señora, you decide so quickly. It is a joy to have you in my shop."

"I know exactly what I want. If it's right, it says so to me."

"Most women do not listen that well."

"If somewhat misogynist, I know you meant that as a compliment. Thank you, señor."

The proprietor of the next furniture store said, "Señora, you are composing a beautiful house. I have paintings on consignment from Yucatan for very little; saints and angels by the nuns of Merida to grace your walls, at a very good price."

"Señor, I have many artist friends in Laguna. They would be distressed if I came away from here with the work of other artists, however deft these sweet nuns must be."

"Four small panels, only. Fifteen dollars for the four."

"Well, let me look. What wonderful faces they have, the flocks of sheep are very well drawn, and so many clouds and birds. I mustn't be tempted, though." She kept looking at them, then turned to walk away.

"Ten."

"I'd better take them or you will sell them to a well-meaning housewife for five dollars, with nothing left to go back to the poor nunnery. Yes, I'll take them. They seem right for Santacasita."

Tin lamps with pierced tin shades. Three large rugs of bleached cotton with wide green stripes for each of the main rooms, a small rug with no stripes for the bathroom.

At noon, she lacked only the chairs for the front porch. The bamboo ones she preferred all came from China, the wooden ones from Mexico were too square-edged to be really comfortable. At the last stop, she found some leather seated chairs with curved backs. Perfect for watching sunsets on the hill above the sea. They made an agreeable squeaking noise as she tried them out. She rechecked her list and crossed out the last items.

David and Donovan had deserted her after the first two hours, so she walked to the park to find them. They were nowhere to be seen, so she sat and waited on the bench under the statue of the Archangel with a trumpet. She counted out what remained of her furnishing money, just over three hundred dollars when she started. There were eight dollars left. More than enough for a lunch for three of tamales and enchiladas at La Posada and their carfare back to San Miguel. What a successful morning.

Anna then remembered asking the boys to wait at La

Posada and there they were, sitting silently together at the table.

"Well, the shopping for Santacasita is done, everything being sent down to Laguna. What do you think of that?"

Donovan said, "David has a stomach ache. Maybe we should go home."

"Of course. We'll go right now." She felt David's forehead and made apologies to the waiter. At the streetcar stop the car for San Miguel was waiting so they stepped aboard, David drooping noticeably. Anna had David sit next to her and she cradled his troubled head against her shoulder.

David fell almost immediately to sleep, and Donovan asked Anna, "Is it all done? Do you have everything for the house?"

"Almost everything. The Mexican goods have a spirit all their own, maybe because of the hands that made them."

"I like the colors they use. Bright colors."

"Donovan, I had sense of your connection with Mexico in those shops. I am sure you will marry a Latin beauty, sparkling dark eyes, a joy to look at and, a sweet, pliant thing, following your every wish."

"You really think so?"

"I'm almost sure."

David appeared to have recovered somewhat on their arrival home, but Anna asked Donovan to walk with him to his home. Donovan said as they walked, "If you feel like it, we can go into the mausoleum at night sometime."

"All right. I'll bring my flashlight."

"Let's do it next week. Mr. Erasmus is always in the cemetery on weekends."

"Okay. Tuesday or Wednesday night then." With a promise of a new exploit, David's recovery was almost complete.

High Position

At breakfast on Monday, Anna announced to Donovan and Grandfather Merrill that she had invited Wo Fong for tea that afternoon. It was too cool to have it on the porch, so she asked them both to meet in the sitting room about four thirty. Wo Fong, according to his delighted brother, had found a position at the city hall.

Grandfather Merrill said, "I cannot be there, my dear, as the vestry is meeting to decide upon the new stained glass window. There is opposition to using the vestry money that way, so we're going to iron our differences. I may miss dinner as well."

"Oh, bother," Anna said. "I so wanted you to spend some time with Wo Fong."

"Perhaps I can leave the meeting for a moment and look in on you."

"I would like that, James."

The winter storms intensified as January progressed. The usually balmy winter days in Southern California had turned to chilly dark ones, many people using their fireplaces every day. Anna arranged with Ah Fong for a fire in the sitting room hearth, dried eucalyptus logs that popped and crackled with an exotic aroma. Except for the tea pot, the completed tea tray sat on a center, low table with chairs surrounding.

Donovan arrived at four thirty and dried off after his walk home in the rain. He stood with his back to the fireplace. "David isn't mad at me anymore. Marjorie took him to see her father's office, too, so things are better."

"She's a wise girl. Equality is a noble trait in dealing with other people."

"I thought you would like to know."

"I'm glad for David. He hurts easily and his friends should take care not to bruise him."

"You aren't wearing your Chinese robe."

"No. When my thoughts are twisted and ornamental, like the winding entrance to a Chinese garden, I prefer the robes. Mind and cloth are one. At other times, like today, my outlook is like a straight arrow. Look, there's Wo Fong out on the porch."

Donovan opened the door while Wo Fong shed his raincoat and umbrella on the porch, shaking off the water. He made a small nod to both Donovan and Anna, and presented them with a string bag filled with vegetables, as he promised, celery and carrots sticking out from the strings. Li Fong, who had appeared with the pot of tea, took the bag back to the kitchen. Anna seated him in the chair next to the fire.

She said, "I saw lovely carrots peeking out of your bag, like young girls' legs on a hayride. Thank you, Wo Fong."

"You are most welcome. Mr. Donovan, have you been well?"

"Yes, sir. We went to Laguna."

"I understand you did. Did you like it there?"

Anna intervened to explain to Wo Fong about the building of the house and their trip to Olvera Street to furnish it. All would be in readiness for them soon.

Wo Fong said, "So you will spend the summer there?"

"Part of it, anyway. I love the people, artists and thinkers, and the climate there is the best along the coast. People compare it to Menton on the coast of France."

"The Fong vegetable farms are just inland from Laguna. Perhaps I may call on you at next time I am there."

"We would be delighted."

"I have news of my position with your city hall, as an assistant clerk at the Registry of Deeds."

"How wise of them to recognize your abilities."

"I must record all the details of deeds into a large book, very like what I did back in Nanking. It is important for the Fong family to have one member in an exalted position."

"Your brother has a high position with us, as you know. To be a gardener has no less status than to be a clerk, here."

Wo Fong was somewhat offended by Anna's apparent lack of respect for the high position of a clerk. "In China, people bow lower to a deputy clerk on the street. It is in the scheme of things, to have a few very high and most lower."

She backed away from the argument with, "I am sure it is so."

"You do not wear your beautiful Chinese robe."

"Not today. My mind is on Western thoughts." She poured out the tea into the cups and passed them. Li Fong's sweet rice cakes were next, on matching small plates.

The conversation came to a pause, so Wo Fong looked

around the Merrill sitting room. He remarked on the Clyde Forsythe oil painting of clouds and Anna's collection of green and white Capodamonte in the vitrine. Then he saw Anna's yellow bowl standing high on its seven-legged stand.

He took in a sudden breath when he saw it and stood up to inspect. The bowl was entirely yellow with a slight overtone of brown. He did not touch it, but leaned low to look at it, inspecting all sides and looking down into it.

"A large Imperial Yellow bowl. Very, very rare. You have a choice item from the Palace, now spread so far around the world."

"Surely not from the Palace."

"The Summer Palace was sacked in eighteen eighty by western forces. Nothing was left from their looting and items now turn up in commerce everywhere. The pride of China was spirited out of the land, to be sold and resold by the world's shopkeepers."

"I should return it."

"Alas, the imperial family is gone into ruin. What remains of the Summer Palace is used for cattle and goats and the Japanese are taking what little is left. The western troops who pillaged it are all dead by now, so there is nobody to blame, nowhere to return anything."

"I had no idea."

"You must not think yourself personally to blame. It was a sad time."

"I liked the bowl simply for its beautiful lines, but I will look it with more respect, now."

Grandfather Merrill arrived for his brief appearance, Donovan noting how he paused at the doorway until the others turned to notice him. He made his apologies, taking Wo Fong's hand into the warmth of his two hands. Charm was the resource that Anglican ministers could turn on like a floodlight, to dazzle visiting dignitaries and to cosset rich parishioners. Donovan observed that his grandfather was especially radiant with city officials of high station and old Mrs. Pallon, who had contributed the money for the stained glass windows and other embellishments. It was curious to see the forces of Christian charity in action. Although the holy ghost part of religion escaped him, Donovan understood intuitively the other part which involved the extracting of money from the rich and favors from the powerful.

Grandfather Merrill said, "So, tell me, Wo Fong, how is the lot of the Chinese family in San Miguel?"

"Much improved, Doctor Merrill."

"I would imagine an educated, well-placed man like you would be an able leader for them."

"It is so, Doctor. As the eldest, I am the one who bears the duty to head the Fongs in this land."

"You must come to our services one day. I should like to introduce you to our parishioners, who would delight in meeting the leader of our Chinese community here."

Ah Fong beamed and bowed. Grandfather Merrill shook his hand and took his leave. As he walked down the hall to the back door, Donovan thought he could see his grandfather's charm light turn off, no further waste of inner energy.

The tea was officially over. Wo Fong bid them goodbye, put on his hat and opened the umbrella, and he was off into the rain, quickstepping around the puddles.

Black Eyes

The next day, Anna said, "Donovan, your McBeale grandparents have summoned you for a visit. Since it is the weekend, you may stay tonight and tomorrow and I will return for you early, before school on Monday."

Donovan packed his wicker case with a few clothes and they were off to the McBeale house. Grandfather McBeale's new house was a much smaller two-story version of the turreted, shingled mansion all the McBeales had lived in since the 1890s. Anna left him at the curbside and he rang the doorbell.

"Hello, young man. Please come in," Grandfather McBeale said. He waved to the departing Anna.

Donovan went in and kissed his other grandmother, who was waiting just inside. She told him to take his case up to the guest room and wash up. They would be having a late breakfast of pancakes and melon slices in a few minutes. The guest room had the chill he remembered from the last time; Donovan wondered if the spirits of his brothers had come there, hiding from the cold darkness of the Catalina bottom.

At the table, his grandfather asked, "We want to know how

you're getting on. It's been some months since the unhappiness and we think of you every day."

"I'm doing fine, thank you. School is different in San Miguel, but I'm getting to like it."

"You're so lucky to have the influence of your Grandfather Merrill. A very spiritual man."

Donovan wondered if he, in fact, had any influence. He trusted his Grandfather Merrill, but his lofty position was too high to have any effect on Donovan. It was Anna who was in the middle of things, making decisions and giving advice, but he knew that the McBeales did not favor Anna.

"Yes, sir."

"As you know, the Depression has taken a toll on the McBeale assets. The ranch is being subdivided, but with war coming on, people are not buying home sites. We'll just have to wait and hold on."

The McBeale ranch was only a hundred acres, presided over by a three-story shingled mansion with cone-roofed cupolas, imaginative brick chimneys and a high circumferential porch with turned posts and gingerbread brackets. The passage of time had turned the acreage into prime land for development. The citrus trees diminished in importance.

"Can we go over to the ranch house?" Donovan asked.

"I need to go by there this morning, so you may come along. But you must be prepared for what you'll see. We had to tear down the ranch house as the land was needed to complete the subdivision. There's nothing there but the basements."

"It's gone?"

"Yes, but it's all for the better. California needs new houses and the groves were over fifty years old, nematodes and insects galore. We're naming all the streets for you grandchildren, there's a Cynthia Drive, Gareth Drive, Jameson Street, and if we continue, a street for you and one for Whiting."

"Can I see my street? Donovan Drive?"

"It's not been engineered yet, son, but I need to go over to the ranch house on other business. You can see what we're doing there."

After they finished their pancakes and the peppered cantaloupe slices, Grandfather McBeale drove them the few blocks to the site of the destroyed house. The curving drive lined with magnolia trees was still there, and a circle of date palms with their lions' manes of expired leaves and jacarandas outlined the brick-lined basement where the house stood. Workmen were taking down the wire fence surrounding the tennis court and another crew was dismantling the two-story barn. As they watched, the crew ran out of danger as the walls to the barn collapsed, no longer held firm by the roof-beams. A cloud of dust arose over the pile of fallen timber, and the cast iron bell rolled away in an eccentric path, clunking a muffled peal.

Behind the ranch house site, on what Donovan remembered as a grove of Valencia orange trees just a year ago, several streets of the new subdivision were already paved and one small house in the first stages of construction. Beyond that, tractors with mechanical claws pulled up the orange trees and piled them upon the bonfires while engineers staked out the streets and their corners.

Donovan had never really understood what Grandfather McBeale did besides being a lawyer with his father's firm, but here a large sign announced that this was a McBeale Brothers Development, "The Newest Place in Alhambra." The lettering went across a band of orange blossoms and a rising sun.

After Grandfather McBeale talked to some of the men working, he came over to Donovan, sitting on the fender. "What do you think, son?"

"I remember playing in the barn. It smelled like hay inside."

"We'll salvage some good timbers. Redwood and Douglas fir from Northern California, some six inches thick. We can re-use those in the new houses."

"Why did the ranch house have to be torn down?"

"The old ranch house was old-fashioned and inefficient. Nobody lives that way now, with rooms for the Irish maids in the attic, wood-burning furnaces in the cellar and a staff in the kitchen. We had to hire a man full-time just to split and stack the eucalyptus logs. No, the house had to go. Besides, this will leave a better estate for you grandchildren."

"But I would rather have the old ranch house."

"Don't question so much, Donovan. The adults know better."

Donovan did not think so. He had strong memories of Christmas Eve dinners with the extended McBeale clan, dozens of people of all ages who gathered in the old ranch house to celebrate the holidays. It was the only time he saw his second cousins, and a bachelor grand-uncle and a very tall spinster grand-aunt who lived together in San Francisco. There were many unmarried McBeales all over California, often living with their married siblings.

There were also people who were only identified as Cousin Matty or Cousin Lionel, and a severe, very old woman who was called Mrs. Bonesteel, "your great-great-grandmother," with the thinnest haze of white hair, pink from the exposed scalp, and a black ribbon around her neck.

She only ate dark meat, in small portion, and a single caramelized carrot, and much was made of serving her correctly. Everybody seemed afraid of her because she appeared to be angry. Donovan had watched her across the table on the Christmas Eve before last while she picked at her food like some exotic, caged water-bird and he felt a chill when she looked up suddenly straight across at him, black eyes with white flecks focused perfectly upon his face. He would miss those Yule gatherings, always ending in a night of headache from the hard sauce on the plum pudding.

They got back into the automobile and drove down Cynthia Drive. There was a new house at the end being put together by contractors, others showing only the slab foundation with pieces of plumbing. Farther down the drive, the parcels had sidewalks running in front of them, with four-foot high trees planted in the median alongside the concrete street. This was the new California, Grandfather McBeale said. Houses and land for everybody.

Grandfather McBeale was a handsome man, a full head of white hair, and a well-tailored man who always wore suits with vests, the coat unbuttoned to show a heavy gold watch-chain going from vest-pocket to vest-pocket. He had also had the same black eyes of Mrs. Bonesteel and her small hands. Donovan wondered why he did not feel close to either of his grandfathers. Grandfather McBeale did not tell the truth, he was sure, and the other did not want to know the truth, hiding behind his churchly obligations. Maybe that was all you could expect from grandfathers.

Since these two men could not agree on the particulars, no memorial service was held for Donovan's family. Anna had a square marble plaque with the four names installed without ceremony beside the gravestones for her other children.

Static Electricity

*I*n late February, Anna said, "Friday is the first of March. Mr. Mendoza will have completed the house and Donovan and I should go to Laguna to pay him. I am sure he has gone into debt to finish it."

Grandfather Merrill said, "Shouldn't you call someone in Laguna to be certain that it is done?"

"Mr. Mendoza told me last fall that it would be completed."

"I cannot accompany you, with the sermon to be written. But, surely, Ah Fong can drive you there and then come back here."

"No. The streetcar works very well for Donovan and me. We won't stay long, just until things are settled, to feel that Santacasita will be safe until we get back. Why don't you have Ah Fong drive you down on Monday? You haven't had a proper vacation in years."

"Is it wise to take Donovan out of school?"

Anna said, "He knows more than the other students.

Another week away would do no harm. You should reconsider and come down. Santacasita needs a benediction."

Grandfather Merrill considered that for a moment, then said, "I believe I can come. For a short stay, only, however."

"Good. I will cook a housewarming dinner for you and my artist friends. Is Monday night all right with you?" Grandfather Merrill nodded assent and buttered another piece of toast from the stack without crusts.

Donovan said, "I promised David Messenger that he could come to the housewarming. Could you and Ah Fong bring him down to Laguna, too?"

Grandfather Merrill said, "Of course. What about his schooling?"

Anna said, "You must call his mother, Paulette Messenger. She works at the newspaper and she can write a note to the principal."

"I will see to it."

So the housewarming dinner was set, with Grandfather Merrill and David to be in attendance. Anna wrote a letter to the principal of Donovan's school, again not waiting for reply. Donovan had worries about missing school on their first trip, but now he knew that Anna's note was like an Open Sesame to foreign lands. She packed the wicker bags and a lunch hamper the night before. Ah Fong delivered them to the Mission streetcar stop and they were off on a late morning departure.

They arrived at El Delirio just as it was getting dark, too dark to walk up to Waterbird Lane.

In the morning, the fog pressed into the windows of Donovan's room, tendrils of it slithering silently into the room itself when he opened the French doors. He dressed quickly, listened to make sure Anna was still asleep, and then he dashed down the stairs to the beach.

The storms had washed away much of the sand, the beach was now much narrower than before. He stayed close to the cliff all the way down to Latraviata's promontory. The wooden stairway was gone and in the fog he could barely see up to the snag where it had been ripped away. Two steps stuck out into nothingness from the rocks. Latraviata's studio was not visible up in the mist, no Russian chords descending.

There was a scrubbed quality to the beach as Donovan walked back to El Delirio. No piles of seaweeds and no broken branches like before, only hard-packed, damp sand all the way from the water to the cliffs, swept clean by the waves.

In the dining room, Anna and Donovan listened to the waiter's tale of the storms, how the water surged up the concrete stairways right into the lobby and dining room. Some waves were so strong that the crest crashed against the windows on the upper floors. He was proud that concrete and steel El Delirio had survived. If it was a plain, uninspired building, it was also a sound one.

"All seems quiet now," Anna said.

"You're lucky. No storms predicted for a while."

"Donovan, I've ordered your oatmeal and orange slices."

After breakfast, they set out in the fog to Santacasita. Anna held onto Donovan's arm as they walked up the hill, past pines and eucalyptus dripping with dew. Parts of the dirt roads were washed away in big gullies and rocks littered the trail. They came up the last stretch of Waterbird Lane, and Donovan was the first to see the dim silhouette of the house.

"Look. There it is."

Anna did not respond as they walked down the front path, everything glistening wet from the dense fog. The dark house was dripping from the eaves as they opened the unlocked front door. A carved wooden sign next to the door said in neat block letters: Santacasita.

The furniture and rugs from Olvera Street were all in their places; the Mendoza women had moved everything in. The beds in the bedrooms were made with the green spreads and pillows. Curtains hung at the windows, towels on bars in the bathroom; the nunnery paintings were in a perfect row in the sitting room, like a project of the altar guild. Anna turned on the lamps as she went around the house and opened the French doors to the porch, now looking out on the white void.

Mr. Mendoza had even laid a fire of eucalyptus logs in the fireplace, with the cylinder of hearth matches sitting nearby, waiting to start them up. Donovan touched the round rocks of the fireplace and they were cool, solid.

"Well, if it is possible to have perfection on earth, the Mendozas have come very close to it," she said. "However, I see a need to rearrange those chairs, and I am sure the kitchen wants my fine tuning."

Donovan unpacked his small suitcase in the guest bedroom closet and sat on one of the twin beds, looking at the foggy window. The fog reminded him of his brothers and mother and father and the events of last summer. It did not hurt as much to think about them now, but he still felt a deep, underlying blame for what happened. Would that ever go away?

There was a knock at the front door. Mr. Mendoza arrived with a canister of Mexican coffee. Anna asked him to sit down while she prepared it, then they would talk. In a few minutes, she came back with a tray with two cups of coffee, in her Mexican green dinnerware.

"I can't tell you how happy I am," she said. "Everything is perfect."

"I'm so glad. My whole family had joy working on this house. Every day we came to work, we watched your house grow and grow, and then it was done. I will miss working here."

"The house is just as I imagined it, dark and nurturing."

"Let me show you how the windows work." He opened a pair of casements to the fog outside and inserted the hooks to keep them open. He also showed them how the door locks operated and the trick to the fireplace damper.

"I have your money here." She went into her bedroom and returned with a parcel wrapped in brown paper, encircled with the ubiquitous rubber band. She unwrapped the pile and started to count them all out.

Mr. Mendoza stopped her from counting. "I am sure it is all here. Twenty three hundred dollars."

"It is. Now, to a matter of some importance. On Monday night, I am having a housewarming party for all my Laguna friends and my dear James. Donovan will be here too, as well as his friend David. I would very much like the whole Mendoza family, everybody who worked on the house, to come as well."

"Mrs. Merrill, it would be awkward for my family. We do not go to Anglo parties here. It is better that way."

"Then, I will do another party on Tuesday afternoon, especially for you and your family. No Anglo friends."

"That is kind, but you must not. Building the house was thanks enough."

"I must insist. A house cannot be born without a proper celebration, a fiesta for those who built it. It is written somewhere, I know."

"Very well. Tuesday afternoon." Mr. Mendoza rewrapped his pile of bills and left.

On the weekend days, Donovan walked around their part of Laguna Beach, up Waterbird Lane higher into the hills and over to parallel lanes, while Anna worked in her new kitchen. She made cookies and cakes for the housewarmings, and special *bisquochitos* for the Mendoza family event.

Grandfather Merrill and David arrived just after noon on Monday, the morning fog having thinned into a winter haze, a milky blue sea just visible in the distance. Ah Fong would stay with his vegetable-farm cousins over the hill. Donovan gave them a tour of the house and grounds while Anna continued in the kitchen. She made potato salad with chopped onions and celery, pimentos, mayonnaise and mustard. There was a cheese bread and biscuits, fried chicken and asparagus in hollandaise. She sliced the ham that she had baked the first day and the table was covered with platters just as the first guests arrived.

Simon was first, with an armful of wildflowers. "At last, Laguna is complete."

"Simon, this is James. He drove down today just for the house-warming."

Grandfather Merrill turned on the charm light, but Donovan noticed that the wattage was low, no doubt because funds for a stained glass window or a new rectory were not involved with these Laguna people. He shook Simon's hands with his two-hand special.

"Mr. Grunewald, your fame as a painter has even reached San Miguel. One of my favorite parishioners, Mrs. Pallon, has several of your striking paintings in her sitting room."

"Ah, the lovely Mrs. Pallon. A smart lady who always asks for the better price, even from poor artists."

"She does not waste her money."

"This is my son, Portman. He runs the business part of my studio."

Grandfather Merrill gave him a one hand handshake, not to waste his powers.

While the adult guests talked enthusiastically, Donovan and David sidled out of the French doors to the porch, and slipped over the railing. Donovan showed him the boulder adjoining the house and they quickly found an agreeable ledge where they could watch the entry to the house and hear the festive noises from inside.

David said, "Have you seen the machines in Marjorie's house? The ones in her father's office that look like big vacuum cleaners?"

"Yes. But we didn't turn them on."

"We did on Friday. Marjorie wanted to be the doctor and me the patient. So I lay down on the bed. She put on her father's white coat and turned on the machine. She used a wand with a flat piece at the end, and it made a tickle on your body with a buzzing noise."

"Did you take your clothes off?"

"Yes, she wanted me to. It tickled until she turned it up a bit, then it was sort of like a sting. It hurt, but not too bad."

"Did you get excited? You know."

"Sort of. I liked it. She said that lots of people come to her father for treatments, and most of them leave with a smile."

"I wish I had been there. I didn't think I was going to miss anything by coming down here."

"Marjorie said she would let me be doctor next time and wear the white coat."

"You get to do all the good things."

"I know."

Donovan and David watched as the guests spilled out onto the porch, chatting and pointing. Simon and Anna sat down in the leather backed chairs, while Grandfather Merill remained in the house.

"Your James is a very kind man, perhaps a holy man," Simon said.

"All his parishioners are impressed with his qualities."

Simon noticed that Anna did not include herself in those impressed. He said, "I believe that holy men, and I have known a few, never sit with an ease upon this earth. In their rush to get to their reward, they can do foolish things in this world."

"Do you think James is foolish?"

"No, but I sense he is anxious."

"I wonder that if loving others, providing solace for others, is to give yourself strength and wisdom, rather than taking it away. Is he really anxious to get to his reward?"

"We'll see." He patted her hand and smiled. It was evident to all that Simon had grown fond of Anna, exceedingly fond.

Inside Latraviata talked to Grandfather Merrill as they sat in the circle of chairs around the fireplace. She said, "Your Anna is a remarkable woman, James. She will find Laguna like a new river of energy, green leaves and blossoms where you least expect them."

"Most of our friends think that she is a handsome flower as she is."

Latraviata noticed that James did not include himself in those admirers. She said, "I had a neighbor, a woman in England who opened a studio for herself in Cornwall, right above the raging Atlantic. She had never had a single thought about art or form or beauty before, looking after her rackety family in Hampshire, but within in a couple of years she was sculpting the most heavenly pieces, white marble totems in every size, abstract icons, incredibly powerful pieces. This simple, sweet woman harbored a talent as large as Rodin. Critics came, buyers bought and the art world was at her feet, and the Hampshire family had to let her loose, let her soar. I think a similar woman hides within Anna."

"A sculptor?"

"No, of course not. It was a parable, James, as you well understand. I meant that she will find something new, something exciting here in Laguna. I am sure of it. Who is that divine young boy with your Donovan?"

"David Messenger, Donovan's best friend from school. He drove down with me."

"I must talk to him. I need a model for a series of paintings I have in mind. A young shepherd with his flocks in the hills above Laguna, deep grasses, wildflowers, craggy hills, glimpses of the nurturing sea. Neo-biblical renditions for these unsettled times." She left Grandfather Merrill and walked briskly over to the two boys. Both were so startled by her forceful approach that they ducked their heads, not knowing what to expect from such an onslaught.

"Donovan, your friend must pose for me. Let me see your face, David." She took it in her hand and turned it this way and that, as if inspecting it for purchase. "He has the most glorious blonde hair and will be perfect as the shepherd boy in my new paintings."

David smiled nervously, but said nothing. Donovan said, "We are going back in a couple of days."

Latraviata was not to be put off, however. "This summer, after school is out, I am sure Anna plans to bring you both down here for a long stay. I will wait until then. I can paint the hills and the trees and leave the shepherd boy portion alone. What joy to have found him. I will have the canvases stretched tomorrow."

"We'll have to ask his mother."

"I am sure she will agree. David, please leave me your address so I may write your mother. She can't say no to your being immortalized on canvas, trapped forever in your tow-headed youth."

Donovan did not understand his own reactions to Latraviata's excitement over David. Couldn't he be as good a shepherd boy himself? He felt left out, but tried to be happy for David.

"I guess you would like that, David?" Latraviata asked.

"I don't know. Can Donovan model, too?"

"No. Don't be a silly billy. I need only one shepherd boy."

David and Donovan spoke lowly together, looking up from time to time.

Latraviata cut through their conjectures with, "Don't give

it another thought. It's settled. How curious that you are named David already."

Anna's party drew to a close with the guests departing in twos and threes, until they were gone. She and Donovan cleared up the glasses, cups and dishes scattered around the house. Grandfather Merrill disappeared into the bedroom for a nap and David sat out on the porch, rocking the leather-backed chairs enough to make rhythmic squeaks.

Egg Rolls, Chopsticks
1970

*T*omas's dinner was going better than I expected, with the guests already seated when I arrived. There were five round tables for ten, white cloths to the ground along the pool terrace. He had picked up on my Chinese paintings with an elaborate Peking dinner, ducks roasted in a coating of red mud and salt, curious crisp vegetables of all sorts, red rice from the upland terraces, rice wines and a squadron of waitresses in high collars. He ordered real ivory chopsticks with the name of the occasion engraved along the shafts: *Donovan Merrill- New Paintings -July 1970.* I noticed that his eyes were dilated with excitement; he wanted the dinner to be commensurate with my paintings, to exhibit that he was an artist of equal measure, not just a painter's anonymous companion. The guests were edgy, however, sensing my tardiness held some unknown portent, so I kissed Tomas on the mouth with a long, theatric gesture, and the guests applauded.

Carole sat next to me, Tomas on the other side and the gallery owner, a patrician woman of sixty, just across. A small mesa of spring rolls sat on the revolving stand in the middle of the table and the guests, no doubt relieved at my arrival, set the stand spinning as they served themselves, chatting enthusiastically, clicking the chopsticks, dipping the rolls into dark sauces and downing the rice wine quicker than it could be readily replenished.

Carole said, "I know what made you late. You were studying your paintings. No?"

"Exactly. Do you do that, too?"

"Always. I would rather not have this sort of party afterwards, just so I can spend some time looking. See what's wrong, what's good. It's too late the next day."

"It makes me feel better about disappointing Tomas."

The meal went faultlessly through its courses, the women in Chinese dress expertly carving, serving and passing each succulence as it came from the kitchen. I could not help but think of Anna, her love of all aspects of the Orient and how she would enjoy the meal that Tomas had arranged.

Cousin Mary was a keen observer of our grandmother from her years growing up in Laguna, and she thought Anna yearned for a Chinese husband mainly because she wanted to refer to herself as Madame Fong at the Laguna grocery stores. *Hello, Madame Fong here, are the ripe apricots in?* Although she had not taken Simon's last name when she married, I observed the sparkle in her eyes when she called herself Frau Grunewald at the grocery. *Hello, this is Frau Grunewald, can you take my order, please? Guten Tag, this is Frau Grunewald.*

You're not Frau Grunewald, I would tell her, *you're Anna Merrill.* But she was many people, I grew to know. The parson's widow was a role she used to effect when it was called for, a painter's companion, a market-savvy investor, a placid cook, a friend to the oppressed lesbians of Laguna and a fierce opponent of the vestry back at the Church of the Holy Spirit back in San Miguel, who could do nothing right, in her eyes. Anna slipped unnoticed from one persona to another, always confusing those who sought to follow.

Carole observed my expression as I mused. "What are you smiling at?"

"Anna. Tomas and I go to her place tomorrow. A command performance at the family hillside."

"Can I come? I always liked your Anna."

"Not this time. She was charmed by you also years ago and would be only more impressed now. She thought I should marry you."

"A smart woman. I think that, too."

"But the Fates intervened."

"I suppose you could include Tomas among the Fates. Why the command performance?"

"I don't really know. It probably has to do with the estates she manages. At eighty-nine, she and Delores control a vast fortune from the kitchen table. We cousins, two generations away, hear about it only when changes are brewing."

"So why were you smiling?"

"I was thinking about her wars with the vestry at Grandfather Merrill's church in San Miguel. They don't like her plans for an Old Testament rose window, too Jewish they said, wanting her cash contribution instead. She claims they can't be trusted with money."

"Is she winning?"

"I would never bet against Anna when she decides upon something."

Tomas required some attention on my other side, so we talked about our trip to California in the morning. He said he would look forward to swimming again in the sea at Laguna Beach, even though it could be sixty some degrees in July.

"Thank you for the beautiful party. I'm very lucky."

"Very lucky, very late." He was, indeed, a Latin beauty, with a full head of shiny black hair and pale brown eyes looking so defenseless and unhappy. Did I cause his unhappiness?

"Do I make you unhappy, Tomas?"

"Sometimes."

"Is it my obsession with painting? Do I spend too much time in the studio?"

"No. I respect that. It's when you treat me like a servant or just a paid assistant. I go crazy with quiet rage. Like now."

"I love you very much. I was late because I wanted to look at the paintings by myself for a while, to make sense out of where I'm going."

"You couldn't do that tomorrow?"

"You know not. We've been through that."

"I didn't understand it then and I still don't."

"I told you from the beginning that work was the most important love in my life, but that you were next, ahead of everything else."

"I just didn't know how far down the ladder the number two was."

"That is nonsense. I can't imagine life without you."

"Right now you seem to be doing very well without me."

"Can I make it up to you?"

"I'll think about it. I have something to tell you. Important. But not tonight."

174

"Good important or bad important?"

"Important."

Carole leaned across and interrupted. "You must talk to your other guests, you two. They're feeling neglected."

I could not find a time alone with Tomas again until the evening was over, the last guest driving down the gravel driveway and off into the night. He said he was too drunk and too tired to talk. Tomorrow he said.

Flock of Blackbirds
1939

The morning after her house-warming, Anna asked Grand father Merrill, "Don't you like my new friends? Aren't they interesting?"

He did not smile as he replied, "They are a different sort than what we are used to, Anna. I can see you are taken with their creativity and iconoclasm, but we as church people should revere the established order, reinforce the layers of tradition. They do not."

"Gracious, you don't like them? I saw you talking to Latraviata; she must have made your ears burn with her bohemian ideas."

"She thinks you are ready for a major shift in your life, very like some friend back in England who left her family high and dry to sculpt white marble on the Cornish coast."

"How annoying. I have no such plan, I assure you. White marble, indeed."

"And Simon Grunewald says you are like a bird trapped in a crude, slatted cage, needing to soar high to find your true self. I believe all your friends down here think I that I keep you trapped in the rectory, like some Victorian novel."

"Oh, my. How difficult they are. I will speak to them about such ideas."

Donovan and David ate their oatmeal in silence, not looking up. The only sound was the clank of spoons on pottery bowls, all four of them thinking about last night's party.

Anna said, "Well, the Mendoza family shouldn't make you feel ill at ease. Let us enjoy them and make them feel welcome."

That afternoon, they arrived all at once, pouring out of four black cars packed to the gunnels. Mr. Mendoza, carrying a seedling Norfolk Island pine in a pot, did his best to introduce them one by one as they passed the front door, but Anna stood aside to let them all in. There were several sons and daughters, each with their spouses and children, Mr. Mendoza's two brothers and their lineal descendants. Two very old women in black shawls appeared to be the twin spiritual centers of the clan, the others favoring them and getting them seated. The house was bulging and echoing with the quick cadences of the Spanish language.

A grand-daughter, Delores Mendoza, came over to stand beside Donovan with her back to the wall. Taller than her cousins or aunts, she had given up the customary long hair for a short-cropped bob, almost uncombed.

She said to Donovan, "Grandfather let me work on the house. Did you know that?"

"No. What did you do?"

"Some of the stone work and I painted the trim. Do you want to see?"

Donovan assented, and David caught up with them as

they went outside. Dolores took them around to the north side of the house where the stone base-walls of the house stood higher.

She said, "There. I put those stones in, with mortar. All these river rocks have one flat side, grandfather showed me. See here and here. If you line up the level sides to the outside, it makes a flat wall of stones. There is a lot of bad stonework in Laguna where they don't pay attention to the flat side."

"So you want to be a stone mason?" David asked.

"I don't think so. Grandfather is happy when I help him. I wanted to do it, to show I could do it. Like swimming, I can swim better than all my brothers and cousins."

Donovan said, "When we come back this summer, let's swim in the surf together. I tried it last year and it is hard, but I liked it."

"Yes. I'll show you how and also where the abalones live on the big rocks."

Mr. Mendoza and Anna were watching them from the porch as they walked around the house talking about the stone walls. He said, "I worry about Dolores. She doesn't like the kitchen work or the sewing. Her mother tries, but it does not take. She wants to build houses, like her brothers, and she can climb higher in the trees than anyone else. She wants to be better than all of them."

"She is more like an American girl. You can tell just by the way she walks," said Anna.

"I want her to be an American girl, but not to lose what we had for generations in Mexico."

"There will be many changes in the next few years for all of us. I don't know if there is anything we can do about it."

"Maybe she could come to you this summer and do some work here? She might learn cooking and the like faster from you. You are a modern woman. She won't listen to the women of our family."

"Certainly. I will let you know when we are coming and she can help me from time to time."

Grandfather Merrill's white collar attracted all the Mendoza women in a circle around him, listening to what he had to say about his church in San Miguel. A married priest was a novelty for them and Anna could hear many embarrassed giggles.

The table Anna had laden with platters of fried chicken, biscuits and ham emptied within an hour, a time that everybody sensed was long enough. Like a flock of blackbirds, without consultation they all stood up and left at the same time, slightly bowing to Anna and Grandfather Merrill as they passed. Mr. Mendoza spoke for them all, a message of thanks. The black automobiles started together, turned around in tandem, and, like a church procession, moved slowly down Waterbird Lane towards the sea. David and Donovan planted the pine tree on the far side of the boulder.

Grandfather Merrill said, "I am exhausted talking to all those women. A surfeit of fun."

"At least they are not revolutionary artists," Anna said. "Lovely family, don't you think?"

"Lovely, yes. The Roman church has a way of welding their families together that I wish we had. But now the sea air asks for a nap."

Strange and Divine

Back in San Miguel, life on the surface returned to normal. The tides of church matters ebbed and flowed, Sunday services making the pinnacle in each week. Grandfather Merrill wrote a series of sermons about the true nature of the Pharisees, the evils of iconoclasm, the breaking up of the temples and the upsetting in the order of traditional things. It was clear that he did not approve of Anna's house in Laguna and her friends there, and Donovan understood that the sermons were a part of their conversations, one of the few times she could not respond. The sermons were Grandfather Merrill's way of empowering his side of the discussion with church trappings and the power of the pulpit. Was Anna such a power that he needed bolstering in their give and take?

The green of spring turned into the dried grasses and ochres of early summer. The Merrill's second son, John, and his family, who lived in San Francisco, came for a visit on the first of May. John had a wife, Suzanna, and two daughters, the eight year old Annabelle and Mary, just one. All would stay at the rectory. Anna asked Donovan to sleep on the sitting room sofa to allow his girl cousins to have his room, and John and Suzanna slept in the spare room.

While the adults drank coffee in the sitting room and caught up on family news, they asked Donovan and Annabelle to get acquainted outside.

Aunt Suzanna said, "Donovan, you and Annabelle are exactly the same age. You must have a great deal in common."

"Yes, Aunt." Donovan felt there were few things he and Annabelle would ever agree upon. She looked sullen and closed.

"Ask Annabelle about her spelling prize," Suzanna said, and herded them both out onto the front porch, away from adult matters.

Annabelle's light blonde hair was in tight braids, with butterfly clips of white plastic and her dress was perfectly pressed. She sat upright in the bamboo chairs with a hand firmly on each chair arm. "You don't look much like Uncle Jameson. Are you sure you are his son?"

"I am his son. Everybody said I favor the McBeales."

"Papa says you killed his brother's family."

"I didn't. It was an accident."

"Not what I heard. They would have been there before the storms, but you made them late. That's the same as killing."

"That's not true. Anna says that bad weather is nobody's fault."

"Papa said to me that Uncle Jameson took all of Grandmother's attention away from him. She only had eyes for her first-born."

"She loves me and I'm not the first-born."

"Papa says you are an albatross around their necks. You

should be in an orphanage." Annabelle smoothed out the skirt of her dress.

"But I'm here, aren't I?"

"I think Papa is secretly happy that Jameson is dead."

"How long are all of you staying?"

"Only until tomorrow. I don't like you."

"Me neither." He left her on the porch and walked to the cemetery. If today was going to be unpleasant, Mr. Erasmus was a more preferred source of unpleasantness. He walked right past the cottage with no emergent Mr. Erasmus and went all the way to the back of cemetery, where he and David had come over the wall.

He lay down in the grass by a large, granite obelisk and looked at the sky, clouds moving slowly in from the sea. He knew he must not say bad things about Annabelle, because she was popular with the adults. She knew how to smile and to make the sort of talk that the adults liked to hear. He would just stay away from her until tomorrow.

He slept for a while, his back on the grass, and when he woke up he heard voices. Without sitting totally upright, he got up on one arm to see. It was Anna and Grandfather Merrill, sitting on a bench near the obelisk. They must be escaping their guests, too. He did not want them to see him, so he squirmed around to the other side of the obelisk. He could hear them talking but he could not understand the words.

After half an hour of their muffled talk, Anna stood up and said in a louder voice, "I'll go back to the rectory, now."

He said, "I'll stay here for a while, my dear. I can sort out my thoughts."

She walked a few yards away, then turned to look for a

long time at Grandfather Merrill as he sat on the stone bench. She turned again and walked back to the rectory.

Then Grandfather lay down on the grass like Donovan, looking straight up at the clouds. Donovan got up and walked towards him, assuming his eavesdropping had not been discovered.

"Grandfather…"

"Oh, you startled me, Donovan. Sit down, if you like."

Donovan sat, cross-legged as Grandfather Merrill turned over on his side, his head propped up on an arm. He looked younger, more accessible on the grass. He said, "Were you listening to us?"

"Yes, sir. I couldn't help it."

"Did you hear it all?"

"I don't think so." He did not tell his grandfather that he had heard nothing intelligible.

Grandfather Merrill said, "I think your Uncle John's visit has, in some unfortunate way, resurrected Anna's grief for your father. She loved her firstborn totally and has walled away her tears since he died. Maybe seeing John alive and knowing your father is dead is too bitter a pill."

"Do you think I killed my father, too? Am I to blame?"

"Did Annabelle say that? She's a naughty girl. No, it was God's will, Donovan. An accident. Even if you are a budding agnostic, a serious lapse in itself, you aren't a killer."

"But how can it be God's will to make a storm that kills people?"

"We cannot comprehend His will. It is strange and divine."

"I don't understand."

"I do not understand, either. But God loves us, nonetheless. It would be better if you don't question everything so much, son. Faith is the lack of questions."

Donovan wanted in the worst way to please his grandfather by understanding these contradictions in religion, but he could not. How could God love us and kill us at the same time? There were contradictions in Grandfather Merrill to match. He was a very holy man, but also a manipulating money-raiser. Donovan many times watched as his sociable, spiritual grandfather made people laugh with simple anecdotes about the Anglican church, but he knew there was inside another man, a very different, more complicated man. What else awaited, still covered from view?

"I think I'll go back, Grandfather. Why was Anna so upset?"

"I told her things she could not have wanted to hear."

"About me?"

"No, son, about us and some others. It will mean a big change in our lives soon. We will tell you everything, perhaps next week."

"A big change?"

"Yes, son."

The remainder of the visit of John and his family went without further incident. Anna cooked a farewell dinner and Donovan engineered not to sit next to Annabelle, nor did he even have to talk to her again. She glared at him several times across the laden dinner table, but he just looked down at his plate. The others talked about church affairs and family incidents long ago, while Donovan watched his other cousin, Mary, in her crib next to him. She was a happy infant, smiling up at her cousin and gurgling. Donovan wondered how the two sisters could be so different.

Anna did not talk very much, looking down at her food most of the meal. Grandfather Merrill kept the conversation going, tales about the silliness of the high church, incense and vestments with golden embroidery, and the great, simple wisdom of the low church.

When Donovan reassumed the ownership of his room, he opened wide the windows to get out the smell of the girls. He flushed down the toilet a hair-ribbon of Annabelle's that he found on the floor. He looked around for something to burn or to stomp into bits, but nothing presented itself.

Nobody Sleeps

L ike a continuation of the winter storms, the waves of sadness did not give up their dark rhythm. Grandfather Merrill died suddenly the next week in the vestry meeting in the church's special meeting room. Mr. Sanborn came over to the rectory with the word.

"James has had an attack of some sort. A heart attack, we think."

"Is he still alive?" Anna asked.

"My dear, we tried to revive him but he has gone. It happened like a bolt from the blue; he was seated at the end of the table, talking to us about ordinary vestry business. Then, he made a strange noise, clutched his chest and fell over out of his chair. Dr. Jarman, a member of the vestry, you'll remember, was there and he immediately rubbed his chest and hands. He sat James up, crossed his arms and rocked him back and forth."

Anna said nothing, but held onto Mr. Sanborn's hand as he talked and looked intently into his face.

"It became clear that there was nothing to be done. Dr.

186

Jarman formally pronounced James dead and is now filling out the death certificate he had in his bag. I am so sorry, my dear Anna. They are sitting with him, now. May I take you over there?"

Anna nodded and took Donovan by the hand. They walked over to the church and Donovan was aware of the strong aromas of the church as they walked in. Was there also the smell of rotting seaweed, death, among that of musty hymnals, the altar guild's furniture wax and the lingering candle smoke? In the vestry, the men had lifted Grandfather Merrill onto the table and crossed his hands on his chest. They stood in a row, silent, against the wall like guilty schoolboys, as if they were somehow to blame for the events there. Grandfather Merrill's skin had turned a whitish, greenish gray, his eyes closed but his mouth slightly open, almost a crooked smile.

Anna kissed him on the forehead and with one hand tried to close his mouth. It would not stay closed, so she kissed him again and continued to hold it closed. She did not cry, but Donovan could see that she was stunned, not aware of what was happening.

Anna asked the vestry to leave. She and Donovan sat with Grandfather Merrill for about twenty minutes, saying nothing. She held her husband's limp hand the entire time. Finally, Mr. Sanborn came back in when the mortuary people arrived and gently led Anna out.

Donovan hardly slept that night and he could hear Anna crying in her room. The next day the rectory was filled with people from early until late. Friends and relatives came and stayed, bringing flowers and food. The sound of hushed voices in sad converse resounded in the sitting room. Was this the big change that Grandfather Merrill talked about; did he actually know he was going to die?

In a few days, a bishop and a suffragan bishop came to officiate at the funeral services with their white robes, miters and polished staffs like golden fern fronds. A long procession of lesser clerics and ill-shod choir boys preceded them into the church past massive vases of white flowers. Parishioners sat uncomfortably close together in the packed rows while the organist played a slow-paced dirge. This bishop was tall with a sharp nose; his delivery was that of a shrill tenor, not the reassuring deep tones of Grandfather Merrill. After the Bach, the Handel, and the culmination of many voices from the choir, they all walked back out into the sunlight with a single note from the church-bell ringing and ringing. In the hushed talk around him, Donovan heard phrases like... *such a good man... sorely missed...never the same again... an era was gone.*

Anna did not talk directly to Donovan for days, but made her presence to him known by holding his hand for long spells. He would not have known what to say to her if she did talk, so it was an acceptable solution.

John, Suzanna, Annabelle and Mary came for the services, but they did not stay in the rectory this time. The graveside ceremony, family and close friends only, was held the next day in Mr. Erasmus's cemetery, the jacaranda trees called into bloom by another death.

A dozen people were in a circle around the grave, the coffin held up on boards across the opening. Anna stood by herself in a thick black veil, no part of her face visible. Mr. Sanborn held Donovan's hand for the entire ceremony, uncomfortably moist towards the end. He saw Annabelle scowling at him across the coffin and wondered if she blamed him for Grandfather Merrill's death, too. Mr. Erasmus, in the back row, also had an accusing look. Had the bodies of his own family, never found, been eaten away by the fishes at the bottom of the sea? Did the fishes eat all the bones, too?

Finally, the people were gone and life at the rectory was quiet once more. Li Fong came each day to cook their breakfast and lunch, and now she made the dinner meal as well. Anna and Donovan sat together at one end of the dining table and said very little. It was not at all awkward or unnatural to be silent with Anna, even when they looked at each other.

"Were you mad at Grandfather Merrill before he died?" Donovan asked.

"What a question. You just might see too much, Donovan, as I did when I was your age. Yes, I was angry with him and maybe I am still. He gave me distressing news just before he left us. Now I cannot talk about it with him or find a way to accept it."

"What was the news?"

"I can't bring myself to tell you, right now. I will later, though."

"Do you think he left us on purpose?"

"I don't know."

A few days later, Anna said, "Mr. Sanborn is coming by now. He has news about where you and I will go, now that a new rector has been appointed."

"A new rector?"

"Yes. He's a young man from the East Coast, only a few years out of divinity school. He and his family will need this rectory."

Mr. Sanborn arrived with a long face, an unwilling bearer of news. They sat down in the sitting room, Li Fong brought glasses of iced tea. He said, "Anna, you and Donovan must vacate the rectory, where we have had so many good times together. The vestry has rented you a small house in San Miguel for a year."

Anna asked, "For only a year? What about after that?"

"There is a retirement home for the widows of Anglican clerics and their families in Santa Paula. Walnut groves all around, I believe. It will take time to find an opening for both of you there, but everyone says it is very satisfactory, all expenses paid. The church is very proud of its facility there."

"And what about the widow's pension?"

"It will take a while for that to start, as well. Meanwhile, the vestry will send you a check each month. You will not want."

"Where is the house you have rented for us?"

"On Harrison Avenue, near the center of San Miguel. It is not a bad house, but it is very small. I am so sorry, my dear."

Anna took the news without emotion. She and Mr. Sanborn talked about other things for a while, then he left. She asked Donovan to come sit beside her.

"Donovan, I don't want you to worry. We shall stay together."

"That's good. I want to be with you."

"We will move our furnishings over to the new house on Harrison Avenue. But, as soon as possible, I want us to go down to Laguna and stay. There is a reason that house is complete and waiting for us there. What angel saw to that, I wonder?"

"I would like to live in Laguna."

"David can come for a long stay this summer. Latraviata is most insistent on his being the shepherd boy of all shepherd boys. Simon has written us a beautiful letter, his official invitation to come and be his friend. So I think we should plan to go there. Soon."

The death of Grandfather Merrill stayed in Donovan's mind for a long time. With another member of his family gone, would the rest shortly follow? Would each death bring a similar major disruption in all parts of his life? New house, new school, new city, new friends? Was it a punishment upon him, for being so disbelieving with his grandfather, for knowing that there was no God? How could God punish you if he did not exist?

Biblical Lightning

Moving day was a bustle for the Fong family, back and forth from Harrison Avenue. The rectory finally grew empty of furniture, only a few boxes of china and kitchen goods here and there, a fire-screen against the wall and a dry pot of cactus. Anna had dressed up for the departure, wearing a black dress with long pearls and a black, broad-brimmed straw hat with a whole wing of black feathers attached. When the Fongs had taken out the final boxes, Anna took Donovan's hand and walked straight out to the automobile. Without lingering or turning for one last look, she backed out of the drive and down the church lane, pepper trees waving in a slight breeze.

Harrison Avenue was only a few blocks away on the map, but it was a different world in spirit. The house was a small cottage on a typical city lot, fifty feet by ninety feet, the street lined with camphor trees that almost touched to make a green tunnel. Most of the houses had no garage, so there was a car parked on the street in front of them. The neighbors, sitting in chairs on their porches, watched the pageant of Chinese people carrying boxes and furniture into the cottage.

Their cottage did have a garage, barely wide enough to take the car. Anna drove right in without diffidence. In the house, she took off her hat and directed the unpacking of boxes and the placement of furniture. Li Fong sorted out the whole kitchen without supervision, but for the books and ornaments she needed help. As Ah Fong moved the last chair into its position by the fireplace, he said, "Miss Merrill, we will work for you here as long as you want."

"I have no money for you, my dear Ah Fong. You must go back and work for the new family at the rectory. Donovan and I can look after this small house on our own."

Li Fong had come out of the kitchen to listen. Anna continued, "And my Li Fong. We had so many good years. I can't think how I will ever be happy in a kitchen without you."

She gave them each a folded bill from her purse. There were tears and hugs and they walked back to the rectory, Anna's auto no longer theirs as well. Donovan had his own room, but he would share the bathroom with Anna. The kitchen was smaller than the one at the rectory, and the dining table sat at the side of the sitting room. There was no spare room for guests.

Anna and Donovan unpacked their own personal items in their rooms. Then Anna came to Donovan's door.

"I have a crazy notion, Donovan."

"Do you want to go to Laguna right now?"

"What a good mind you have. How long will it take you to pack?"

"Ten minutes."

"Then we're off. I will write your school from Laguna. It

would matter about your schooling, if you weren't such a gifted boy. Real life is the best school, anyway."

They pulled the shades on the street-front windows and locked the entry door. It took several tries to back the car out of the garage and onto the street, but Anna, with her black hat in place, was in full control as they started down Harrison Avenue. Well after noon when they left, the four hour trip would get them to the sea by sunset. Anna gave Donovan the map and showed him roughly the route with her right hand as she steered with her left hand.

"You know, Donovan, at some point I must give Santacasita back to the church. I promised James I would do so. But not right now."

"When, do you think?"

"I don't know. I believe it will shelter us for many years."

"I like it there."

"I know you do. What I really mean is that I do not have the power to bequeath it to you when I die, as I would like. We have it for my life, only."

With only two wrong turns for the entire trip down Rosemead Boulevard, one near the berry farms and the other at the Balboa turn-off, they were there at five o'clock, driving slowly up Waterbird Lane. Since there was no garage, Anna turned the car around to face down-hill and parked right in front of the house. Donovan told her to turn the wheels to the curb, which she did without comment.

After they unpacked in their rooms, Anna said she was driving over to Featherstone's store for groceries. Thus the design of their Laguna days began, Anna in her kitchen much of the day and Donovan sweeping the porches, cleaning up in the garden. Simon and Portman came to lunch the next week.

At the table, Simon said, "Anna, how are you doing?"

"The days pass and I am not idle."

"It will take some time, of course."

"I understand the value of time; it sends things farther away from you, like a boat going to the horizon, but time's fabled healing qualities are highly overrated. It does not diminish in any way the hurt and unhappiness in my mind."

"Of course, my dear. I am sorry if I implied that it did." Taking a different tack, he said, "Donovan, I still need an assistant in my studio. You would clean my brushes and scrape clean the paint table. Also I would train you to stretch my canvases the way that I like them, hard and taut. Are you interested?"

"Yes, Simon."

"My paint table is in sore need of a scraping. You'll start tomorrow, then. A few hours for three days a week only, as I don't like anybody else in my studio for very long. Even Portman must leave me alone."

Donovan could walk the distance to Simon's studio, a half mile uphill into a grove of eucalyptus trees. The house that he and Portman occupied was small, the studio the obvious structure of importance. It was crafted of dark brown wood, with windows on three sides, the entrance on the side facing away from the sea. The view from inside was better than from Santacasita, encompassing the whole coast and a prospect of the Channel islands on clear days.

Inside, Simon had several easels, each with a painting in progress. Finished canvases hung on the spaces between the windows and in an array on the entry wall. The ceiling, walls and floors were all stained a dark brown, giving the well-fenestrated room a curiously dim quality. Simon's paintings, however, exploded with color, almost creating their own light.

On Donovan's first day, he pushed the young boy hard. After a couple of hours of scraping off the dried oil-paints from the marble-topped paint table, he set him to work on the brushes in the adjoining wash room.

First, Simon demonstrated how to rinse them energetically in a bowl of turpentine, back and forth as the imbedded color released itself, and the whole process again in a cleaner bowl. Finally, he cleaned a single brush in warm water and soap himself, gently opening the bristles with a fine toothed comb to get rid of all trace of the linseed oil and turpentine. Then he left Donovan on his own to finish the brushes while he went to work at the easel.

Simon painted with long brushes, stepping back to look often. He held them straight out, almost exactly square with the canvas, rubbing them up and down. His large canvases were aswirl with circles and triangles, intersecting and overlapping. If there was an embryonic landscape in his composition, it was deeply hidden in these strong, geometric designs. Several of the completed paintings that hung on the walls contained biblical lightning bolts right down the middle, sharp and white, with undulating designs radiating out from center to represent thunder.

When Donovan was finished washing and drying the last brush, he came to the door and waited for Simon to notice him. He heard the old man wheezing as he worked and humming a single melody over and over.

"Ah, Donovan, you are done. Come sit here and watch for a while."

"Doesn't Portman want to clean your brushes?" Donovan said.

"He did when he was younger, but he handles my business affairs now."

"What are you painting?"

"After this one time, you must never ask such a question. It is bad luck, endless bad luck, for a young man to ask an old painter where he is going. But, this once, I will tell you. I went to school in Paris, learned to paint the luscious flesh of women, and then afterwards, I spent a few months at Giverny, watching the work of the master. I learned that Monet's vision was not my vision. So I went home to Berlin, where I found an exciting new movement, a small group of painters who called themselves *Die Kunstbauerns*."

"What does that mean?"

"It means the 'art builders', but that doesn't matter. It was just a title, a name like the *Der Blaue Reiter* in Munich or the Pointillists in Paris. We reduced the outside world to geometry: lines, circles, rectangles, squares and we painted them as if each shape was fighting a war for survival. See here?"

He pointed to the canvas on his easel. A wide band of gold circled around the upper canvas, but smaller, darker shapes intersected, sometimes blotting out the gold entirely, other times working their way behind it. The definition of the gold circle was clear, but edges were crumbling, or being overlapped.

"This is the one dominant shape, the yellow circle, a fair-haired symbol of completeness, trying to survive attacks from every source. It could be God being brought low in an agnostic world, or just a man being harassed by his own troublesome family. It is an idea, rather than an actuality. The idea of survival and assault, the outcome of which is yet to be known, the battle afoot."

"Why do you have windows out to the sea if you don't paint the sea?"

"I just like to see outside, but painting comes from within. When things get too intense at the easel, I can look out and calm my mind. Now, no more questions. I must work before the momentum is lost. Until tomorrow." He swirled around on the high stool, faced the canvas on the easel, resumed painting with his subdued hum. Donovan, completely dismissed, quietly left.

It was exciting for Donovan to be in Simon's studio. He did not understand the paintings, but he knew they were strong, worthwhile. Anna asked him how things went that night.

"Simon paints big circles and small boxes that want to eat away the circles."

"He is a well thought of painter in California. I think you could learn a great deal from him."

"He sent me outside to plant the eucalyptus seedlings he had grown in pots. He asked me not to ask any more questions."

"I should think so. His time is too valuable to make answers for a boy. You must just be silent and watch. Much can be learned that way."

"I will, because I like being there in his studio. It feels good there."

"In time, you will have your own studio, I know. Beside

the water, somewhere, with thick, cool walls."

That night, Anna had invited Latraviata to dinner, just the three of them. She arrived after dark, dressed in a long, flowered robe with a belt, her hair hidden beneath a tightly wrapped turban, this one a scarlet red.

"I didn't have time to dress, dear Anna. Just left the easel a moment ago. It went so well today, I didn't want to leave."

"Sit down. Dinner is all ready." She brought platters from the kitchen stacked with fried fish coated with cornmeal, lemon wedges, rice and green vegetables. Anna served them each from the platters.

Latraviata said, "Donovan, what news from your friend David? I hope he is coming here soon, as I have the shepherd boy paintings, four of them, all completed except for him. I could probably paint him from memory, but it will give the paintings an authentic presence if I use a sitter."

"We haven't heard from David," Anna said.

"If you give me the address and I will write his mother. She mustn't be afraid for the boy. I will pay him a good fee."

Anna said, "Donovan has started helping out in Simon's studio. We were just talking about his not asking too many questions, as it bothers Simon."

Latraviata said, "Simon can be such a pill. He's a marvelous painter, though, so pay attention, even with your lips on the zipper. I think both of you should meet more of our artist community. I'll pull myself together and have a party."

"Maybe later, Latraviata. I'm not in a jovial mood."

"Of course. Why am I so thoughtless? We will wait until this winter. I cannot think how you must feel, Anna. So many deaths in your small family."

Anna said, "I don't think James liked Laguna, so it's curious that we've ended here without him. As if he went on so we could be here."

After the dinner was over, Latraviata did not tarry over coffee but stood, ready to go. "Anna, my love will not replace the love you lost, but I want you to know it is there. And, you, as well, Donovan."

She kissed Anna, squeezed Donovan's shoulder and briskly walked out.

Shallow Water
1970

I asked Tomas, "Wouldn't you rather stay here? I can go to Laguna by myself."

His eyes flickered as he responded. "Oh, I'll get some sleep on the plane. I'm just paying for that fucking rice wine." The caterers were folding up the tables and sweeping the evening's detritus from the terrace as we left for the Albuquerque airport, sixty miles distant. Tomas was silent, morning not his time and especially not a morning after a major event.

"I feel like a meteorite hit me. You can drive this once," he said.

Tomas was the better driver and usually preferred to be behind the wheel, feeling safer from the automotive ineptitude that I seem to have inherited from Anna. He dozed most of the way. We parked in the airport parking and arrived at the gate just as they were boarding.

The flight was an hour and half to Los Angeles. I sat by the window and watched the long stretches of desert and dry hills while Tomas immediately fell asleep again. The parched land below brought up thoughts of a late September trip to Mykonos, a few years ago, also dry and dusty.

The island was sere and thirsty for the rain that was still several months away, but the Aegean waters were warm from the summer sun. Tomas drove us in a rented Jeep early each day to a beach on the south coast, empty of people at eight in the morning, only a beach attendant raking yesterday's bottle caps and cigarette ends from the sand. It was good to have the beach to ourselves for a couple of hours, before the denizens of the late night discos woke around noon, downed some Greek coffee and straggled down to the beach. While I swam close to shore, Tomas went quickly out into the deep water, the splash from his strong strokes disappearing around the headland.

This was early on in our years together when he was writing the stories. After our mornings on the beach, we would return to the simple hotel in the Venetian district and while I read, he wrote and rewrote. I went through the stack of paperbound books that I had lugged all the way from Santa Fe. I thought that a collection of classics, some never read and others to revisit, would see me through the month. Day followed day without a change in form, swimming in the morning, work and naps in the afternoon, long dinners of grilled fish, large salads and Greek white wine in the harborside tavernas. If paradise existed, it must have hovered, winged and waiting, somewhere very close to Mykonos that month. I had already finished two of Sinclair Lewis's earlier novels, Kazantsakis's *Saint Francis*, and *Pride and Prejudice*, once again.

One afternoon, as the temperature reached its zenith, I was re-reading Flaubert and just about to give it up as the wrong book for the Aegean, when Tomas looked up from his writing and asked me, "You're reading Madame Bovary. It's about infidelity, isn't it?"

"Yes. A woman caught up in her desires."

"Why are you reading that?"

"I liked it when I read it first, at university, but now she merely seems like a foolish creature, selfish beyond measure."

"Do you think infidelity is always foolish?"

"Mostly. It's a trap that people make for themselves, and it is always selfish."

"A trap? Is that what Flaubert says?"

"I'm not sure. He writes very sagely about human nature, and foolishness and unfaithfulness are just part of that. Why?"

"I'm working on a story about a man, a professor of mathematics, who sneaks around on his wife, then also on his girlfriend and eventually when he is discovered, in deep remorse, drowns himself in the lake Xochimilco, or falls by accident drunkenly out of the dinner boat, the reader doesn't know which. The water is so shallow that even small boys can stand in that part of the lake. To die in shallow water is more demeaning than a deep sea, don't you think?"

"I suppose. That's a cheery tale."

"But I knew him. Filiberto Morales, and he did exactly that. He was highly educated with many advanced degrees and my father told me that I must always call him Doctor Doctor Morales. I guess he was, in the end, foolish."

"I think I won't finish the Flaubert. Somehow, provincial French infidelity and hot Mykonos afternoons are not compatible."

I had not thought about that conversation in several years and it occurred to me there was no story in Tomas's collection about an unfaithful mathematician who dies in the shallows. Did the story just not work or was there never such a story? Why was Tomas thinking about an unfaithful man?

It was not a road I wanted to continue upon. I cleared my mind by looking back down at the row upon row of barrancas and dry arroyos as Arizona slipped by under us, then the even drier, hotter dunes of the California desert and finally the reward as we angled down through the root-beer colored smog into the Los Angeles airport.

Mary was waiting for us out front at the arrivals building, her four door Mercedes cool in the summer sun. We piled our luggage into the trunk and she headed out to her house in Benedict Canyon.

Fallen Soufflé
1939

David arrived by streetcar, proud to have negotiated the entire trip from San Miguel through the complicated connections in Los Angeles by himself. Anna and Donovan waited for him in Newport at the palm circle for the twenty minutes the streetcar was late. David smiled when he saw them and ran their way with his cardboard suitcase.

"I hoped you would wait. There was an accident in Huntington Beach. That's why we are late."

Anna said, "We had a good time watching the seagulls here. It's no matter."

They drove back to Laguna, and Donovan showed David the bed he would use and the drawers he had cleaned out for him. They went outside to the rock behind the house and sat on the ledge.

"Marjorie wanted to come, too," David said. Maybe her family will rent a house down here later."

"Did you see any more medical books? How about the electric machines?"

"We did play doctor again. This time I was doctor and got to wear the coat."

"Did she take her clothes off?"

"Yes. It was fun, but her father came into the room. He was mad."

"What did you do?"

"I took off the coat and ran out. He tried to chase me, but not very far."

"I'm glad that was you, not me. Delores works for Anna now. She wants us to go swimming with her sometime."

"Okay. What about the old lady painter, Miss Johns? She wrote my mother a letter and said she would pay me five dollars a day."

"That's a lot. We're supposed to go over there tomorrow."

"I'll share the money if you stay with me. Two for you, three for me."

"I have to work for Simon Grunewald on Wednesdays but I can go with you tomorrow."

Anna left the boys on their own for the whole day. She cooked and served them a dinner, and David was almost asleep at the table, tired from his long day. They all turned in early that night.

In the morning Anna said, "I saw Wo Fong at the grocers this morning; he is here visiting his family at the vegetable farms. I have invited him to dinner. I thought I would surprise him with Simon and the others, so he could meet some of the artistic community here. Don't be late, Donovan, as I want you to set up the table."

"Wo Fong came by the house to visit my mother," David said.

Donovan had a sudden image of David's mother dancing nude for Wo Fong and other Chinese businessmen, bumping her breasts up and down as they smoked sweet-smelling cigarettes and sipped hot tea from cups without handles.

"Really? I wouldn't have thought they would get along," Anna said.

"She didn't cook or anything. He just came by."

"When was that, David?"

"Last week. Wo Fong told me outside when he was leaving that I have a very talented mother, and very pretty one, too."

Anna's face showed no reaction as she watched Donovan and David walk down the hill toward Latraviata's studio. Donovan asked him if his mother had danced for Wo Fong, like the others.

"No, we just sat together talking in the living room."

"Why not?"

"I don't know. I think she likes him more than the men who come late at night."

Arriving at the studio, they could hear Latraviata's loud music from several houses away, and after walking through the front tropical thicket, they arrived at the open door.

She must have heard them coming because she walked through the house toward them, talking. "What a joy to have my shepherd boy here, at last. Donovan, you can help him get dressed in the spare room over there. I have laid out your costume."

It was a white short tunic with a yellow border, and

a woven leather belt. The sandals were hard to figure out at first, but Donovan found a sketch on the bed of what the outfit looked like. The long laces of the sandals criss-crossed up the leg to mid-calf. A narrow leather band was to be worn around his forehead. When they had pulled the outfit together, both boys laughed as they looked at David in the mirror.

Latraviata was impatient at the door. "Come, come. Let's get going."

She led them to the studio, where the Rachmaninoff still played. "Donovan, you must stay quiet over there. You can sit there and read those art magazines. David, I want you just like this, pointing up to a flock of birds." She showed him her sketch of the pose. It was not a pose for a beginning model, but David tried not to wiggle too much. Latraviata drew his outline on the canvas with charcoal, then erased the sketch entirely and redrew it slightly larger. When she was satisfied with the charcoal cartoon, she painted in the colors in thin oil washes.

Donovan read his magazines without talking, looking up at her progress from time to time. Each time the concerto ended, he returned the arm with its ivory hand to the beginning without being asked. He was impressed how quickly Latraviata worked, and with total control, not wasting any motion as she went from palette to canvas. After an hour, she gave David his first rest of the day.

"Donovan, would you get us some water from the kitchen. Please put some ice cubes in the glasses."

David came around to look at himself in the painting. He knew better than to make a comment. Donovan returned with a tray of clinking glasses, and the three of them studied the emerging shepherd boy with one arm akimbo and the other pointing high. He thought her rendition of David still looked like an addition, a paste-on in the larger painting.

"I could be done with this pose in a couple of more hours," she said. "David needs to be blended into the whole, which takes some thoughtful solutions. Can you hold that stance for that long?"

"Yes. I sort of get locked into it after a while."

She painted another hour on the canvas, melding the new image into the existing work. Donovan could not tell where one started and the other ended. She feathered the background colors together with a fan shaped brush and stood back to look.

"Let's all go outside for a minute. I'll see things fresh when we come back," she said.

They walked out to the terrace and looked down. Mr. Mendoza and his sons were rebuilding the staircase down to the sea. The upper portions were already finished, and now they hammered nails into the wooden steps down by the sand.

"I saw the sea take away my stairs," Latraviata said. "Because I heard a cracking sound above the storm, I came out on the terrace in a slicker. The rain was coming down like steel rods. I got here just in time to see the whole staircase break into pieces and tumble into the water. The next wave crashed the pieces against the rocks and it turned them into so many toothpicks. With the third wave it was gone. So much for the kindness of Mother Nature. I wanted to rebuild immediately just to show her who's who."

"Were you afraid?" Donovan asked.

"Petrified. I felt the storm really wanted to destroy me personally, but the studio was too far above the water. It was still light and I could see in the cove where the waves were hitting the hotel's upper floors and beachside cottages were sitting at crazy angles."

"Could the waves really come up this high?"

"In my heart, I thought so, they seemed malignant and alive. It was as if now that they had bested the hotel and the cottages, they wanted the crazy Englishwoman who comes out in bad weather. I spent the night up the hill with Simon and Portman. When I came back here the next day, after the storm, I found a great fish, a marlin I think, had been deposited on my terrace. Six feet long with blue skin, looking peacefully asleep, and there were smaller fish, as well. Offerings, I reckoned, from Neptune for the inconvenience that he and the other sea gods had wrought."

The boys, now chilly with tales of near-death, gladly went back inside. Latraviata worked another couple of hours fine tuning the details of David's tunic and bits of colors all over the canvas. She stood back with arms high and announced it done. Donovan was pleased that she had solved the problem of the shepherd-boy looking like a last minute addition. He now blended seamlessly into the vast scene she had painted previously.

As the day ended, David did not seem tired at all. Donovan noticed that he had taken to the idea of being a shepherd boy, as he pointed skywards this way and that, in Latraviata's pose, on their walk home. He paid Donovan his two dollars and said, "Maybe next time, it should be four dollars for me and one for you." How quickly art took hold of ego, bending fairness and modesty.

When they got back to Santacasita, Anna and Delores

were working in the kitchen. Delores, wearing a white apron, was chopping vegetables into small cubes. She looked like some unfortunate military recruit, trapped into kitchen duty for a small misdeed. Anna was sautéing chicken as the two talked.

"Delores, David has been posing this summer for Latraviata," Anna said. "A shepherd boy in the Laguna hills. How was it, posing for a famous painter?"

"I like Miss Johns. She works fast."

"That's all? She works fast?"

"Yes, and she plays loud music."

"I can hear the music when I swim near the abalone rocks. Everybody on the beach knows when she is working," Delores said.

"Delores is helping me get ready for Wo Fong's dinner tonight," Anna said. "He, Simon and Portman, Agnes and Mary Louise are coming in about an hour. Latraviata was busy. So both of you wash up and light the fire. It's going to be chilly."

Both boys preferred their ledge on the rock to the sitting room. After washing and getting the fire to a high blaze, they left the house for their perch.

Without talking, they sat and watched the chimney smoke as it crossed against the sunset. Delores, done for the day of kitchen servitude with Anna, came to join them.

"How was it, being in an apron?" Donovan asked.

"I was mad at first, but Anna is not like my mother and aunts. She doesn't talk to me as if I were a child."

"That makes a difference."

"Donovan, can we go swimming this weekend? Like we talked about? I have to work for Anna for the rest of the week."

"I work, too, for Simon. Saturday, then."

"Let's go early, right after it gets light. David, you can come, too."

At dinner, the round table would be full. Donovan retrieved the chairs from his bedroom to fill out. Simon and Portman were first to arrive, then Wo Fong. Anna introduced them and got them seated around the fireplace. The eucalyptus logs felt warm and reassuring. Simon was first to speak.

"So Mr. Fong, Anna tells me you have an important position at the city hall in San Miguel."

"How kind of Anna to say that. Yes, I am Deputy Registrar of Deeds."

"That does sound important. How do you like working there?"

"The Fongs back in China held similar positions, so it is right that we continue them here."

"High position is its own reward."

"Exactly. Tell me, is Grunewald a Jewish name?"

"It certainly can be, and in this case, it is. Is Wo Fong a Chinese one?"

"Of course. What do you do here in Laguna? Do you trade gold and lend money?"

Anna interceded, "Wo Fong, that is a highly unpleasant cliché that Jewish people are solely money lenders and currency changers. Simon is one of our highly-regarded painters. An artist with many awards and collectors."

"A painter? A Jewish painter?" Wo Fong said. Simon's initial surprise and amusement at Wo Fong's attack was wearing off. Anna could see that he was just about to say something.

Anna said, "Simon is an artist, Wo Fong. He has a beautiful

studio up the hill and his paintings are sought after across the nation."

"In China, scholars and high bureaucrats are forbidden to consort with artists. They are no different than household help, and there were Jewish gold traders in the market in Nanking. I remember the signs over their shops, but we never went in to talk to them or even to look at them. People are happier when there is a strict order to things, when everybody knows his place."

"But here we do consort with artists, happily so," Anna replied. "It makes no sense to continue those narrow minded traditions here in America."

"Alas."

"Wo Fong, I thought you would enjoy meeting Laguna's most creative citizens."

"Perhaps I should come back on another night."

Simon had endured enough. "I think, Anna, that you must let me defend myself. Your friend is a small minded bigot. Curious considering what his people have been through. Portman and I should not waste his time. We will come back when Wo Fong is busy with the filing away of his important deeds. Come, Portman. Take me home. It is not your fault, Anna, dear."

He kissed Anna, and as they left, Agnes and Mary Louise were just arriving. Simon said, "Turn around Agnes, there's a man inside who hates Jewish artists, and I am sure he hates lesbian artists even more. We'll take you to dinner at El Delirio."

Anna was left with Wo Fong and the boys.

"Maybe the City Hall did us all a disservice by giving

you a titled position," she said. "It seems to have gone to your head, made a change in you. Or perhaps it just uncovered an intolerant nature that was always there."

Wo Fong said, "You seem to have changed also. It is a surprise that an Episcopal minister's widow would consort with such lower echelon people."

"I guess, Wo Fong, that I must call off our dinner. Simon and the others are dear friends, and you have sorely insulted them. I can't have that. You must leave immediately."

The three remaining sat down for dinner together at the table with too many chairs. Anna said, "That didn't go very well, did it? I should have known that something bad was brewing when the vegetable soufflé collapsed into a small, hard pancake." She passed it around and they ate for a while in silence.

"The soufflé *tastes* good, Anna," Donovan said, hoping to move on to cheerier matters. He thought about David's high-flown notions after posing for Latraviata, and realized that it was the same as Wo Fong thinking he was better than all others because of his city hall position. Ego was probably better left in the bottle, tightly capped.

"I will call on Simon and Agnes tomorrow to apologize. How humiliating for them."

Donovan was relieved that Anna's fascination with Wo Fong was over. He had been afraid she would go off with him to Hawaii, Chinatown or China itself, and how could there be a place for him in the fields of the Fong family farms? It was much better this way.

The Elusive Abalone

Anna went to Simon's studio the next day to make her apologies. The painter was working on a new canvas and Donovan was busy washing a pile of old brushes in the adjoining room, the sound of running water audible through the door.

"Simon, I am so sorry. I thought Wo Fong was an interesting man, but wasn't I a poor judge of character?"

"My dear, he is a priggish bureaucrat."

"I will make it up to you."

"You mustn't worry. I have learned to get up and leave when things go wrong. That's why we left Berlin, things going wrong. Leaving saved us from a greater wrong."

"But I put the evening together. I should have known."

He motioned for Anna to take a chair beside the easel and he continued to paint as he talked. "From what you and Latraviata have told me, I suspect that you were interested in Wo Fong in some romantic way, a Nineteenth Century type of attraction, like a bit by the Bronte sisters. So this let-down is more than just a disrupted dinner party."

"I don't think so, Simon. I respect the Chinese as a people and a culture."

"I know that, but your attraction for things Chinese distilled into the idea of one man. One that could look after you now that James is gone."

"I never thought of it that way."

"I think I do. You saw Wo Fong as the head of a large Chinese family, a strong-willed patriarch who could replace your James without directly competing with his memory. Wo Fong is clearly the sort who seeks a Western wife from the highest caste, and you would be an unrivalled catch. A bold man without principals who viewed you as nothing more than a major boost in his climb up the New World ladder."

"Perhaps you're right. He did seem overly interested in his own position right from the beginning."

"But your motives are more complex, I suspect. Just another minister or well-placed white Protestant wouldn't do. You needed an exotic man to look after you, someone incomparable. Your perfect sense of style is acting itself out; it might as easily have been a Hindu diplomat with colorful turbans or an Egyptian poet, descended from the pharaohs, but an ordinary man wouldn't do."

"Am I that complicated? And am I really Nineteenth Century? How backward."

"If I'm right, you were looking in entirely the wrong quarter." He mixed up a strong crimson red and started to color a large triangle in his painting.

"I'll have to reflect on that, Simon. You are so easy for me to talk to, but these are matters that I have never put into words before. I am not at ease talking about my inner thoughts. I know you have my best interests at heart, but exposing my very soul is hard."

He continued filling the triangle with color. "In Berlin, most of our non-painter friends were psychoanalysts and psychiatrists. They were interested in artists, and we were interested in them, so we talked at dinners many nights about inner feelings, psychoses and the wanderings of the human heart. It is right for us to try to discover the truth about what lies below our actions."

"I know that now, but I was taught to keep everything under cover, tightly lidded. A placid front even on stormy seas."

"So, it is time for a change. You are in a new chapter, and it befits you to exercise your mind, to be more open. With a new life, comes new freedom. In that regard, I have a question of some importance for you." Simon paused as he took the top off a tube of yellow, which he mixed vigorously with the remaining crimson on his palette.

"I know what it is, Simon."

"Do you, indeed?"

"I am sure of it."

"My bold Anna. Then what is your answer?"

"I must have time to consider it. To marry again so soon, it means so many changes."

"You bristled when I said you need a man to look after you, but perhaps that is too general a statement. You need someone to love you, and I do love you. From the moment you joined our table at El Delirio last year. And in the long unfolding of love, I knew I would shelter you, see that you are happy. I am old, but not depleted. I think you know that we would have a good marriage."

Anna stood up and kissed Simon on the forehead. "Give me a few days, Simon. Just your asking me has made me very happy."

"We've been together only a few times, a dozen at the most, but they were enough to make me sure that we belong together. It may appear to be a short time ago that we met, too short, but in my mind it has been an eternity to this day. It's a shame we did not meet thirty years ago."

"It has been a short time, but there is a connection. I felt it right from the beginning."

"Since I did, too, I do not want to waste precious time."

She turned to leave. "I must go and think about it. And Donovan, you can come out, now."

Donovan came to the doorway to the adjoining room, holding the last brushes from his cleaning project. He was embarrassed, but smiling.

"It is right that you heard everything, as you would be involved too."

"I will wait your answer with nervous spasms," Simon said.

Anna had driven the up to Simon's studio and she gave Donovan a ride back to Santacasita. They were both silent and when she had parked in front of the house, she turned the wheels to the curb.

"So, my dear, what do you think I should do? I depend a great deal upon you now."

Donovan knew that this was the continental divide in the way things were between Anna and him, that the rivers would flow in opposite direction from now on. It had always been Donovan who had asked Anna what to do, and here it was turning around.

"I like Simon," he replied.

"I do, too. Could we make a family with Simon and Portman? Would you feel good about that?"

"I think so. I don't know Portman very well, but he seems okay. It would be fun to live right next to Simon's studio."

"All this information needs time to percolate. I shall worry that you might feel that I have abandoned you. Is that in your mind?"

"No, Anna. I think you would be happy with Simon. He always smiles when you are around." It was amusing to Donovan that Anna could not read his thoughts when matters were really important, only when he had committed minor infractions.

"He loves me. I know that."

They did not discuss Simon for the rest of the day, or at dinner that night. Donovan and David talked about Latraviata's studio and her paintings. David understood how important he was to her project and relished his central position.

"Mr. Mendoza finished the new staircase down to the sea," David said. "We took some time off from the studio and walked all the way down to the bottom, trying it out. She asked me to jump up and down in places. It didn't shake."

"Could you see where the old staircase was?" Donovan asked.

"No. Not a sign."

The next day was Saturday and the boys woke early to meet Delores on the beach in front of the hotel. It was a clear day, without fog, unusual for midsummer. She was there already, sitting at the edge of the water.

"Do you want to swim out?" she asked.

"Yes. But David thinks he'll watch from the beach, instead."

"Let's go." She took off her jeans and tee shirt, down to a black, one piece bathing suit. Donovan stripped to his trunks and they ran straight out into the surf. He watched Delores as she pulled ahead, then dove down below the next wave. He did the same, surfacing behind the wave. There were two more waves to go under before they reached the calm out past the line of breakers.

She called to him, staying always ahead, "Let's swim over to those rocks."

The midsummer water at first seemed colder than the Balboa Bay water he was accustomed to, but after a few minutes it felt warmer. They both swam toward the headland, where rocks jutted up out of the water. Delores stayed some distance from the rocks where the surf collided. She led them through a calm channel between two of the rocks, and suddenly they were in a still pool, clear enough to see the sand on the bottom. The surf surged around the pool, but not directly into it.

"Let's dive down," she said. She took a gulp of air and descended in the clear water. Donovan followed her down, but it was not as easy for him to be underwater as on top of it. He saw her point over to a submerged rock and they surfaced.

"Abalone, right on that rock. Let me show you how to get them."

Underwater, she stood on the rock with the abalone between her feet. It was a shell the size of a small saucer, with a foot attached to the rock. Inserting her fingers under the shell's slippery foot, she pulled sharply up and the abalone came loose. On the surface again, she said, "You've got to do it quickly. A quick pull up. I've heard that if people are too slow, the abalone sucks down on the fingers and you can't get away. They drown. Do you want to try?"

"Yes. Let me get my breath."

In a few seconds, he swam down to a place nearby, where he could see another of the abalones and put his feet on the rock. He bent down and easily slid his fingers way under the foot, and he could feel the abalone constricting, pulling down, trying to stop him. He had a flash image of joining his brothers in a watery death, patrol boats sending down divers to prise the shell off his fingers and pull up his lifeless body, swaying back and forth in the tide. But as the abalone pulled down, he yanked up with all his force and it came loose from the rock. He thought he heard a thwacking sound under the water. It floated around in the current until he could catch it and go to the surface.

"He almost got me." He laughed as he caught his breath.

"You nearly waited too long. I would have saved you, though," Delores said. "When we swim back, hold it this way, with the shell side against your body."

They swam out of the protected pool and along the breakers, then a sprint back through the surf to the beach, clinging onto their catch the whole time, using one arm to swim. Delores was testing him, but Donovan knew he had passed with good marks as she proudly related their adventures to David waiting for them on the sand.

Delores gave her abalone to Donovan. "Take these to Anna. She'll know what to do with them."

Island of Zen
1970

Mary made the quick turns away from the airport necessary to access the boulevard for Beverly Hills. I had forgotten what a good driver she was, an ability that had forsaken me in the years away from California, if I ever really had it. The freeways now intimidated me, made me think twice about trips across the state. I would just achieve the middle lane, the preferred position of safety, with much signaling, racing ahead, braking, slowing down and lurching, when the middle lane turned without notice into the far left, fast lane, and I would have to start all over again. It was the curse of Sisyphus in modern dress.

"So, what is Anna's gathering about?" I asked.

"I would suppose it's about money in some major way. The market has been down for a few months, but her portfolio has done very well. Neither she nor Delores confide in me about their investment choices. Amazing women."

"And then Annabelle will disagree with everything that she suggests and you and I will approve, as usual."

"Exactly. It's not worth fighting with Anna."

"What a curious family we have become," I said. "A grandmother as sharp as J.P Morgan with three willful grandchildren, on their own agendas, and nobody on the levels in between. No fathers, uncles, aunts. As if a great dragon had eaten out the middle of our family, leaving only the top and bottom."

"I don't know that I like your casting me as the bottom rung of the family," Mary said. "I called Delores to let them know that you would spend the night with me, then drive on down in the morning."

"Delores has become very important to Anna, more than just a companion. It's a good thing, don't you think?"

"Yes. I watched them at the kitchen table on my last visit. Two women who have rebelled totally from their former dependence upon men, looking after a vast fortune, issuing buy and sell orders while they cook chicken necks for Greenwood. They still have an old dial telephone and a mechanical adding machine, and they make little of my suggestions to update."

"I wouldn't try further, since they've done so well just as they are," I said. "It's a good image, though, the aroma of chicken necks wafting around debentures and gilt-edged bonds."

Mary was quick to see the humor of our situation. Three adult grandchildren, cosseted and spoiled beyond measure by a kindly, but eccentric grandmother who prospered at doing things exactly her own way. Greenwood was the current Irish wolfhound, a breed that Anna saw and liked at Agnes's house. He was the fourth or fifth with the same name, a constant companion to Frau Grunewald and her companion.

"How's your house coming on? The renovations?" I asked.

"You'll be surprised how well. I've got all the hot Mexican colors painted out, the happiness of off-white restored. I'm just starting on the gardens. The abundance of California left unchecked is a thing of horror."

"What have you done with your house in Pasadena? Sold it, I suppose?"

"Oh no. I still have it. Anna gave me a lecture when I asked her about it. Rent property, lease it, lend it, leave it empty but never sell it."

As we drove up her steep driveway to her new house, I said, "I remember these hedges and topiary pines from the last time. You've been working on them."

"I let the gardener do the hedges, but I've built a scaffolding with wheels and a brake so that I can trim the pines myself. I saw a photograph of the first owner pruning from the same sort of contraption, a blue-stocking sort of woman who went to Mills College. I knew I could do it, too. Did I tell you that some of those pines are forty years old? Mrs. Winterer planted them to a garden plan from Kyoto. They look much better now, but we're not there yet. All the old gardeners tell me that bonsai and topiary must be looked at in progression of years, not weeks or months. Patience. Patience. And a ceremonial bow."

Mary had purchased the house a few years ago from a Mexican woman, reputed to be the girlfriend of a former president. The bright yellow ceilings, electric blue walls and orange doors made her feel at home so far away from Mexico City. The scholar's chairs, temple sideboards and tulipwood hibachis were given to the Salvation Army, replaced by motorized reclining chairs and glass-topped coffee tables from Barker Brothers.

She returned to Mexico after a few years, and the house languished on the market for years, the daunting task of re-restoration too great for prospective buyers, until Mary saw the beauty that lay beneath. Green tile roofs and the original paper-paneled doors now adjoined the finely pruned flatness of the Black pine trees, an island of Zen on this hurly-burly street.

Tomas and I headed for the guest house, a pavilion by the swimming pool. We dumped the luggage on the floor and, after changing into our swimming trunks, dove into the deep end of the green tiled pool. Not so large as our pool in Santa Fe, it was beautifully proportioned, long and narrow, its clear, green waters perfect for swimming laps. Mary's spare, but elegant taste was starting to show everywhere on her property as she addressed new aspects and cleared away thoughtless additions. There were matching green towels at each of the poolside lounges. We swam laps for thirty minutes or so, then lay in the afternoon sun. Mary soon came to join us.

"Mary, come sit by me. I have questions," Tomas said.

"What?"

"First, I want to hear about your love life. Is there an Italian hunk waiting off in the bamboo?"

"Nobody right now, Tomas. I had a boyfriend in the years after college, but he went to Europe and didn't come back. I thought that since Donovan prefers men and Anna had a woman for a lover, maybe I should follow the family bent. I tried that, but there was something lacking."

"I know what's missing, it's..."

Tomas interrupted, "We don't need your levity right now."

"I've been very busy at work and restoring this house fills

the other hours," Mary said. "I guess I've replaced a flesh-and-blood lover for one made of wood-frame and roof tile."

"Donovan tells me about you and the family. I want to know how you felt about living with Simon and Anna."

"I loved them completely. They took me in when my mother remarried, after Dad died. Mother wanted to start a new life in San Francisco. Annabelle was off at boarding school, Donovan at university in Paris, so I went to Laguna to live."

"Did you ever want to be an artist like Donovan?"

"No. I realized that I was hopeless."

"But you are very artistic. Just look at this house and what you've done."

"But having a good eye, which I do have, is quite different from actually being a painter. I knew in my heart it would never work."

"Did you feel Simon thought you were not worth the effort?" Tomas asked.

"No, it was me who gave up on art. I prefer working around people, in the middle of things. Painting is a lonely endeavor, I learned. Long hours in the studio with your own thoughts."

"Like writing."

She went on to describe how Simon never actually gave up on her. He said that painting could be learned, like swimming or handwriting, but that you needed to really want to learn it. Mary believed that she did not really want it for herself, merely enough to please Simon. She said that Simon told her that I took to it immediately, like a baby turtle swimming away from the coast, never looking back.

I knew that Tomas was pursuing his bête noir, the notion

that his accomplished family, authors and poets, just gave up on him. He was not worthy, not worth their time and effort to convert him from a soccer student to the bookish son they wanted. He blamed them, and felt strongly that if they somehow had tried harder, had more patience with him when he stumbled, that he would be a more successful writer now. I thought with humor how unusual Tomas's plight was, how many bookish students yearned to be the soccer stars their fathers preferred.

I don't believe I can attribute my mishaps to Simon and Anna, or going back further, to my mother and father. Flights from the nest are one's own. I enjoyed finding the quote from Lincoln where he said that every man over forty is responsible for his own face.

Tomas continued, "What about Annabelle and your mother?"

"Mother is dead now, but she vaguely disapproved of me, called me a tomboy. After I went to Laguna, she seldom came to see me. So it's only Annabelle and me. The English say different as cheese and chalk, and that's definitely it. She is only concerned with herself and her children. You'll see this weekend. People who don't really know us well say I'm so lucky to have such an elegant sister, always the picture of grooming and fashion, the perfect mother."

"Donovan doesn't like her either."

"With good cause. Her blonde good looks conceal a very dark and selfish nature."

Mary cooked like she decorated, with a spare and simple elegance. She offered up salmon filets grilled with lemon slices over charcoal, a green salad and a loaf of sourdough bread with butter. The open bottle of Pinot Grigio was already on the table.

An apple tart for dessert from a local deli, coffee after that. It felt good to be with Mary again, her no-nonsense approach to life making mine seem complicated and needlessly ornate.

Tomas was already asleep when I finished drying the dishes in the kitchen with Mary. Whatever important announcement he had simmered slowly on a back burner, a pot that would be unlidded later.

Sister Disappointment
1939

Anna did know how to prepare and cook the abalones that Donovan and Delores had pried from the rocks. She carved the soft portion out of the shell, trimmed the edges and cleaned the dark matter out under running water. The results were two oval steaks of pearlescent white, about three-quarters of an inch thick.

Donovan watched the process, proud as a frontier father who had delivered a brace of game or a winter supply of venison. Anna said, "Now comes your part. You must pound the steaks with the edge of this plate to tenderize them, or they will be like small white, manhole covers. Tough."

"Like this?" He thumped the steak back and forth with the plate, and Anna motioned for him to continue. After five full minutes of this, she inspected the abalones, bending them this way and that. She decided that another five minutes was necessary, this time with the plate hammering across the other way. At last they were ready. She immersed them in buttermilk in a shallow plate and put them away in the icebox.

"They need a time to rest and cool. Abalone are very tasty,

the pride of the Pacific shore, they say. The danger is how tough they can be. We'll have them tonight, sautéed in butter with capers and chives. Meanwhile, sit down for a moment."

Donovan, with trepidation, sat at the kitchen table. Anna pulled out a folded piece of paper and smoothed it. "I've been making a list of all the couples I know and whether or nor they are happy together."

"Is that because of Simon's proposal?"

"Partly to find some direction and partly just out of curiosity. I come up with two 'Yes, they are happy' and nine 'No, they are not.' The 'No's' include 'Maybe they are not' or 'I don't know.' If my calculations are right, Simon and I have an eighteen percent chance of being happy together."

"Who are the unhappy ones?" Donovan asked.

"Myself with James, I put that in the 'I don't know' category. Mr. Sanborn and Frieda, I think they aren't really happy. Latraviata and her husband, Derrick, definitely not. Simon and his first wife, she was lost at sea while he was looking the other way. How could they have been happy? Our John and his Suzanna, they're both miserable. Eugene and May, no again. Mr. Mendoza and his wife, who can tell? Ah Fong and Li Fong, also I don't know.

"And who are the happy ones?"

"Simon and Elsie, at least Simon was happy. And Agnes and Mary Louise, they appear to be contentedness itself. So the vast majority aren't content or happy. I guess they marry or bond together because of lonely nights. Simon and I must strive to beat the odds." She crumpled her list and threw it in the waste basket.

"So you're going to marry Simon?"

"I'm still thinking, but probably."

Latraviata asked David to pose for a few hours on Saturday afternoon. Donovan walked with him down the hill to the promontory, music encircling them as they approached. David was posing for the third of her shepherd boy paintings, and for this she had arranged a different costume. The tunic was of the same design, but a deep crimson color with a lighter border around the bottom. The sandals and the headband were the same, but she provided him with a well-turned bow and a quiver of arrows.

"In this panel, you'll be preparing to shoot the hawk, up here, because it is homing in on this flock of doves," she said. "Stand this way, and hold the bow just so. The young saviour of the helpless symbols of peace."

It was a sunset scene, with an orange sky behind the Laguna hills, dotted with rows of pink clouds. The trees and hills were suffused in the golden light, long shadows angling up the steep hills. David's figure would have an extended shadow too. For this she had arranged for David to stand in front of a low, strong flood lamp, his shadow cast up on a sheet, cleverly angled up to serve as a hill. Donovan sat in his usual corner.

She adjusted the flood-lamp to a lower angle, then said, "Perfection. I must work fast or you will get exhausted in this pose, poor dear. The shadow pulls it all together. How exciting."

So the process was repeated, a charcoal sketch right on the canvas, then a thin wash of turpentined paints, and finally the finished form and colors. Donovan understood that this was the proper, academic way to paint a painting, each stage done completely before moving on to the next. The excellence of the finish was in this painstaking preparation.

As the work was almost complete, Donovan knew he could ask a few questions without inciting Latraviata's displeasure. Anything asked in the middle of her work always elicited a prompt put-down. Now was the window of opportunity.

"Latraviata, did you go to art school?"

"As a wee girl, yes. But never to a proper school like the Royal Academy or the Beaux Arts in Paris."

"How did you learn the different steps in painting, the way you do it now?"

"Well, I had some trouble figuring it out. There were many months for the tears of frustration. At last, I saw some progress. And then, one day, a painting went from beginning to end like a perfect day, sunny, windless and without a cloud." As if to emphasize her point, she painted a thin scarlet line around the middle clouds.

"Would you teach me?"

"Absolutely not. Nothing against you, dear Donovan, but I abhor teaching. I can talk you through the steps, then you must go to your own studio and struggle through on your own. It's the only way. The Royal Academy could shorten the process, perhaps, but I doubt it could change it in any real way."

"So you think art school is a waste of time?"

"If you are determined and know that the art monster has gnawed at you beyond healing, it probably is a waste." David's tunic needed some purple shadows, which she painted in with quick, short strokes. She took her finger and blended them together.

"Am I determined, do you think?"

"I shouldn't think so. At ten I was a silly little girl who

only wanted to please my papa. A very pretty girl, mind you. Determination comes later, with disappointments and sighs."

"What about David? Is he determined?" David turned his head, ever so slightly.

"Don't move, David. Maybe so. He has a serious demeanor that masks something deep. A somber lad who hides his boiling ambition and make-it-to-the-top resolve. His glorious hair makes up for the naturally gloomy facade, however."

Donovan liked it that Latraviata talked to them as if they were adults. Most of the time he could not completely decipher all that she was talking about, but he knew she was not talking down, using simple words just because they were ten years old.

"Now, give me a few minutes of silence to bring this to an end."

She finished the painting in her allotted time and they all three stood back to inspect and admire. It was a large canvas with the florid colors of sunset washing everything. Donovan had learned not to say that he merely liked it, because Latraviata had brought him down for that. Be specific in your comments, she had said.

"It's very orange, almost like firelight."

"Good. I wanted a warm glow for this piece. I think it works. Thanks to both of you. Take one of the umbrellas, as there is sure to be a shower on your way back."

David did not dare reduce his payment to Donovan this time, as his conversations with Latraviata made the time easier. Two for Donovan, three for David.

On their way back, it started to rain. There was sun light coming in under the clouds from the west, but the rain was heavy. Donovan told David that Anna might marry Simon.

"Would you move up there to his house?" David asked.

"I don't know. I think Anna would keep Santacasita, no matter what. It means a lot to her."

"Could I visit you up at Simon's?"

"I think so."

The rain stopped just as they were walking up the front. Anna was out on the porch and they joined her. She motioned to them to sit down.

"Donovan, I have been thinking all afternoon about Simon's offer. I am sure you told David of it?"

"Was that all right?"

"Yes. I just saw the most complete double rainbow and it seemed to end right where Simon's house is behind the trees. Do you think that was an omen?"

"Is that yes?"

"I think so, because of that and because it seems the right direction for you and me. I think we need to be a family again, and, as you say, Simon loves me. That's a very good start. I'll tell him in the morning."

"Can David still stay with us?"

"Absolutely yes. Now it's time for your abalone steaks."

Donovan had expected to be gloriously happy with a meal of abalone steaks pried off the rocks with his own hands, a young hunter-gatherer on his first providing for the clan. They were hard to chew, alas, and without taste. Another visit from Sister Disappointment. Why did everyone go on so about abalone?

Falling Angels

*T*he next morning David went back to Latraviata's studio for another day of shepherd boy. This time he was on his own. Anna had announced to Donovan that the two of them were invited to Agnes's studio. It was late morning when they started in the car down the steep hill to the coast highway, exact destination unknown but instructions from Agnes on a piece of note paper.

"After leaving your house, turn left at the main road, go through town to the far side, then turn left again at the gas station with the large palm tree, go a half a mile up and we're the redwood buildings on the right, the sign says Brown and Howland. It's in the shape of an Irish wolfhound. You can't miss it."

Anna drove up the bumpy, dirt drive to the house. The studio was a large, separate building with a multi-paned window, the redwood siding weathered to a cool gray. Agnes was standing at the Dutch doorway when they pulled up, wiping brushes in a cloth as dogs barked behind her.

"Joy. I have the two of you here at last. Come in, please."

"Hello, Agnes." Donovan shook her hand with a serious look. They went through a small vestibule into the main studio room, this one larger than either Latraviata's or Simon's. The flotilla of dogs circled around them with curious sniffings. The room had a twenty foot ceiling, with the one window looking out to the west, the morning sea quiet and flat. The other walls were hung with the work that Agnes Howland was known nationally for, biblical tableaux with heroic-sized figures in staged settings.

The largest was on the wall facing the studio window, a depiction in many shades of blue of the Annunciation, the angel, black-winged with orange eyes, hovered above the ground as he made his startling pronouncement to the upturned faces of the frightened gathering below. The sky was stormy and a white-walled city with turrets and domes burned in the distance. Agnes talked as Anna and Donovan looked at the painting, but neither heard much of her commentary as they studied the disturbing details of the large canvas. Was Gabriel, hovering with menace above Mary and her entourage, a demon or an angel?

In another canvas, Agnes had depicted the angels falling from the heavens, a whole cluster of them upside down, feathers from their wings making baroque currents in the sky, the viewpoint from above to accentuate the stony harshness of the ground below.

"You mustn't be put off by these pieces," Agnes said. "I have some cheerier paintings in the racks over there. Seraphim and cherubim above green Holyland hills, sheep and shepherds in long shadows, but I must admit, they're a bit too sweet for my taste. The horror of the Christian faith is my recurrent theme.

What disillusionment it wreaks upon the innocent."

Donovan thought it a strange mixture, this small, white-haired woman in overalls, and these dark, violent canvases. Simon was very similar to his work, a person could easily predict the painting that he would create, and Latraviata was, too, but no one could foretell what this rosy-cheeked, optimistic-appearing woman put on canvas.

"I'm stunned at their strength," Anna said." I think I have always believed what I can see here, but I was too weak to speak out. Now here it is."

"I hope they resonate where it counts. What do you think, Donovan?"

Again Latraviata's words about commenting upon art rang in his head. Pretty and nice were not acceptable. He paused and walked close to her depiction of the falling angels.

"They look like they are afraid. It's so far down."

"It is far down," she replied. "A discerning observation. Now let's go have lunch. Mary Louise has it all ready over at the house." They walked over to the cottage, small and cheery in comparison to the hulking studio and Mary Louise was waiting for them on the patio where she had been reading a book. When she heard their voices, she put a worn leather bookmark in and motioned for them to come up on the terrace. She was a small-boned, elegant woman with a straight, classical Greek nose and a pile of salt-and-pepper hair. Lunch was already prepared, under a white tea towel, protected from flies and birds.

"Sit down and tell me what you think."

Anna and Donovan repeated their comments about Agnes's paintings, unwilling to venture much further into the fine points of art. Lunch consisted of cheese sandwiches, ripe oranges and iced tea on the terrace. These women had a grand view of the sea, a three-foot stone wall circling the terrace for sitting and viewing.

Anna started her questions. "The two of you are so happy together. Where did you meet?"

Mary Louise answered. "In New York. Agnes was having an exhibit at Pierre Haspin's gallery on Madison Avenue. I was headed to a cocktail party farther down, and just by chance I looked in on her opening. Her work stunned me, we talked and planned dinner the next night, where she asked me to come live with her in Laguna."

"Did you accept that very night?."

"No. I had some work to finish, a book I was writing and some editing I had promised to do. We exchanged letters for a year, my book was published and after that I said yes."

"When was that?"

"Twelve years ago. Laguna was a more bustling art colony then, although very rustic. We had to drive all the way to Newport to get books and the like. I learned to order most things from Los Angeles or San Diego, to be delivered." Without conviction Mary Louise swatted one of the wolf hounds who was edging his nose into her plate as she talked.

Agnes added, "There were a number of painters here then, more than now. On any one day you could see a dozen French easels set up on the hills and rocks above the sea. Most of the men wore suits and ties and the women watched from the sidelines. It was a ferment of activity. Many have moved on, since collectors vaporized in the bad years after nineteen twenty-nine."

"But you have survived here," Anna said. "Agnes's

collectors haven't disappeared, it would seem."

"I have some very loyal admirers from Chicago and Cleveland," she said. "They send me annual checks and then come here on Boxing Day to take their pick, two paintings each. I then paint a small red square to mark their selections and I can sell the rest wherever I can."

After another half hour more of conversation, Anna and Donovan left the two women on their terrace and drove slowly down the hill.

"Someday you will have a studio like these Laguna painters," Anna said. "I know you will succeed, it hovers like a deep yellow aura over your head."

Donovan looked up for any trace of such an aura, but as he suspected, he could not see it.

"I will leave you now at Santacasita. I have private things to discuss with Simon," reaching over and giving him a kiss.

Shortness of Breath
1970

As Mary expertly negotiated the freeways south, I realized how much California had changed since I was a boy in the waning days of the western paradise. Now there was no open land, few adobe houses, fewer globe-shaped orange-juice stands, no Chinese and Japanese farms, no rows of ripe berries, few rows of eucalyptus. It underscored the impossibility of my ever living here again.

This time Tomas sat in the front seat with Mary. He said, "You missed a wonderful exhibit and a so-so party, Mary. I gave your chair away to a woman who wants to spirit Donovan away."

"Probably a better solution, despite the danger. I like your friends there, but the artistic world is so different from mine."

"Being one of the few women investment bankers in LA must please you."

"It does." We drove along in silence for a while. She said, "Do you ever see David Messenger anymore? You never mention him and I always liked him."

"We drifted apart while I was in Europe. I wrote him

several times asking him to join me, but he wrote back to say no, he had everything he wanted stateside. David never left the dreamy boyhood that we both enjoyed so much; he is a textbook example of the California man-child."

"What does he do now?"

"Nothing, really. His mother and his stepfather have both passed on. The royalties from his mother's books are still coming in, getting larger as the years go on. Someone told me a good cookbook can have as long a shelf life as the Bible. I still see her ethnic cookbooks featured in bookstores, and she was before her time with organic food. He lives in the same family house on El Molino. It's almost creepy."

"Donovan, most people in the world live in their parents' house," Tomas said. "There's nothing particularly creepy about that."

"Maybe not in India or provincial France, but in California there is. Everybody else I know has moved on, moved away, created a new life."

"Did he marry?" Mary asked.

"Yes, I guess that qualifies as a new life. He married our friend Marjorie Eastover."

We were halfway to Laguna, to the middle of the new Orange County. Rows of red tiled roofs marched in serpentine rows up the hills on one side of the freeway and down to the sea on the other. Domestic prosperity had replaced the orange groves and berry-bushes. Mary said, "So you haven't seen him since you were boys?"

"He and Marjorie came to Santa Fe about ten years ago and we were all hoping for a big, rewarding reunion. They had been married for some years, but the three of us hadn't gotten together for various reasons. But from the start, their visit didn't go very well. They stayed at La Fonda and I waited half an hour in the lobby for their appearance. After the short walk to the Pink Adobe, Marjorie said she couldn't breathe up at our altitude, wanted to have an early evening. When, during the dinner conversation, I talked about the ease of gay life in Santa Fe, they both were quiet for the longest time."

"That really should not have been a surprise. You've never hidden that. And besides, I always thought David was gay, too."

"I think he is. That may be what made Marjorie's shortness of breath even more severe. Or an overdose of static electricity when she was young."

"What does that mean?" she asked.

"Too difficult to explain. David was my best friend when we were young, and I was his. I will always be thankful to him for getting me through the loneliness of those years. I never really tried to make other friends, as our friendship was all that either of us wanted or needed. It saddens me that our closeness did not survive."

"Do they have children?"

"No."

"He sounds unfulfilled."

"I think he is. Marjorie invited me to their wedding in Pasadena, but I was in Paris. I sent them a Baccarat ice bucket with a letter explaining that I could not come back for just a few days. She has acted hurt and unhappy with me since."

"David may not be the husband she expected," Mary said.

"No question of it."

Tomas interceded, "I think that David, from afar, is still in love with Donovan, and Marjorie is, too. Maybe that is what the two of them have in common."

"I don't think so," I said.

"Donovan, all the women love you. They want to convert you, bend you to their will. Carole Francis, back in Santa Fe, still carries the torch and wants you for her very own. Delores in Laguna watches you with an intent, Latin eye that I understand. I think your tall build and big hands confuse them. You act so straight that they all think a good woman is all you need, and presto, gay no more. But it's too late. Tomas de la Pena has no intention of giving you up."

We were driving past the area where the Japanese and Chinese farms used to be, now more acres of red-tiled shopping malls with date palm esplanades. I could see the first glimpses of the water off to the right. My spirits rose, as they always did, at the first sight of the bluff above Balboa and Newport. It was still pristine and undeveloped. Balboa Island looked the same from a distance, more yachts in the harbor and I always had to look down the still waters of the channel between the two jetties to the white-capped sea beyond. The blue-black sea that took away my brothers.

Into the Black Sea
1939

Simon was delighted with Anna's decision. He insisted that they have an announcement dinner that very night at El Delirio, since that was where they had met. He booked a large table for all their friends and ordered lobster dinners for everyone.

Latraviata was the first to arrive. "Simon, dear, I found three bottles of champagne in my cellar hoard. Curious they haven't been used before now."

"We'll put those on ice," Simon said.

Agnes and Mary Louise were next, and several more artists straggled in.

The staff at El Delirio pulled out all the stops for Simon, setting the large round table in the center of the dining room with a massive bouquet of ginger, heliconia and other tropical blossoms.

Anna was seated to Simon's right and Latraviata to his left. David was just beyond Anna and Donovan next to Latraviata. Portman and the other guests filled in around the other side, some hidden behind the flowers. When the lobsters were finished and the buttery fingers all washed off and dried, Simon stood up in announcement mode.

"When a man reaches my great age, he has no expectations of the sublime joy that came my way this morning. Anna has agreed to become Mrs. Grunewald. The third Mrs.Grunewald, to be sure. We have not set the date, but it will be sometime soon, whenever Anna decides. I believe there is champagne for everyone."

Latraviata was the first to offer a toast. "Simon, you have shown the great wisdom to choose Anna. I can't think why she chose you, when there is a long queue forming for her hand, including one she least suspects. And how were you so absent minded as to misplace two former wives?"

He answered, "My first wife fell overboard into the Black Sea on our honeymoon. We were so young, I can barely remember. My second was the incomparable Elsie, Portman's mother, who died long before we left Berlin. I loved her very much. If the third time is likewise charmed, and it surely seems so, then Anna is like the end of a long eclipse, a sun coming into my shadowed life."

"Golden words, but let's not forget, a fabulous cook coming into your forgotten, dusty kitchen. I must question your motives, Simon," Latraviata said.

"Succulent meals may be the mortar that will hold it all together, but my motives are lofty and pure. Even before I knew whether Anna could tell a saucepan from a whisk, I fell in love with her right over there. A rush of love, happiness and warmth I had not felt since long ago in Berlin. I said to myself, Simon, this is your lucky day."

All the guests broke into applause. He sat down and took

Anna's hand, with a whisper. "And I didn't tell them how I saved you from the tortures of Confucius."

Anna forced a smile, stood up and pulled out a small piece of paper. "I wrote down some thoughts. Second and third marriages should be decisions of reason, rational conclusions for two people to live together. But I think Simon's is pure emotion, that he does indeed love me. And I feel like a thoughtless, but lucky girl, to marry in such haste."

Latraviata interrupted, "Have you forgotten the 'repent at leisure' part of that quote?"

Anna replied, "Nothing is more auspicious than a double rainbow, which I saw yesterday arching into the roof of Simon's studio. I suspect, Latraviata, you are just being a troublemaker."

Donovan wondered if there was something stronger under Latraviata's tart remarks. Was she yet another of Anna's admirers?

They finished the champagne and left, one by one, leaving only the boys and the engaged couple. Simon sat down by Donovan. "What do you think, Donovan?"

"Can I have a room of my own?"

"I expect we can find a room for you."

"Can David come to stay, also?"

"Of course."

"So we can go to school in Laguna this fall?"

"I hear it is a very good school and the art teacher there is a long-time friend. You will be required, however, to listen intently to your step-grandfather when he tells you things about painting and painters."

Sharp Pieces
1970

Mary turned left onto the Hill Road and up past the crowd of summer cottages to the Grunewald compound on the crest of the hill. The eucalyptus saplings that Donovan planted behind the houses were now soaring giants. Anna and Delores sat in the deep shade of the front porch with a pitcher of iced tea and a tray of glasses. Greenwood lay flat on the porch between them, awaiting events.

Although it had appeared that as I grew taller over the years, Anna grew smaller, I knew that Anna had grown in ways I could not begin to understand. She greeted Tomas first, ever perceptive of the feelings of the one with the least stature.

"Tomas, welcome again. He gets more handsome with each year, doesn't he, Donovan?" She hugged Tomas, then Mary, then me, holding my arms as she surveyed my face for the changes and lines that would reveal who I had become. "I have iced tea for all of you. Let's just sit a while before you get settled. Delores, will you pour, please?"

"Anna, I've brought you the catalogue from my show," I

said. "I knew you would not leave your hillside for the opening night, so I asked the gallery to produce a record of the show."

She paused as she looked through the catalogue, turning the pages slowly. "Donovan, you've become a fine painter. Such beautiful work. I would love to see the paintings themselves." On some of the pages she looked for half a minute or so, studying the images closely. She closed the catalogue and gave it to Delores to look through.

"And...?"

"The yellow bowl. So many memories you've packed into those paintings. Do the broken bowls stand for something important? Simon would have known instantly, but the psychological significance is lost on me right now."

"All the bowls come from my upper mind and are involved with my devotion to my grandmother."

"And do the broken ones reflect a deep-seated anger?"

"Their meaning was not clear for me, either," I said. "I knew I wanted to include the object that for so long was central to our lives, so much a part of you. As I reworked the objects on the table, one of the larger yellow bowls fell off and broke into a dozen shards."

"So you paid attention and used them."

"It seemed right at the time. The sharp pieces went well with the shiny, rounded porcelain shapes, gave a counterpoint, made angled shadows. I can't think why I would be angry."

"You're talking like Anglo-Saxon Protestants now, everything polite and guarded. Shutters closed," Tomas said.

"It may be too late for us to change that, Tomas," Anna said. "Simon told me that successful painters' lives were never an even, upwards incline, but rather a series of plateaus, each one higher than the last and separated by dangerous ravines with jagged bottoms. This new work tells me you've made your way across another treacherous gulley. I would like to have one of these paintings for the house here. I think they mark a turning point in your work."

"Most of them have already been sold, but I will let you know what's left and you can choose," I said.

"I would like for you to select it."

The First Tuesday
1939

*I*t was the last day of August and the summer people had
left when Anna drove David and Donovan back up to San
Miguel. After depositing David curbside at his home on El
Molino Street, they opened up the house on Harrison Avenue,
musty from being closed all summer. It seemed to Donovan like
a stranger's house, never having absorbed any of their energy.

At lunch the next day, Anna said, "I would like for you to
go with me to the vestry meeting this afternoon. I will do the
talking, but I need your support."

He dressed in his suit with his black, Sunday school tie;
Anna was in her black dress, pearls and large, befeathered hat,
denoting something important about to happen. They drove
over to the church, not stopping at the rectory, and she found
a parking place next to the church, a dozen other cars already
parked.

Anna said as they walked into the church, "The vestry
meets the first Tuesday of every month, so I know that the men
are here. I'll knock, but we'll go in without waiting."

The door to the vestry room was on the right side of the

church, under the lectern. Anna knocked sharply and opened the door, gently pushing Donovan ahead of her into the room. There was a long table surrounded by men in business suits, with the new, young rector officiating from the head chair. Glasses of water and papers spread across the table.

"Mrs. Merrill. We are having the vestry meeting," the rector said, standing up. All the other men stood up, too, and nodded to Anna. She gestured for them to sit down.

"I know that, gentlemen of the vestry, but I have business with you. I've come to tell you that I will be vacating the house on Harrison Avenue and you may cancel your rental arrangements there."

Dr. Jarman turned around in his chair, clearly the spokesman more in charge of things than the young rector. "Anna, is it not suitable?"

"We are moving to Laguna and won't be coming back here."

"Oh, we're sorry to be losing you. Will you also no longer be requiring our monthly check?"

"I will need it until the pension starts."

"Also, Anna, there is the delicate matter of the house on Waterbird Lane. James led us to believe you would be deeding it over to the vestry soon, since it was built with churchly fees." With many years of vestry duty behind him, Dr. Jarman knew how to play a melody on the strings of guilt.

"No, not soon. I'll have to use it for quite a while longer."

"Can you put a date on that?"

"No, Alex. I cannot. Those churchly fees, as you call them were James's gift to me, not a loan from the vestry, as you suggest. Such a gift to a pastor's wife has ancient precedent, as you well know. The land itself was a gift from my dear friend, Partridge Sanborn. I plan to honor my promise to James, but not on your schedule."

"I will ask our lawyer to send you a letter of agreement to that effect."

"Forget that. The return of Waterbird Lane will be on my schedule and I come from a notably long-lived family. And where is Partridge Sanborn, by the way? The senior member of the vestry, as I recall?"

"Partridge resigned last month. He had differences with the vestry consensus," Dr. Jarman replied.

"How strange. He would be last to resign, I would have thought." Several of the other members of the vestry cleared their throats and looked down at the table.

"But there it is," said the doctor.

"Well, thank you, vestry, and Alex, for your concern over my welfare, however fleeting it may be. I will let you know when I have vacated Harrison Avenue."

Peasant Toes
1970

As Anna asked Mary about her work in the financial tower and Tomas about his writing, I took the time to look at Delores Mendoza. She had grown into a tall, Latin beauty, her formerly short hair now long, done up in a tight bun. Her mannish stance was underscored by the black slacks and simple black shirt she always wore. She resembled an androgynous bull-fighter, slim and poised for action.

At first, her role at the Grunewald establishment was informal, but continuing. Now, she beamed the confidence that her permanent position as the companion to the grande dame afforded. If Anna's world was a court, Delores was its Cardinal Richelieu. Delores smiled at me and took my hand. Greenwood stood up at attention, shook himself and surveyed me with a new interest.

"Donovan, I'm glad you're here. There is much to tell you." She kept a hand on Greenwood's collar.

Anna cut across my conversation with Delores, "Tonight, all will be revealed over dinner. Not so much as an inkling beforehand."

"A chicken dinner? Roast Chicken with brown potatoes?" I asked.

"Absolutely. Annabelle is coming for dinner only, then back to Newport."

We went to our rooms in Simon's big house and unpacked. The house still had the dark look of a California bungalow from the early years: pale, weak light from the small lamps, turned on even during the day, and dark, well-crafted wood in the beams, paneling and window seats. Simon prized his window seats, installing new ones with the slightest encouragement from Anna, each still stacked with the same pile of dark velvet cushions from the early days. If the dim light of his house and studio grew claustrophobic, he could look out to sea from an ever-nearby window seat.

There was more darkness in the furnishings, all heavy and oaken; even the rugs were forest green and deepest brown with a border of stylized pine cones, perhaps acquired in the estate clearance of the dead leader of a woodland society. I realized that all of Anna's houses had been green and brown with welcoming rooms, unchanged sanctuaries from the modern world.

Every space that could hold a painting, held one, usually with its own horizontal, cylindrical light so that the deep colored walls glowed with the lighted pictures. Several were Latraviata's paintings, David Messenger with a golden crook and an immortal smile. Others were paintings by Simon and his Berlin contemporaries. The place of honor over the mantel was reserved for a single Marsden Hartley, a design of badges and medals of his Prussian officer, a purchase by Simon while he was still in Europe.

Tomas and I went to my old room, preserved as it was. Did I really live here for so many years? Twin beds with a massive metal lamp between them, where I read late into the nights. That was what I remembered most about that time, happy, foggy nights with the dark house creaking and groaning, as if we were all on a wooden ship through mysterious waters.

When I first moved there, the war was just starting in Europe and we listened in the dark of Simon's living room to the crackling news from the radio each night after dinner. As the Allies bombed farther and farther into the Third Reich, Simon described the former glory of the gutted cities, one by one, with stories from his boyhood travels to each of them. He told about attending concerts in Dresden with his grandmother, all Beethoven symphonies on successive evenings, *Apfelkuchen* with whipped cream at the interval. With a bachelor uncle, who tired of the gray winters in Berlin, he traveled by private railroad car, dinners cooked and served from their own kitchen, to a villa with palm trees on the Black Sea. Europe was a fabled land where black clouds gathered, but we were safe, far away in the rustling eucalyptus.

Tomas lay down on the bed and asked, "What do you think is going on? Anna seems to have some major plans afoot."

"I expect it's a change somehow in the family financial patterns. She'll be selling some treasuries or debentures and buying some common stock. If it's like other meetings, Mary and I will agree and Annabelle will noisily disagree, insisting on a change in ownership in favor of her family. She thinks that women who produce children are more deserving than others, but Anna will hold the line."

"So, no surprises?"

"I don't expect any."

After a light knock on our door, Anna came in and sat erectly on the side of one of the beds. Tomas lay across the other bed, his head propped up on an elbow, admiring Anna.

Her personal style had changed from the gray crepe de chine dresses with white collars from her parsonage days and the black from her mourning years. With a Laguna seamstress, she designed variations of a tailored long robe in solid colors, belted with a high collar, part Chinese and part ecclesiastical. She had a day version, black or white with a shorter hemline, but at important occasions in the Grunewald compound, she used the evening edition with bolder colors, tonight's a deep-purple with an amethyst brooch. She deservedly looked like the Pythia from Delphi, an exotic personage at home with her family.

"It's good to have you back here," she said. "I still believe that the two of you belong here next to the sea with me in Laguna, not the dry desert of New Mexico."

"We have the big pool," I replied. "Some people call it the Seacoast of Bohemia."

"I know, but it's not the same thing. That isn't what I want to talk about."

"What, then?"

"I sense a distressing tension between the two of you, a strong undercurrent that was not there on your last visit, something hurtful and unpleasant."

"Maybe it's the stress of the solo exhibit," I said. "I've been spending extra hours in the studio and that effects us both."

She was not convinced. "So, Tomas, what is it? Donovan would never tell me in a thousand years. I think the three of us talking about it, here and now, might put an end to it." Her years with Simon had ingrained a delight in group therapy and the wisdom of opening up your thoughts, most assuredly the thoughts that hurt the most to divulge.

Tomas sat up, cross-legged on the bed. "You're right, Anna, Donovan never wants to face anything unpleasant. I was trying to tell him something the other night, but his face looked so closed and unreceptive."

Anna said, "I first need to tell you both something about my past, a matter that happened years ago. But in a way it flavored all the years to follow. I promised to tell you, Donovan, but I never found the right time. It may answer many questions you may still have."

I wondered what could be in Anna's life that I did not know. She was always so open and quick to confess even small misdeeds. I thought I knew more about Anna than I did about myself.

She continued, "Your Grandfather Merrill had a mistress, Donovan. You will remember Paulette Messenger, not a wicked woman, only a foolish and vain one. She made her first play for James in San Miguel while we were down here moving into Santacasita."

"Paulette Messenger? I can't believe it."

"James told me while we were sitting in the cemetery, taking a rest from our house guests. I thought that you had overheard us, but somehow the years erased it all from your mind."

"No. I never knew, but it sounds so totally unlike Grandfather Merrill. How did it happen?"

"At first, I did not understand. James was on the surface

a holy man, so how could the weaknesses of the flesh get such a strong hold on him? I now believe that it was my fault. My determination to find a new life for us in Laguna was a threat to James. He thought I was abandoning him, and I suppose he unconsciously protected himself by finding a way to love someone else."

"Were we abandoning him?" I asked.

"I guess so. I only wanted summers away from San Miguel, but Laguna grew in importance for me."

"Did he actually love Paulette Messenger?"

"I don't know. He said the earthly world crashed in upon him, and he was weak, could not resist. He hoped that it was all over, in the past and would never happen again. He apologized to me and I had no reply."

"That was just before he died?"

"Yes. You can't imagine how I've regretted not forgiving him."

I thought about Paulette in her living room, dancing in front of Grandfather Merrill, smiling lecherously back at her with his white collar askew. It was a grainy black-and-white German movie, the evil Lola-Lola luring the good *Doktor* forward. How was it that he was not there on the sofa on the nights when David and I peeked through the plum-colored curtains? What would I have done had I seen him there? Had David seen them in a feverish embrace? Was that what brought the coolness between David and me?

She continued, "I felt a knife in my side and the breath go out of my body. We sat there in silence for the longest time, and I left him sitting in the cemetery."

"When Annabelle and Mary were visiting?"

"Yes, and that's what kept me from taking you and driving away that day. They finished their visit and James's heart attack came at the next vestry meeting, so there was never a moment of stillness between us. When we moved to Laguna I confided my unhappiness to both Simon and Latraviata. Their love and understanding allowed me to heal. I came to know that I was not the only victim of betrayal in the world, and in the whole scheme of things, it is not so important after all."

"Did you ever forgive him in your mind?" Tomas asked.

"Perhaps. It was so hard after he died, no way for us to discuss things. I was ashamed how trite and cinematic it all was. I have wondered many times what would have happened if Laguna had not come into my life."

"What did Simon think about it all?" I asked.

"He saw right from the beginning the cosmic humor in Paulette's being all things to all men, a Circe in modern dress. James viewed Paulette as a nubile temptress of the sort he had been forbidden as a man of god, her physical beauty worth risking his well-placed life.

"His death seemed like a sudden, biblical punishment. It was a fair measure, I thought; there might be more to this Christianity than I had realized. Sudden death for dalliance, punishment from on high. Now I wonder if it wasn't the other way around, that he was given a brief, sensual holiday before the ultimate, unchangeable end."

"You must have a reason for telling us this now," Tomas said.

"Yes." She looked at Tomas.

He said, "Donovan has told me that he thought you could see right into other people's thoughts, so you must be looking into mine. I saw another man this spring while Donovan was working day and night for this exhibit. It seemed that Donovan did not want me any more, he was crabby at dinner and locked away in the studio during the day. We did not make love very much and I felt alone again. I thought he was hiding from me in his work, that he couldn't face telling me the truth. That he did not love me."

So there it was, the important something Tomas wanted to discuss. I felt a constriction in my chest and my throat closing. I could not talk. Tomas confessed to things often when we were with other people, usually matters vastly more minor than this, a dent in my car, forgotten telephone calls, knowing that I would not berate him in public. With Anna here, he knew I could not ask the questions that whirled around in my mind. Who was he? Did you fuck in our house? When? Was he handsome? Was he better than me in bed? Why did you really do it? Will it happen again? Is there any hope for us?

"I'm sorry, Donovan," Tomas said. "The man has moved away and the affair is over; I will never see him again. I did not want to lose you, mad as I was. This secret has been festering in me ever since. I knew I had to confess it to you, but have dreaded doing it. I couldn't find a time to tell you. Now, it's the only way I can move on. Too many years in Catholic school, I guess, where confession is the gate to going ahead."

I still could not talk or look at either Anna or Tomas, only down at his feet on the bed. Wide feet, feet of a country peasant, not the long, narrow feet of an intellectual. Big toes. Sensual toes. I loved those toes and, now, hated them, too.

"Donovan, can you start to forgive me?" Tomas asked.

I never liked talking about myself, even in a one-on-one

situation, but with onlookers it was impossible. Especially with Anna. Tomas was more at home in this type of group therapy than I was, probably because of his probing, bookish family and the obligatory confessions to his priest every week. Hide. Fuck. Run. Confess. Everything okay.

I measured my words. "I think I know what drowning feels like. It crushes in on you, memories and pain. I guess all that I want to know is, Tomas, do you still love me and where do we go from here?"

"I love you even more now. It was childish of me to feel hurt when you neglected me for the studio, but I'm the spoiled one, the one wanting all your attention."

"Tomas would not have told us this unless he loved you, Donovan," Anna said.

With that, she left us. There was an awkward silence. Tomas came over to me and kissed me, warm and long. I responded, but sensed a thick layer between us now, as if an opaque, heavy curtain had been drawn on the open window. Would that be there between us for the rest of our time?

The story about Grandfather Merrill and Paulette Messenger stuck in my mind. I wondered if he had actually sat on her living room sofa, draperies pulled, while she danced in front of him, perhaps rubbing her breasts on his white collar, and both of them laughing, in the throes of obsession? Did he sneak out quietly in the night, like me when I met David, creeping across the garden to meet his paramour? It could have been a Mozart opera, grandfather and grandson bumping into each other in the dark on separate missions, a duet of two voices, one a low bass and the other a boy soprano.

Did they embrace on the sofa, quietly lest David awake, in

hot passion while he mumbled prayers of contrition, his collar pulled off on the floor? Now Tomas had done the same thing, romping about our house with a mysterious, sensual male, from time to time peering out the windows to make sure I was still at work in the studio, foolishly unaware. Anna's sad tale was engineered to spare me the hurt she knew was coming, that such things had happened before, but nothing could lessen it at that moment.

Song of the South
1939

At Harrison Avenue, Donovan and Anna tried to recapture the notion of being a family on their last days there. Donovan lay on his bed, reading with the door to the bedroom open. Anna made noises in the kitchen, preparing for the evening meal. She called Partridge on the telephone. Frieda answered.

"Hello, Anna. Are you back for good, then?"

"No, Frieda. I will tell you all about it in person if you can come to dinner tonight."

"We'd love to. Partridge will be back from his errands soon, and he will be delighted."

"Thanks, Frieda. See you about seven."

Just as she put the receiver back on its cradle, the telephone rang. It was Grandfather McBeale.

"Anna. You're back from Laguna. I've tried to ring you several times."

"Is there news?"

"Yes, I'm afraid."

"Bad news?"

"Yes. The company Eugene Jr. works for, Allied Assurety, went south."

"What does that mean, went south?"

"They are in bankruptcy. Eugene no longer has a job."

"Well, I'm very sorry."

"There is also the matter of Donovan's annuity. Since the company was dissolved, his annuity is worthless."

She lowered her voice so Donovan would not hear. "Worthless? You and Eugene, Jr. said it was rock solid."

"So we thought. We are blameless here, Anna. These are hard times and many others were taken in, too."

"So Donovan has nothing, now. What about Jameson's car? It seemed to disappear handily when you returned from Balboa."

"Well, Eugene, Jr. has it. He needs it to look for work now."

"I see. What a mess you've made of things, once again."

"I'm sorry, Anna, to bring such news. So many unhappy tidings recently."

When she hung up the telephone, she looked into Donovan's room and saw that he had fallen asleep reading, a book on his chest. Anna thought she would wait to tell him about his annuity, maybe after they were back in Laguna. The poor boy can only absorb so much.

She worked in the kitchen all afternoon preparing the dinner and took off her apron just as they rang the front bell.

"Come into our small house. I hope the food will be the same."

"It smells so good," Partridge said.

"Please sit before dinner and tell me about your resignation from the vestry. I couldn't believe it."

"The vestry has gone expansion mad," he said. "We had just paid for the new stained glass window, exhausted all our surplus, and they want to double the size of the church. Alex Jarman is fomenting all this, actually. I believe he wants the Church of the Holy Spirit, a community church, small and nurturing, to compete in size and magnificence with the cathedral in Los Angeles. I could not put a stop to things, so I knew I had to leave."

"How sad, Partridge. After all those years."

"I know. But Frieda and I want to travel more, so it gives us more time. We're going to London next month on the Queen Mary. Frieda will go over to Berlin to retrieve some of her mother's valuables; the Hochgarten properties have been confiscated, but jewelry and gold are safe with relatives. I will wait in London. I have not been able to get a visa for Hitler's Germany, but we understand Frieda can come and go with impunity. After all, she's still a German citizen as well as a US citizen."

"Well, let me serve the dinner. Then we'll talk more." Anna brought the platters from the kitchen and she served them. Just at the end of the meal, after slices of lemon meringue pie, Donovan asked to be excused.

"I told David I would come by tonight. Is it all right?"

"Yes, dear. Be home by nine, though."

When he had left, she cleared the table and served the coffee in the sitting room. She poured them each a cup and said, "Partridge, we have money problems. Donovan's annuity has come to nothing with the company's bankruptcy. We have the income to live on now, but his schooling was going to be paid with that annuity. Eugene said it was rock solid."

"Annuities are only as strong as the company itself. Not good in the long run if the company isn't."

"So we've discovered."

"Maybe, it's time to sell your bowl. The Imperial Yellow. It has great value, you know."

"Really? How much value?"

"I don't know exactly, but I can find out. When I had the jewelry business, I often dealt with a Chinese merchant in Los Angeles: Mr. Shangho, who had beautiful pearls and emeralds, and fine Asian antiques. He is an honorable man with a small store in Chinatown; he always bought and sold the most exquisite pieces from China. I could call him, if you would like."

"Yes, I would like."

"Then, I suggest that you buy certificates of deposit from good banks and treasury bills or bonds. They would be much safer for Donovan than an annuity."

"I will worry about your trip to London and Berlin, with war looming. Europe does not seem a place to be right now. Frieda, are you sure you cannot arrange things by mail or telephone, rather than actually going there?"

"I wish I could, Anna," Frieda said. "I will go in and out on the same day, so it should be safe. Not to worry."

"Nonetheless, I will."

Anna did not tell Partridge and Frieda about her marriage plans, which somehow seemed insignificant and distant. They said goodnight, knowing that it might be a while before they were together again.

Chinese Cookbook

The next morning Anna said to Donovan, "Your school begins in two weeks in Laguna, so we have much to do before we can leave. First, we need to go into Chinatown to meet Mr. Shangho. He will advise me on selling the yellow bowl."

"But that is your favorite bowl."

"It was part of another life. Life in San Miguel with James."

"Are you sure?"

"Yes, I'm sure. Right now the less that reminds me of our time at the rectory, the better. There were certainly some good days, Donovan, but there were sad ones, too. The yellow bowl was at the center of life there, so I am positive it will be better now to let it go. It may find a new happy life with Mr. Shangho."

"I won't mind moving on, either."

"We'll drive into Chinatown this morning and see if he is the one to sell it or buy it. Then, I'm going to have a big house sale here. We'll let go of everything, since the Laguna house has all we need. I need to keep only a few small items."

"When will you have the sale?"

"I think this weekend. I can run an ad in the newspaper and you can make signs to put at each end of the block. Estate Sale, I think sounds best."

Anna preferred taking the streetcar into Los Angeles, but the automobile was called for with their important cargo. She let Donovan carry the blue, cloth-covered box and he placed it safely on the back seat. Anna still drove slowly, inciting the ire of drivers who passed around her noisily.

By ten, they parked on the street where Chinatown began. Partridge said that Mr. Shangho's store was in the middle of the first block, on the left and that he was expecting them. They found the store easily, and the chime of the temple bells attached to the door announced their entry into the incensed interior.

A young man behind the counter looked expectantly at the box that Donovan was carrying. "Mrs. Merrill, please come through."

He led them down a doorway hung with strings of glass beads, down a dark hallway to a small room at the back, Mr. Shangho's office. He was waiting, inside, alert and seated at a round table with carved legs, lions feet with claws.

"Mrs. Merrill is here." He seated Anna in the only other chair, leaving him and Donovan to stand. Mr. Shangho nodded, while the younger man did the talking.

"My father expects you. You have a bowl to sell?"

"I do have a bowl," Anna said. "But I would like to discuss price before deciding to sell."

Father clearly understood more English than his silence indicated and bowed slightly. The son took the box from

Donovan and placed it in the middle of the table. The father gently took off the top and placed it beside the box. He lifted the bowl out gingerly and looked for a long time at the bottom. Then he set it gently on a cloth and rotated the bowl slowly around, feeling the entire lip of the bowl.

He said something in Chinese to his son and the son replied in Chinese. They continued, touching the bowl and inspecting the bottom again. The father talked in Chinese for almost half a minute, the son looking at him intently but not reacting in any way. Anna said, "I also think, as both of you apparently do, that it is very, very good. At least, it holds a strong place in my heart."

Both of the men opened their eyes with surprise at Anna's grasp of their conversation. The father realized that their language shelter was gone and said in English, "It is a very large, very good Imperial Yellow Bowl. The Wanli period of Ming Dynasty, perhaps dating from around fifteen ninety. What price will you be asking?"

"I don't know exactly. I will know, however, if you tell me how much you are thinking of paying me."

They whispered to each other, put off that Anna could understand some of their back and forth. Finally the older man said, "Six thousand dollars."

Anna waited a minute, then said, "Twelve thousand, please."

The old man smiled and said, "Nine, please."

"Ten thousand, I think. I will sell it to you for ten thousand dollars." There was a finality in her voice that made the old man nod.

"Very good. Please wait," he said.

His son quickly walked out and they waited for his return. Every time that Donovan looked up at Mr. Shangho, he smiled, nodded and patted the rim of the bowl. The son returned with an envelope of money. Anna counted it and shook hands with both father and son.

"I have other Chinese items. Would you be interested in them?" she asked.

"Are they also from the Imperial Palace? We deal only in the very finest."

"I don't think so. Only good porcelains and fabrics."

"We can suggest other shops and dealers."

As they walked down the street back to the car, Anna said, "My kitchen Chinese came in handy. We should have lunch here in Chinatown, don't you think? A small celebration."

"Remember that David got sick the last time?"

"You will like it. Just here is the Peking Palace."

They were seated in the last unoccupied booth in the busy restaurant, near the front door. A paper lantern with a dim electric bulb hung over each booth and somewhere, there was the rustling gong of wind-chimes. Anna ordered for them, MooGoo Pork with Fried Rice, Yellow River Chicken, Egg Rolls and Egg Drop Soup. Without asking, the waiter brought a pot of green tea and cups.

Donovan asked, "Do you think that your bowl was worth more than ten thousand dollars? They agreed to buy so quickly."

"Of course. Otherwise Mr. Shangho could not make a profit."

"How much more?"

"A great deal more, Donovan. I could not think about

that, only the price I would be willing to accept. Ten thousand dollars was it. A two story house in Pasadena sells for five thousand, so I wasn't taken. Imagine a bowl worth twice more than a house."

Anna poured green tea for them both and looked around the room. Across on the other row of booths sat Paulette Messenger and Wo Fong, having lunch together. Paulette saw Anna and leaned over to say something to Wo Fong; then she came across the room to their table.

"What a surprise to see you here, Anna. I'm so sorry about James."

"We all miss him terribly, as you might understand."

"Yes. How are things going for you?"

"I'm recovering, Paulette. We made a quick visit to Chinatown this morning. Is that Wo Fong with you?"

"Yes. Did you hear that we are to be married?"

"No. What news."

"I have a favor to ask you. The wedding is in San Francisco next week, and I have worried about David. I think he would rather be with Donovan than in the big city."

"What do you think, Donovan? Can David come to stay?"

"Yes, Mrs. Messenger."

Wo Fong did not look their way, and remained seated in the booth, chopsticks busily bringing rice from bowl to mouth.

"Splendid," Paulette said. "Did you know I have written a new cook book, classic Chinese recipes adapted for American kitchens? Wo Fong and I will be traveling the country for the publisher, a book tour, they call it. I will speak to ladies clubs and groups interested in cooking. The book is titled *Peking Duck for Western Ponds*. What do you think?"

"You are a clever woman, Paulette. A Chinese husband just lends your book credence. I wish you the best. The book and the marriage."

"It's all an adventure, isn't it? By the way, could David stay until next year? I would send you money for his keep, so he wouldn't be a bother financially. There's really no place for him on the road."

"Yes, of course."

Paulette adjusted her dress and walked back to Wo Fong, who did not look up as she sat down. Donovan could still not help seeing Paulette naked, dancing wildly with bouncing breasts and he looked up at Anna with guilt, hoping she could not see into that portion of his brain.

Apparently his mind was temporarily opaque, unviewable, because she skipped over that and said, "Who would have thought? Wo Fong and Paulette."

The strange couple was done with their lunch before Anna and Donovan. Paulette waved over to them as they walked out, but Wo Fong looked only straight ahead. Donovan knew that Anna was still sad that things did not work out between her and Wo Fong. It was better, he thought, to leave the matter alone.

Sail Away

The estate sale was a grand success. Donovan printed large signs that he nailed onto the camphor trees at the street intersections at either end of the block. *Estate Sale, 9am to 2pm. Choice items from all over the world. Priced attractively. Saturday Only. 910 Harrison Avenue.*

Ah Fong and Li Fong came to the house before sunrise to help them move the furniture out onto the lawn. Anna had written out a price tag for every item: *Linen napkins from Portugal, Five Dollars; A Good Porcelain Bowl, Three Dollars.* Donovan thought her graceful handwriting lent validity to the prices; who would dare question writing so eloquent? *Footed Pottery Compote, English, Two Dollars.* The tables were filled with china, lamps and pots, and even the chairs and the sofa had baskets and books piled upon the seats. Clothes, kitchen goods, towels, bed sheets and all the black-and-white framed engravings of European cathedrals. *French Vermeil Candlestick (Gold over Silver) Seven Dollars.* The full service of sterling silver forks and knives were individually priced, and the silver vegetable dishes had a separate price from their covers.

The crowd started before nine, rushing to buy the choice items, and they kept up in a steady succession until noon, when everything was gone except for Li Fong's cleaver.

"I wonder if you priced things too low. There's nothing left," Donovan said.

"I would rather view it that I priced everything exactly right."

Donovan held up the bamboo rake he had hidden away from the sale, "I'll rake the lawn where the grass is all pushed down."

"Do it quickly, because we'll be taking the cleaver and the whisk, and leaving Harrison Street for good in about ten minutes."

"Won't you miss some of the things?"

"No. The cleaver is an interesting remembrance, as well as the whisk that I saved out in the kitchen. We're going to a new life, Donovan. No strings from the past, except the money from our sale."

Anna had the ability to drive away from unhappiness like a British yacht steaming full speed out of a pestilential, foreign harbor. Donovan saw that she did not even glance into the rear view mirror as they steamed down Harrison Avenue onto Rosemead Boulevard, their inland passage to Laguna. All the possessions Anna had treasured for so many years were gone, sitting on other people's tables and dressers, being admired by other eyes. How could she be happy without them in Laguna?

When they arrived they did not go by Santacasita but drove directly up to Simon's house. Anna stopped the car at the beginning of the drive and they both looked up the road to their new home. She reached over and kissed his cheek.

The wedding between Anna and Simon was a civil ceremony at the courthouse in San Diego. Late one morning, two cars from Laguna drove down there in tandem, Anna's with Simon, David and Donovan, Latraviata's with Portman, Agnes and Mary Louise. They were all refugees from someplace else in the world, gathering to start the building of a new Laguna family. It was imperative for them to nurture the ceremonies of this new clan, to give confirmation to its existence. For most of them, it would be a stronger family than the one they had left, and a happier, more productive place than the actual homeland. The wedding dinner at the best hotel was followed by a procession with paper streamers back up the coast, eight exhausted people in their beds way after midnight.

Anna entered into the studio-centered life of Simon without fuss. She took over the workings of the house from Portman, who was glad to give them up. The kitchen grew in importance, now producing her expert meals on a regular basis, and she arranged the weekly dinner parties for their extended circle. Cleaning and polishing were never tasks Anna cherished, so a woman was hired to do that work under Anna's tutelage. A grand house it would never become, but a certain grace edged its way in. Their friends started looking upon the house as Anna's, the studio still as Simon's.

She developed a new interest in walking. Walking up and down the hills of Laguna and along the cliffside path, she met most of the other villagers, who found admiration and amusement in the sight of this strolling elegant lady, in a variety of sunhats and with her five-foot high walking staff of polished pear wood. She walked almost daily down to the village grocery, but the Featherstone sons delivered what she bought, as she never carried anything back.

Anna pursued the special bond that she felt with Latraviata, the two women doing many errands together, shopping and lunching regularly on the seaside terrace of El Delirio. Neither of them had close women friends before and they took to this new friendship with gusto. During one lunch on the terrace, Anna asked Latraviata, "I feel guilty about our time together, time that you must neglect your easel."

"I was lonely here, before you. Simon is a man, Agnes might as well be, and neither could be the friends we are. Let the jealous easel feel neglected now and then."

"I was lonely, too."

"Don't let us give this up."

"I never knew what it was to have a friend. I had dear Li Fong in the kitchen, but we were happy to be woman and servant. I had a husband, two sons, and some grandchildren, but nothing there is the same as a friend."

"This is different. A happiness of equals being together," Latraviata said.

They talked a great deal about James, his life and his death. There were many issues left dangling when he died that Anna could not resolve. Discussing them with Latraviata on the terrace above the surf took the sting out, started the healing. To leave the ideas that hurt hidden away in the shade, unexamined, was to give them strength. With every lunch, the grief was lessened and the ache of what lay beneath relieved. Anna moved from a strong survivor, hiding the fears that came with that survival, to a woman at ease with herself, feeling strength grow in the muscles she never knew she had.

Donovan became more settled, too. He and David shared

one of the bedrooms, moving their clothes and possessions up from Santacasita. The school was much smaller than Audubon Elementary, with all grades in one building. Despite the small facility, the school demanded a great deal more from the boys than what they had become accustomed to back in San Miguel. Both worked on their lessons at home, with a closeness that Donovan never felt with his real brothers.

Simon saw to it that Donovan and David had extra hours with the art teacher, another migrant from Germany. In the early 1930s when the art colony discovered that the Laguna school had no art teacher, there was a general outburst of indignation, strong enough for the school board to relent and hire young Ernst Richter. It was, after all, Laguna, where art reigned on high and painters were revered like prophets. Richter was the twenty year old son of Hassel Richter, the acknowledged leader of the plein air group in town; a shy, but firm teacher, he brought the high standards he remembered from his own schooling in Berlin and a natural, gentle way with young talent.

Each clement Saturday, he took a group of students, small because of the natural lack of interest in most sixth and seventh graders, to the hills with French easels and paints, provided free by the imbedded guilt of the school board. Each student came back Saturday afternoon with a nearly finished canvas which they were instructed to finish on their own at home. Donovan quickly became Richter's prize pupil, David dropping away early on.

Simon made an occasion each Sunday of viewing and discussing Donovan's work from the day before, establishing it as an important event. Donovan was particularly proud of one scene, a view through a shrub-covered cleft to some high hills beyond, one tall eucalyptus like a sentinel in the left foreground. It was the painting in which Donovan tried to incorporate many separate elements, a more complex effort than any of the earlier ones.

"So why did you choose to place the eucalyptus on the left, Donovan?" Simon asked.

"It was there, so I painted it there."

"And it did not occur to you to move yourself so that it was placed on your right?"

"I didn't think about that. Is it wrong to be on the left?"

"Not wrong, but more difficult for a young painter. A Courbet or a Corot could pull off the left placement of a tree, but, then, they were geniuses. It is essential when choosing a motif to be perceptive, to spend some time and not paint the first thing you see. The Western Eye sweeps from left to right in a canvas, and something as strong as a tree may keep the eye from coming into the body of your picture at all."

Simon talked often about the Western Eye, as if it were a separate organ existing only in people in the Occident. He told Donovan that because we grew up reading left to right on the written page, we in the West view everything, art included, in that grandiose, sweeping manner, left to right. Donovan tried to do the opposite after Simon's first lecture, moving in a counter-clockwise arc, and he found it curiously hurt his eyes. He made a mental note to check for eye movement in the citizens of Hong Kong when he might travel there later in life.

Simon continued, "You must arrange for strictures and schemes to tease the eye into your very admirable scene through the cleft of the hill. All that is worthless if the eye does not reach it."

"Doesn't your eye move around the tree to the scene?"

"No. It stops completely at that dark green blob. Like a solid rock."

"So what must I do?"

"I might make the tree less dense, and perhaps insert a light-colored element in the background, a roadway or a streak of sunlight, peeking through the leaves left to right. Between this section here, and here, here, here. Then the right moving eye just scampers through, led by this path of brightness. The easier solution is to just move the tree."

"Will you make the changes for me?"

"No. You must paint them yourself."

Simon usually found some element or elements of Donovan's plein air work to criticize or to comment upon. Parts of a painting were important. This shrub was out of scale with its neighbors; the hills beyond were painted in strokes too energetic for their place in the composition; the color of this rock was too raw, too unnatural; a bolder sky color might improve what went on below, give it a texture that the milky white one did not.

Donovan began to understand the endless combinations that made a painting. Becoming a painter was a harder task than it seemed at the outset. Simon always stressed that a painting was unto itself, not just a faithful representation of an exact scene. If the painter did not insert himself into the work, he might as well have a Brownie camera on his neck instead of a head. A painting was only an idea, he said. He was quick to praise those parts of paintings that pleased him.

Donovan was now on the road to becoming an artist. He saw how Simon and Latraviata, when she chose to invite him into her studio, forged their ways through painting after painting, new adventures with each canvas, and he saw how right is was to do so. A new canvas on the easel was an absolution from the sins included in paintings that went before, a second chance for perfection, an endlessly renewable second chance.

David, however, found no road to start upon. He was a good student, if an apathetic one, and his quick mind made lessons a breeze. Nothing interested him in great depth. He never stretched himself, never found new skills. He did what was asked, but nothing more. He and Donovan stayed best friends, however, never letting competition ruin their bond. But the almost-brothers were pulling apart, slowly and immutably. While one stayed on the beach, the other was venturing farther and farther from shore.

As 1939 ended, this new family sat longer hours after dinner in front of the radio, listening to the fall of Poland, Czechoslovakia, the Netherlands and the strong possibility of France, itself. The Battle of Britain continued, with the brave aviators defending as best they could. All life in England seemed in peril, no avenue of escape.

They felt safe in Laguna, far from the distant upheavals. The green hillside seemed a fortress against the world, which was falling apart faster than they could comprehend.

Partridge Sanborn returned from England and called to ask Anna if he could come down to Laguna for a visit. Dinner that night was somber as he told his story. Frieda had disappeared into the Third Reich, a vast, dark forest, and no amount of consular effort could find her. It was rumored that Jews were disappearing and Frieda was a Jew.

"I was not allowed to travel to Berlin to look for myself."

"That would have been so dangerous," Anna said. "I've read that Hitler was impounding people daily, anybody that objected. No recourse for them whatsoever. You could well have been taken, too."

"I was beside myself. I spent three months going to the embassies in London every day. Our people could do nothing, they told me. I tried working through the French Embassy, but they were more concerned about the impending fall of Paris. It became impossible to communicate with anybody on the Continent, telephone lines were blocked, mail deliveries cancelled, and private couriers were forbidden."

"Did you ever hear another word? Even from family or neighbors?"

"Nothing. Not a word. The American embassy told me that I must take the last ship to New York or I might have to spend the war in London. I hated leaving with Frieda's fate unknown."

"Was the *Caronia* the last ship?" Simon asked.

"Yes. Talk was that after New York the ship might not return to Southampton, but spend the war in America. Perhaps to become a troop ship, if we get into the war."

"I'm so very sorry, my dear. You must stay on with us. There's an extra room we can have redone as a bedroom for you," Anna said.

Mr. Sanborn's long face neither dissented nor assented. He stayed on in Laguna, sending for clothes and books from his house in San Miguel. So the disparate family grew, all hiding from the storms that were breaking so violently a world away. Simon continued as an even keel for everybody else, painting away at his easel like clockwork, never giving up the very particular duty that was his. If art still mattered, then perhaps sanity and peace still mattered.

Snake on the Pillow
1970

fter I slept for a while, we had a few hours before Anna's command dinner. I said to Tomas, "Let's walk over to Santacasita. We can talk about it."

The exit from the Grunewald compound was the same as it was forty years ago, the eucalyptus trees taller, portions of the estate more overgrown. We turned down the side road which led to Waterbird Lane. Where a single house had been before, now six or seven were wedged into each lot. Laguna had become the poster child of beach communities, every bit of land available was built upon. Lots were subdivided, and re-subdivided to yield the costly, tiny parcels that lined each road. The whole world wanted a Laguna beach house.

Waterbird Lane had a similar crowding of summer houses when we turned into it. I thought about the great expanse of the Grunewald property, a priceless relic from days past. An island in the middle of this urban sprawl.

"May I ask you a question?"

Tomas assented with a nod.

"Do you remember our conversation in Mykonos a few

years ago? You quizzed me about Madame Bovary."

"I suppose so. Why?"

"You were writing a story about infidelity, a professor who cheated on his wife."

"Yes, I remember. It didn't work, so I left it out of the collection."

"Were you thinking about cheating on me as early as that?"

"I've always thought about cheating, Donovan. I'm an unfaithful man."

"So the difference is, now I know that you're that way."

"I can't promise to change."

"So I must figure out how to live with that?"

"Yes, Donovan. I love you, but not you exclusively."

"Does that give me the right to look around, too?"

"Of course, but I can't see your doing that. You're a faithful man. You would never run around on me." Tomas imparted that this was somehow a flaw in my character.

"So we're locked into that. I weep at home like Penelope, while you're the one who has the great voyages of infidelity?"

"You're being too theatrical, but, yes, that's the way it is. There's a saying that goes: 'There's one who kisses and one who offers the cheek.' There is no fairness in life."

"But I think you love me."

"I do. Very much."

We had reached Santacasita. I thought to myself that we should change the name to Bitter End. The house sat well on the lot, the large mossy rock sheltered the small garden behind, a woodland house somehow displaced here at seaside. The Norfolk Island pine had grown to a hundred feet tall. Anna used it as a guest house, allowing the high-end collectors or people concerned with estate matters to stay there. I thought about the discussions that David, Delores and I had had sitting on that rock. Life would be full of promise, anything could be attained.

"So we'll just go back to Santa Fe and continue on?"

"I hope so."

"I'll have a hard time with that. Knowing that any minute you could take off with the next attractive face."

"I'm not promiscuous, Donovan. Just unfaithful."

"I don't see the difference."

"I love you, want to be with you forever. But don't trap me in a cage like a canary. I'm a man. I sometimes have urges that you cannot fill."

"I want our love to work, Tomas. I will try to understand, to pay attention."

We walked back to the house as the sun slipped beneath the horizon. I did understand more than I let on with Tomas. I knew that I had a way of grasping at relationships with too hard a hand, no doubt from all the loss I had experienced. Hold tight, no more unhappiness. Anna had seen this when I was a boy and suggested that I learn to hold people more like an egg, firmly but not hard enough to crush.

We walked back up the driveway up to Simon's estate. Simon, Portman, Latraviata and Mr. Sanborn were all dead now, three of them leaving their entire estates to Anna. She once told me that to be an heir is a curious dichotomy: if a person loved you with a love large enough to make you the heir, the single beneficiary, then it was sure that you would miss them in the same large measure, a giving and a taking, bringing you back to home base.

Portman died soon after Simon married Anna, in a car wreck along the coast. He was never happy in his role as the son of a powerful, successful painter. I tried to connect with him in our years together, but he drew away each time I tried. I do not now believe that he disliked me or was jealous of me, but he could not communicate with anyone other than Simon. Even as a boy I knew Portman would have a sad end, crippled by his lack of any ambition of his own. How many other great painters' offspring never found their way, never leaving the nest until it was too late to learn to fly well. In the end it was an abysmal fall.

At his death, Simon bequeathed to Anna several hundred of his unsold paintings, which museums from Germany and at home coveted, the Laguna properties, which included other parcels adjoining the Grunewald compound, and a handsome portfolio of blue-chip shares. The refugee from the Old World had succeeded handsomely in the new.

Latraviata also bequeathed to Anna her Laguna property, ignoring Derrick Johns and the landed family in Hampshire, and all her paintings as well, museums in the UK being those that coveted her work. Anna kept the house on the peninsula locked, the front gate with a chain and padlock. The tropical gardens, never particularly well-tended while Latraviata was alive, now bulged through the fences and over the walls, a perfect hiding for feral cats and raccoons.

Mr. Sanborn had no real property when he died, here in Anna's sun room. The Laguna friends grew to appreciate his quiet, sound advice on the workings of the financial markets. Even though Wall Street was a continent away from the hillside, he kept a constant eye on opportunities there. He passed on to

Anna another bulging portfolio of investments. No word was ever forthcoming about his Frieda.

These three estates kept Anna busy with correspondence and negotiations in her roles as executor and trustee; Delores proved an able assistant, a keen student of the financial markets. The overgrown five-drawer file cabinet in the kitchen was the only official adjunct to the kitchen table where the two women conducted a business large and extensive enough to justify a suite of corner offices and many assistants. Since Anna never had money in her youth, she was not afraid of it; she could bully it, stroke it and tease it into doing whatever she wanted.

I was immensely proud of Anna. From a simple, if never helpless parson's wife, she had grown personally to an accomplished matriarch for the remainder of her small family: Mary, Annabelle and me. She had nurtured the one asset she had from her own life as Mrs. James Merrill, the proceeds from the sale of the Imperial Yellow bowl. At first she invested only in ultra-safe, treasury investments as war and its uncertainties engulfed the world, then, starting small at first, a dozen shares of this corporation and ten of that. She gradually refocused on the common stocks of growing, solid companies in the post-war years. By the time I was in university she could pay my tuition and expenses totally from dividends, never invading principal. Thirty years of price growth, dividends, shrewd re-investment and compounding brought Anna's own kitchen portfolio to the attention of investment bankers from both coasts.

Are those Old Gods still laughing at the reversals of fortune that continue to swirl around me? The haughty and rich McBeale side of my family lost everything, Grandmother McBeale ending her days in a sunless cottage in Altadena.

Her husband and his siblings, so full of themselves and their inherited lumber money, brought the fortune down to ground, nothing but sepia photographs to mark its rise, only gossip to mark its fall. The curving drive with magnolias remains to this day in Alhambra, a curiosity going nowhere in the middle of a lackluster subdivision, two-bedroom ranch houses pressing against the perfumed blossoms.

Anna's side, so unpromising when we steamed down Harrison Street with only a cleaver and a whisk, had prospered beyond imagination. Were these inherent failings, built-in Greek flaws, and bred-in-the-bone abilities, or was it all a roll of the dice?

My cousin Annabelle now had a husband and children, who also figured in the succession. Anna was clear about dividing her estate into equal thirds, Annabelle to share her portion with her children, Mary and me to each have an undiluted third. Annabelle, of course, thought that her branch deserved the lion's share of income and promise, a full portion for each of her children and children yet to come. But Anna was a dedicated egalitarian who blocked her grand-daughter's repeated legal assaults with a battlefield expertise.

Annabelle arrived just before dinner to have a glass of sherry, all that was being offered in the way of aperitifs. She and I sat together on the porch, while the others buzzed around Anna and Delores in the kitchen. Annabelle had matured into a California trophy matron: tennis, yoga, charity work, eternally slim figure and perfect teeth, masses of blonde tresses. She kissed me with no body contact in the hug. If a fierce and loyal proponent for her children, her love did not extend laterally into the family for Mary and me.

"Donovan. I got your invitation and catalogue. The beat goes on in the Santa Fe art world, I see. Interesting work."

"How nice. Thanks, Annabelle."

"What do you suppose Anna has up her sleeve?"

"Not a clue."

When Mary came to join us, the only sister got the same hug and kiss, devoid of warmth.

Annabelle said to her, "Join us, dear. We're trying to suss out Anna and her plans so important that I must drop everything and come to dinner. I smell the aroma of her chicken dinner, mixed perhaps with the unsettling fragrance of change."

"I think Anna has plans for a building," Mary said.

"Why do you think that?"

"As Delores and I were setting the table in the dining room, I accidentally pulled a cloth cover off something on the sideboard for just a second. I thought it might be a fancy dessert or the like, but it was an architect's model. Delores took the cover out of my hand and replaced it, without a word."

"You made the mistake of fooling with Mrs. DeWinter's things," I said.

"Exactly."

We were called to dinner then, with Anna at her customary seat at the end of the table with covered dishes in a half-circle. She sat Tomas on her right and Delores was always on her left. We filled in the remaining places, in no special order. I, as ever, enjoyed watching Anna in her role as the one who portions out. It was loving and controlling at the same time, her dominance of the table as a visible parallel to the firm, benign rule over the family itself.

"Donovan, here's some white meat, some extra potatoes and a pile of the green beans."

"You haven't forgotten."

"And Annabelle hates green beans and will waste the chicken if I serve too much. No gravy. No potatoes, but some of the purple cabbage slaw. A very parsimonious-looking plate, I'm afraid."

She served each of us, Mary's plate with more meat than potatoes, Tomas getting what I got, and Delores a small portion of everything. Her roast chicken meal still had its power to delight me, to bring me back to every table we had shared from the days in San Miguel. She looked at me across the table, knowing my thoughts.

After the lemon pie and coffee, we continued to chatter in expectation. She cleared off her end of the table, Delores took the covered bowls to the kitchen, and brought the cloth-covered model over from the sideboard. She placed it in front of Anna, where the platter of roast chicken had been.

"I'll expect you know what this is," Anna said.

Mary seldom feigned. "Are you building a new house?"

"No. Something grander, and I hope more inspired." She swooped off the cover and we could see the design model of a many-leveled structure on a stair-stepped base, a stylized wooded slope. If the model trees on the top of the slope were the eucalyptus behind Simon's house, the building was going to be huge. Forty or fifty times larger than the present house.

It was a California bungalow on steroids, the many hipped roofs cascading down the incline with courtyards and open spaces between each section. The architects carved small statues of people to stand about the courtyards, to sit on the sides of the fountains and to point to the sky like the figures in Piranesi prints. I thought that Anna must have summoned the Greene brothers back from the netherworld for one last project.

"It is a house," Annabelle said. "An obscenely large house. Much too grand for you and Delores and Greenwood. What can you be thinking?"

I said nothing, puzzled by something so different from anything I expected from Anna.

Tomas got it, however. "It's a museum. A big one."

"How did you know that, Tomas?" Mary asked.

"It says so, right here." He pointed to brass plaque in the corner of the base. "The Grunewald Museum."

Annabelle made her attack. "So, Anna, you're going to build this gigantic, selfish building with our money? The money that could be going down to the generations beyond. Just for your old Simon Grunewald?"

"Simon was your step-grandfather, Annabelle. However much you wish to ignore it. He made my life easy and happy, as well as Donovan's and Mary's, in the dark years when we all needed solace and support. He understood how adrift we were, and included us in his love. And, my dear, the money is not yours yet, it is still mine to do with as I please. I have the full right to spend down every penny, on anything I choose."

"How much is this going to cost?" Annabelle asked.

"I don't know exactly. I've had estimates from two large construction firms, who were quick to point out that these were only estimates. Probably about two hundred million dollars."

"So what would be left for us?" Annabelle asked.

"It may be considerably less than you had planned upon.

I will probably have to sell some of the other Laguna parcels for the museum endowment and dip rather deeply into the portfolios. There should be many millions left, which must be divided by three, as you know. You will not want."

Mary and I smiled. Anna loved bringing up the division by three and this always brought intemperate outbursts from Annabelle. This time was no different.

"Mary is a single woman and Donovan won't be marrying, won't have any issue. Why should they get more than my children? They are your future, as well, Anna, and here you are undermining it. Since when should the childless ones, barren, no offspring, a spinster and a confirmed bachelor, have more than my deserving little ones? The courts will think differently, I am sure, after you're gone." Greenwood, asleep on the floor between Delores and Anna, woke up to her strident tone and growled.

Anna did not give into Annabelle's angry outburst, but just sat back and listened as she went on and on. Greenwood mustered a few weak barks and settled down to a periodic, showy growl. When Annabelle finally finished, she walked outside without a word, leaving the door to the outside wide open. We could hear her car spinning gravel as she drove out the drive.

"Annabelle will make a noise in court when I am gone," Anna said. " But you mustn't fear her, because I think the will is expertly written, no chance that my wishes are not clearly indicated. No court in America can go against the express wishes of the decedent of sound mind. I doubt anyone would question my mind."

I was not convinced. "Is there even a slim chance that

Annabelle's threat of lawsuits will succeed?"

"None whatsoever," Anna replied. "Even as a girl, she could not share her toys with others. As a matter of information, I may have to sell some of the Johns Peninsula for the museum endowment. Latraviata will have two large pavilions in the museum all to herself, plenty of space for her lovely, large landscapes. Simon will have all the wings on the main level. I thought that the California bungalow was an inspired taking-off point, since most of the paintings were conceived in exactly that sort of building. As we worked with the architects, they scaled the bungalow up to museum size and we loved it."

"Will the galleries be lit better than Simon's old house?" I asked.

"Yes, but dark and woodsy on the outside, white-walled and light on the inside. We already have a nice selection of the California Impressionists for the other rooms, Delores working with their estates. I wanted this to be a center for all the California painters, the plein air impressionists and the modernists, like Simon. It seems only right that the generosity of Simon and Latraviata, both obsessed with painting most of their lives, should go back into a building for the arts. I plan to include a gallery for a Donovan Merrill to be added down the line."

Mary got up and kissed Anna. "Anna, it's a wonderful idea, even if you use all the assets. Donovan and I can surely manage on our own."

"Speak for yourself, Mary. I would like a little left, an income not earned by toil, as the Romans said."

"There will be plenty left, Donovan," Anna said, "for a funded, gentle life for each of you. Mary, that was a strong gesture of support and I thank you."

"Where will it be built exactly?" Tomas asked."Will you have to demolish this house to build it?"

"No, I want both of you to have this house and studio for future use. I will leave it in Donovan's name, but it is yours as well, Tomas. You will have to work that out. It was an artist's house and should continue to be."

She looked right at me as she said, "The two of you will have a long and happy life together, with a only a few rocky times to give the happy ones tone.

"Mary, I've changed my mind about giving Santacasita directly back; I want you to have it only if you agree to continue my war with the vestry all your life. I can't tell you the joy I've had pursuing those smarmy men; it's probably given me an extra ten years of life. Then, you may, only if you wish, give it to the church in your will."

"I agree, Anna," Mary said.

Anna continued, "…and I guess that it's only fair that Annabelle and her clan get what's left of Latraviata's peninsula after I sell some of the undeveloped land for the endowment. I'm funding a trust for Delores so she can stay here in Laguna. I've provided for the cats who have made their home there. And Tomas, in proper answer to your question, the museum will be over there on land Simon bought over the years, ten acres or so." She pointed out the window to the adjoining land.

"You've thought it all out, Anna," Tomas said.

"I've had plenty of time, although there isn't much of it left."

I said, "If you're like your mother, you've got many years left."

"I'm not at all like my mother, Donovan. She lived to a great age, like all of the Bronson women, but she was a dutiful wife. I have rankled my whole life with my inability to obey. It has been the source of all my unhappiness. How much better to be a silent wife, nurturing mother."

"You don't anymore believe that than a Grimm's fairy tale." I said.

She wore a half smile as she said, "There was an omen last week. A rattlesnake coiled on my pillow one morning, its brown-patterned skin menacing against the smooth white linen. I called for Delores to get it out, put it up in the eucalyptus grove, but it was too late. The message was clear."

We tried to dissuade Anna from her gloomy thoughts. How could a snake on her pillow mean anything other than it was chilly outside, the downy softness a welcome change from the convolutions of a cool reptilian day?

But she was right, as usual. The snake had come to tell her that death was near, the discomforts of this life over.

Dark Studio, Now White
1980

This was the first season of my work in Simon's studio, the fog pressing against the dripping windows each morning, so unlike the sunny crackle of winter days in Santa Fe. I had rearranged his studio for my needs, early on deciding that I could not preserve the Schubertian, brown ambiance from Simon's days there. If later curators looked for glimpses from his workspace, hoping to expand their knowledge into the meaning of Grunewald paintings, they would have to scrape away my layer of the palimpsest. White surface, exposing the oaken night beneath.

The old painter's studio was too dark for me. I installed a bank of artificial lights above the painting space and replaced Simon's easel with a taller one, one where I could stand to paint. The strongest image I have of Simon was his sitting at the easel, looking patriarchal and lordly with his long-handled brushes, dispensing wisdom and anecdote. It has never worked for me to sit that way at the easel; standing to face the white canvas, eye to eye, almost as a combatant, is part of what I like about being in the studio.

Layers of white paint, glossy white enamel, now sealed away the memories that his dark walls exuded. It was a task I decided that I must do for myself, without help. A penance in a hair shirt. It took two weeks up and down on a ladder with a wide brush to apply the three coats that were needed to undo every iota of the brown stain. I had a friend who rid his red brick country house in Virginia of nocturnal spirits with white paint, layers and layers of it. It worked for me too, even though the memories were happy, as I needed to wrest the space away from Simon, the ever-present genius from Berlin.

The white walls were such a success that I went on and painted everything else in the studio: the easels, tables, stools, chairs, even the floor. The forest green velvet cushions on the window seats were the last to go, replaced with white canvas versions from a Laguna seamstress. With a ceremonial flourish, I lettered my favorite Restoration quote in a Cursive Italic, three inches high.

> *The crafty duchess, her jeweled ear*
> *to the oaken panel pressed,*
> *did only morsels from*
> *the duke's secret congress perceive.*

It said so much in so few words about what was happening in that unhappy castle, a hidden drama that I continued to attempt to put in my work.

On some mornings when I arrived at the studio in the faint light of dawn, I imagined that I could hear muffled music in a minor key, the dark nostalgia beneath the white surface singing a Dead Sea lamentation for what I had hidden away.

I did not want to exorcise my memories of Simon, as they were always happy and grateful and they will certainly survive my sanitation procedures. I could no more wear his doe skin slippers or his red Chinese dressing gown with the tasseled sleeves than I could use his space unchanged.

As I faced the new canvas on the easel, white with anticipation, I felt that ownership had finally passed into my name, the deed filed away in some great book. Simon could no longer claim the studio.

Tomas believed there was something fundamentally wrong with optimism, his gloomy view perhaps stemming from the strict demands of a Catholic upbringing. So when he called me an optimist, he meant a Panglossian who believed that this was the best of all possible worlds, and if there arose some slight imperfection, then it could with ease be changed for the better. I suppose I did look at the world that way.

Certainly my approach to painting reflected that view. If a canvas was not working, not living up to what I had in mind for it, I took a palette knife and scraped it all away. There was always hope, something to be done. If a painting could be fixed, maybe life could be fixed. Tomas's view was more determinist: people did not change their colors, worlds were headed for destruction, and bad situations seldom improved.

I was about to begin the last of the canvases for a new exhibit, still life paintings of transparent and translucent glass objects on a table top with a covering of crumpled linen. The early morning sun in Laguna was not dependable. I arranged for several low, raking lights to illuminate my motif, strong warm light from one side and cool, mauve light from the other to give glossy, pastel reflections from one object onto another.

I wanted the outside, off-canvas influence to this series to be positive, not threatening, so I have busily set myself to conceiving sunny, top-of-the-hill solutions. Yellow sun dresses and scudding clouds reflected in the glass orb that centered the piece.

I needed to stop thinking so much and start my new canvas. The objects on the table needed rearranging, not the perfect array I had thought them to be yesterday. Several of the empty wine bottles wanted pushing farther back, the crystal charger should be brought forward to overlap slightly the table's edge. If these paintings were going to be sunny, at least they should have a token sense of impending breakage, the threat of shattered crystal. On that theme, I moved everything else around, tilting a few items off plumb and bringing a glass rod precipitously close to falling off the top of the glass cylinder. An aroma of danger lurked. It was working.

Tomas and I had moved to Laguna as Anna had wanted, but it took us several years to make the decision. There was unfinished business in Santa Fe, matters between us that needed sorting out before we could commit to a new adventure. Tomas's continual delight in professing that he was an unfaithful lover proved to be more legend that fact. I wondered if it was not some subverted form of man-on-horseback machismo, brought up from his Mexico City boyhood, to never claim fidelity. True men, even homosexual men, reserved the right to make the young virgins of any gender squeal and flee.

Religions, organized and personal, and their worth were topics that hovered in ever-present readiness in our day-to-day conversations. Tomas's imbedded Catholicism was a source of our continual small disagreements at lunches and dinners about the nature of things, my childhood skepticism having turned into full blown atheism in the adult specimen. Sweet irony surfaced in the fact that the believer, Tomas, was the pessimist and, I, the atheist, was the optimist. There was definitely something in the air over the Laguna hillsides that brought up spiritual discourse; I remembered the cynical and disbelieving motifs that energized the painters there from the 1930s, the falling angels with black wings and the flirtatious shepherd boys with David's tow-headed curls.

Following Anna's dictum that one should never sell real estate, we leased the Santa Fe house and studios to Carole Francis who was looking for a change in her life. Tomas made the observation that if she could not have me, at least she could have my house. Carole's continued devotion amused him, no danger to him perceived.

We took several trips to Laguna to make Simon's house and studio work for us. The changes to the house were completed first, then when I had at last done all parts of the whitewash of the studio, we moved. There were aspects of Laguna that had remained unchanged from my years there, but it was a modern beach community now. The exhilaration of artists at work under shady eucalyptus groves was gone, replaced by an environment of galleries and shops selling art that appealed to the day-trippers.

I told Tomas that other, little-known painters still might live secretly in the hillside groves, away from the daily brawl of the beach and surf, working in their studios to recapture that spirit that I remember of earnest artists fighting the good battle against their own demons. He gave me his world-weary look.

Anna's museum plans were still on hold, brought low by

Annabelle's lawsuits. It could be another decade before anything was built, while Anna's millions sat waiting, collecting interest in escrow accounts.

Mary, Delores and I were called to the probate court on several occasions to testify about the sanity of our grandmother, but I saw that Annabelle was not having success along that road. Anna's last will and testament would hold strong, I felt sure, but it would take time for Annabelle to finish testing every facet for its resistance to attack. The museum had been Anna's war, not mine, and Delores could fight the fine battles and small skirmishes there.

I got going on the new canvas, sketching in the objects with thin lines and blocking in the shadows with a wet turpentine wash. After a couple of hours I knew it was not working. I scrubbed away all the lines and shadows with a cloth soaked in turpentine. Was it going to be harder than I imagined to paint in Simon's studio, to get my work back on track? It was probably better to wait and start again after lunch. Time to go.

Tomas had our cheese sandwiches ready in the main house and I thought of Agnes and Mary Louise, whose many years of lunches never varied. I wondered if Tomas, without prompting, would suggest that he read Proust aloud on these winter evenings. The porches were too cool to eat outside at this time of the year. Instead, we sat in the breakfast room as the weak winter sun broke through the mists.

"Did it go well this morning?" he asked.

"I got the canvas blocked in and an early start to the details, but then I had to scrub it all away."

"You'll solve it eventually, you always do. I went over to Santacasita and got you some more glass objects I remembered were there. Vases and pale green glass plates. They're in the kitchen."

"Thanks." Tomas's black hair had the first signs of white invaders. He ran every day up in the hills behind Laguna Beach, determined to fight any remnant of softening or spreading. If anything, he was more handsome than when we first met.

I had heard the telephone ring during the morning, so I asked, "Who called?"

"Carole. She asked if we would like to go to Mykonos right after Easter? She has rented the villa on the cliff for the spring and summer; you remember it, the one with the lap pool?"

"We could see it through the closed gate?"

"That's it. Carole sold out her show again at the Ludlow Gallery, says the money is burning a hole."

"I always get a lot done in Mykonos."

"It's good for my writing, too."

"What do you think?" I asked.

"Carole's very insistent and very perceptive, but down deep she is willing to spend a small fortune to be next to her darling Donovan."

"You seem okay with that now."

"We all collect around our own demi-god, adoring."

"Let's go."

"Then I'll call her and order our plane tickets. She asked particularly that you bring the blue-and-white jigsaw puzzle. We can at last finish it. I can see us all having ouzo at sunset, still trying to fit the last pieces together."

Tomas had now finally finished his family tome, a novel on the loves and grieving of the de la Penas, and it was published to reasonable praise, good sales. Another collection of short stories got better reviews, better sales and another option from Hollywood. He had completed the first draft of his second novel, which his editor was anxious to receive for the fall lists. The continued acceptance of his writing did nothing to alleviate his anxieties about his own worth or his disbelief in his ability to write.

I had come to the conclusion, an idea that I had not shared with him, that low self worth was the engine that sent him forward. A contented, happy Tomas might never write another word; only the dancing demons of self-doubt, their clicking rhythms right behind made him forge ahead.

If there was an encore to Tomas's infidelity, I was not aware of it, but I had learned to live with the thought of its being there, always possible. Unworthiness also generated a need in him to be loved and a need to be admired, more of each than I could supply.

He had been correct about me, a staid example of pedestrian fidelity. A hopeless, faithful optimist. I was beginning to believe that Anna was right when she said Tomas and I belonged in Laguna at the Grunewald compound. Every day I found more vestiges from my boyhood, like shards from a California that was long gone. I felt new currents stirring, ideas about painting and life. The studio was becoming mine, evidence of Simon's tenure less and less apparent behind the glossy new surfaces. The other parts of my life were just waiting for a similar gloss coat of optimism to seal away the unhappiness of other days.

We talked more about the sojourn in the Greek Islands and the more we talked, the more attractive and possible it became. The waters along the Laguna coast never rose to the balmy temperature of the Aegean in midsummer. Tomas could well finish his novel there, working in a discipline that escaped him here at home. How many books were written in foreign settings, the writer in hiding from the quotidian tides of home life?

I was ready to let the images of the Cyclades percolate into my mind, perhaps to emerge as a series of paintings of the Aegean village. It was a motif that kept beckoning to me down the years, awaiting the right time and spirit to complete. I saw the huddled villages above a purple sea, secure on their hills against the towering clouds of autumn storms. Anna had predicted these clouds in my paintings, getting this one right.

When I returned to my studio for the afternoon session, the blank canvas was still awaiting me. For now the Cycladic villages must wait, even though their shapes were foremost in my mind. I needed to focus my thoughts on the project at hand, the still-life paintings for the exhibit this fall, but there was no reason that I could not include hints of what was to come. Where was that stack of postcards of classical buildings, the Parthenon, the Artemisium, the sea-coast of Delos, the Library at Ephesus? It took me a couple of minutes to find them, on a shelf in the newly-arranged cupboards of Simon's renovated studio. My studio, that is. Two views of peninsular Ionic temples, one in grainy black-and-white and the other in the florid colors of the cheaper cards.

I redesigned the composition on the table to include them, placing the black-and-white card in the middle of the charger and the color one leaning against the glass cylinder. These added the layer of complexity I had been searching for, a looking ahead and looking back at the same time.

Like a camera fixed above everything, I watched as my

hand drew the first, curving line on this new painting, the perfect circle of the glass globe in the center, refracting and reflecting all the other players. Working out from there, the other objects fell into place, their outlines all but drawing themselves, the post cards with Greek temples giving a sharpness to the curvaceous glass. I mixed the thin washes of turpentined color. Latraviata's voice told me that when it comes to painting, a good start and you're halfway there. I was halfway there.

A spring and summer on Mykonos might be the very thing to wall away the past, rough rocks trapped behind a fresh coat of smooth plaster. New ideas and improbable hopes would percolate down through the old brain, gaining strength in their passage, like a handful of golden coins turning over and over, flashing yellow and white, through the clear water to a sandy bottom.

Epilogue
Mykonos, 1981

*T*omas drove into the village for groceries, exasperation still alive from our breakfast conversation, and the white dust raised by the Jeep was just settling in the road. Carole, after several hours of work, set off down the path to the beach with the horse-shoe cliffs, preferring the solitude of a salt-water swim to the long pool on the terrace, away from the morning's discord. We were to all meet for lunch in town.

It was hot midsummer, no breeze with the sun cooking the paving stones early in the morning, still to be felt exuding from the white walls of the house after midnight. We had been on the island since April, three months.

At night we could see the glow from the village, beaming an ochre-pink light in the sky over the hill, but during the day our view was of the unspoiled Aegean cliffs and beaches. We saw little of the adjacent villas, only a pristine portion of the coast, dry terraces from former olive groves walking down the slopes to the sea and the pale silhouette of another island on the hot horizon. Mykonos Town was a short walk over the hill, however remote it appeared.

Perhaps that was part of the problem, the sense of isolation at the villa. When we arrived in the spring, the hills were still green from winter rains, red poppies clustered in the dampness of the low spots. The locals said it had been a wet winter, more rain and snow since even the old ones could remember, and we should expect a notably dry summer, one inevitably following the other.

Those first days were still cool, the sea water bracing. For several weeks we huddled each evening around the corner fireplace, savoring the warmth of the scarce firewood. This was a six month sojourn for us away from our stateside studios.

Tomas planned to finish the novel that sat in draft form on his desk at home, embracing the idea of working on an island, away from Laguna distractions. This summer in Mykonos would put a polish on his book, get the momentum of his career going.

I, having finished the paintings for an upcoming October exhibit, felt free to take some months off, to read, sketch, to renew and think about the series for the following year. I intended to travel to other islands in the coming months, sketching the Cycladic villages that hugged the cliffs, which in mind's eye symbolized sanctuary in troubled world, an icon of safety.

Carole brought along the equipment and supplies to work on her small paintings, interior musings on thick paper with fat oil crayons. She had forsaken the New Mexico landscape per se, bringing up versions of it in her own mind, paintings for which a line of collectors waited to pay out handsome sums. She was generous with her success, paying winter bills for artist friends in need and this, our sojourn in the Aegean. On a rigid schedule, she rarely departed from three intense hours of morning work, and then only for a swim in the fresh water pool. It could be said that Art was now her lover.

That same Art, in one of his many clever disguises, was my lover, too, with whom Tomas had to share affections. It was a role which he did not entirely relish, complaining often to me how low he was on the list of priorities, how alien and unwelcome he felt walking into my studio. It was the tango we had been dancing for years, and the energy in the dance was now no less than when it started.

As we planned our summer, Tomas convinced us to take a ship from the States, the arrival by sea more suitable for an Aegean island. We traded in our plane tickets and booked on a small Greek ship leaving in March from Florida, repositioning for three-day cruises out from Piraeus. It called at Madeira, Lisbon and half a dozen Mediterranean towns before we reached Greek waters. The final port before the mainland was Mykonos and the three of us were on deck for the morning arrival, the sea calm enough for the ship to come alongside.

The island was not expecting us, taxi drivers still asleep or polishing the autos at home for the late afternoon arrival of day trippers. The customs kiosk was shuttered and locked. With seven suitcases, typewriters in cases, and two boxes of art supplies, we stood at the sea end of the dock as the ship sailed on. We watched as it negotiated around the rocky headland and gained speed for Piraeus.

A heavy man on a converted motorbike-truck, the attached flatbed partially loaded with cabbages and carrots from an inland farm, roared down to the pier from the main road towards us, sensing a tip if he could combine errands.

"Vasilios Estate Agents? Do you know the way there?"

Carole asked as he turned up the motor to keep it from dying.

"Yes, yes. We load up." There was just room for Carole next to him on the front seat, while Tomas and I found space among the suitcases, cabbages and carrots on the rear flatbed.

The woman at the rental agency said that Odysseus Vasilios was out at the villa, making things ready. She spoke in Greek to the driver, pointing over the town; he said no problem. Twenty minutes later the motorbike coughed as we chugged with slow majesty up the dusty road to the villa.

The agent's Mercedes sedan was parked at an angle, the villa's front doors propped open with a rock. I paid the grocery driver thirty dollars to compensate for the fresh cabbages now covered with a layer of white dust. He gave a wave of thanks and honked as he retreated down the road.

Carole wrote a check for Odysseus while Tomas and I explored the villa, a large salon, four bedrooms, bathrooms, a kitchen, terraces on all sides, a long pool on the terrace facing the sea, the stone dining table under a slatted porch for meals.

Local developers had long ago mastered the fake Aegean house, whitewashed thick walls with small windows, shutters at every opening, doors giving onto porches with rows of poles to break the summer sun. We met some of our neighbors, expatriates from Northern Europe mostly, a family from Singapore and two men from London, who ran their spice business by daily hours on the telephone.

As I waited for the lunch hour, the morning gave the opportunity to be alone in the villa. I took it to work on the exhibit sketchbook at the shaded dining table. I drew imaginary villages against steep, dry hillsides, cross-hatching the shadows of the houses and detailing the scrubby undergrowth on the land surrounding. The paintings that would derive from these built in my mind, large canvases with textured paint. The image of winter arriving kept presenting itself, dark clouds pressing down upon the island, a suggestion of rough sea below.

As the sketches continued, I wondered if I really needed to travel too far to implant the forms in my mind, shapes that would come forward when I stood at the easel. The villages were more an idea to me rather than actual stone and plaster, a concept of solace and safety, tired sailors returning to first glimpses of home, white houses huddled against the wind-whipped cold.

Tomas said I should not brood about it so much. Just paint. Once I actually started the paintings, I knew that the images would come naturally if I did think it out beforehand, find a rationale for their existence. Carole, also, urged me to let the thought process flow directly onto the canvas. After I patiently listened to the advice from both of them, I knew that thinking and looking were what I liked most about the process of painting, polishing and repolishing the inchoate idea even before it started to take solid form.

We planned to meet at our favorite waterside taverna in the Kastro. Carole would walk up from her swim, Tomas parking the Jeep in town and I would take the twenty minute trek over the hill. I put away my sketchbook, locked the door and headed into town.

I was the first there, sitting down at the table under the awning, the sea smooth and barely lapping against the stone sea wall. A curious school of sardines came close, nibbling the rocky bottom and looking up at me with their protruding eyes.

Carole arrived next with hair under a kerchief, swimming gear in a raffia bag. "Glorious this morning," she said. "The water must be eighty degrees, cool enough to feel refreshed, so much warmer than our first weeks in April."

Her plentiful light hair was still without gray, but the corners of eyes showed the months in the sun, freckles coming to the forefront on her arms. I always thought Carole a very handsome woman, if not a beautiful one.

"I expect Tomas is over his outburst by now," I said.

"It's one of his nicest qualities, the ability to get hopping mad, Latin blood all aboil and then get over it just as fast."

"Unlike us, who retain our injustices in dark corners."

"A Northern European specialty like pickled herring on toast."

"I suppose I shouldn't have brought up his not working on the book. He's so touchy about it."

"Maybe we all need to find our way alone. You certainly do. I can be beastly when someone tells me what to do."

"Okay, I was a shit."

"Yes. Now pour me some wine."

I filled her glass and we both turned to look out over the water, fishing boats coming back into port, the curious sardines gone. The silences with Carole were natural and without strain, so many past words giving a solid horizon for the quiet above.

The last three months were the longest time I had spent with Carole. In Santa Fe we were accustomed to dinners, lunches and short weekends with a crowd, never these weeks of unrelieved proximity. It had been one of my worries when we set off from the States, how would I like being with Carole so many hours of the day? I knew that Tomas and I had come to an easiness together; we could spend a whole day and each feel uncrowded, but would the addition of another strong presence, this Athena of talent, upset the small raft? Perhaps the verdict was still out.

I looked over at her to assist in my judgment. "So what do you think of our Myconian idyll? Are you happy and content?"

"Mostly."

"Me, too I'm glad we came."

Carole and I had forged a friendship on what years ago passed for love. If the fire in me had burned entirely out, I knew there was an ember or two still alive in Carole, perhaps glowing red in the late night breezes. This was an interchange that we had played before, variations on a theme.

At that moment Tomas bounded up behind me, messed my hair and sat down in the chair next to Carole. He kissed her on the cheek. "What have you been talking about? Both of you look guilty. Me? How childish I was this morning? I'm sorry."

"Accepted. We've moved on from that to deeper waters," I said.

Tomas's hair had grown longer and shinier since our arrival, his brown eyes faded to a Turkish honey-hazel in the sun. Heads of both men and women turned with desire when we came to town.

I realized that the three of us enjoyed playing this back and forth trio again and again, a beloved bit from Mozart, each taking his turn at the lament, stage front, while the other two sang a fetching background. We had not come to the finale yet, variations and countermelodies growing in the three months of our island summer, perhaps a theme for years to come.

What promised to be a paradise back in midwinter had proved to be something less as the days played out. Like the promise of spring, it grew into not what we had intended, more a dry disappointment than a turbulent disaster.

Carole continued her work apace, storing away her crayoned paintings between waxed paper in dark drawers as they were finished. I thought of her as an immutable force, painting without deceleration through war and peace alike. If she felt left out of love, unrequited, she made up for it in the sheer force of her work.

I was in a contemplative phase, thinking about the grand design of my Cycladic series, making notes about details as they occurred to me. When I focused on the notebook, my surroundings disappeared, companions turned to stone. Tomas and I had survived years of up and downs and I saw us firmly entered upon a peaceful stretch. The only unhappiness between us now was my obsession with work; when the momentum of my painting for an exhibit heated up, Tomas invariably grew testy and demanding, perhaps mirroring the same qualities he saw in me. I thought of the Black Forest barometers with the witch on one side and Hansel and Gretel on the other; when I hid deeper and deeper in my studio, Tomas felt pushed out against his will into the vagaries of stormy weather.

He was still testing his abilities as a writer. His talent was much greater than he thought, needing only the passage of more time to mature, properly aged vintage in wood instead of the cloudy new harvest. A day would come when this book could be ignored no longer; he would pick it up and work on it steadily through a second draft. Then it would need only a cursory polish, the editors happy again, perhaps fame in the book review sections.

As we finished lunch with cups of black coffee, a cool wind

from the north started to move the awning, breaking the dead heat from the still water. By the time Carole and I had walked back to the villa, the wind was howling around the corners. White-crested ripples ran across the surface of the swimming pool, umbrellas upended and rolling, the doors banging with flapping curtains.

All of Mykonos told us of the Meltemi: a cold wind from the north just as the summer got cozy and warm, preventing ships from landing, cooling the nights to an uncomfortable chill and creating a nervous threnody in all the islanders. It was a remembrance from the steppes of Russia. Tomas was already at the villa, closing the windows and stacking the poolside furniture against the walls.

He came over to me as I walked up the stairs to the terrace and said, "Donovan, I'm so sorry." He gestured to the stone table where I had placed out the Chinese puzzle. It had filled our cocktail silences and morning quiet times with a simple task, something tangible to fill the spaces between conversations. Except for a small section where the willow trees dipped into the river, we had at long last completed the puzzle. A thousand pieces had found their places, a crowd of jigs and jags.

But the puzzle was gone. The stone surface was blown clean, the wind eddies taking up the thousand blue pieces, curved edges, concubine heads, clouds, willow branches, roof tiles, and fish-heads peeking up from the water, propelling them away from us, down the hillside, across the rocky shore and out to sea. As if to say it was now done with me, the puzzle departed on the arm of Meltemi, its new lover, for a first visit to Delos and the faint ochre outline of islands beyond, where adventures waited.